D0375858

© 2010 McSweeney's Quarterly Concern and the contributors, San Francisco, California. By God, it never gets old. We're twelve years into the life of this journal, and there's always something, or someone, that jolts us wide awake again, lest we get at all complacent about the possibility of words on the page. This time it started, if we remember correctly, with a query to Hilton Als: "You ever gonna write fiction?" we asked. See, we've been devout fans of his critical writings and magazine profiles for as long as he's been writing them, and so we wondered—given his lyricism, given his passion, given his ability to paint a moment so beautifully (have you read his profile of Derek Walcott? Has anyone ever captured a person, in a particular moment, in a particular place, so deftly?)—we wondered if Hilton had ever attempted, or hoped to attempt, fiction. Would not his skills be applicable to this form? If Hilton was one of the best prose stylists alive and working in the U.S., shouldn't we get the benefit of him writing fiction? And so we emailed him about this, and he emailed back that he had indeed been working on something fictional. "What, what?" we wondered, breath bated. "Well, it's unconventional," he said, and we said, "Yes, of course, only that, that's all we want or would expect from you." And so began about a year of correspondence, and excited editing and encouragement, resulting in the bold and brilliant and outrageously original piece included in this issue, called "His Sister, Her Monologue." It's only the second piece of fiction he's published, the last being in 1979. So we are proud to have it in our pages, knowing as we do that we exist, and are kept alive, by publishing writers like Hilton at their most daring and unprecedented. And of course then there's Roddy Doyle, without whom the world would be far dimmer. Thank God for him, and for him being reckless enough to entrust us with his stories. Here he gives us another portrait of modern Ireland, an Ireland that would scarcely have seemed possible even twenty years ago. In this issue we also have another instant classic by Mr. Millhauser, whom we have never met, living as he does far away and in the woods (we presume) but whom we also thank for his blind faith in us. Thank you also to a newer writer named Patrick Crerand, who reminds us of the literary humor we used to publish in greater quantity, and thank you also to the nation of Norway. There is a good deal of interest in the literature of Scandinavia right now, the world being in the thrall of Stieg Larsson and Per Petterson (who is included here, on page 249), to name a few. Our foray into Norwegian writing began a few summers ago, when one of our editors spent a week in Oslo, and there he met dozens of writers, all of them serious and most of them experimental, and on the spot asked them if they would put together a section for McSweeney's devoted to all that was happening in contemporary Norwegian writing. The man for the job was John Erik Riley, an affable (wouldn't he have to be?) half-American, half-Norwegian novelist-editor living in Oslo. We're so happy to bring you this primer, in hopes that it will push open the door, just a bit more, to the reading of more new fiction and poetry in translation. Thank you as always for indulging us. INTERNS & VOLUNTEERS: Rennie Ament, Julian Birchman, Samuel Felsing, Jane Francis, Paul Keelan, Jeffrey Mull, Molly Prentiss, Stephen Reidy, Samantha Riley, Max Rubin, Jen Snyder, Sunra Thompson, Rebecca Worby, Hannah Withers, Lauren Ross, John Knight, Tatiana Schlossberg, Katie Wu. ALSO HELPING: Eli Horowitz, Andrew Leland, Michelle Quint, Greg Larson, Jesse Nathan, Meagan Day. COPY EDITOR: Caitlin Van Dusen. WEBSITE: Chris Monks. SUPPORT: Andi Mudd. OUTREACH: Juliet Litman. CIRCULATION: Adam Krefman. ART DIRECTOR: Brian McMullen. PUBLISHERS: Laura Howard and Chris Ying. MANAGING EDITOR: Jordan Bass. EDITOR: Dave Eggers.

COVER AND INTERIOR ART: Jordan Crane.

Printed in Canada.

DEAR TRISH,

Hello from airports again! *GQ* has sent me out on another story and it's a decent hit of cash, and I need a decent hit of cash, so: midnight at JFK, and I don't recognize the name of the airline. This never feels like a good sign. But the beautiful Spanish woman at the gate taking boarding passes has a smile that leaves me calm in the palsy of a schoolboy crush, and confident enough to board whatever dirty burst of fuel and metal these pilots will hurl skyward toward Central America tonight. I'm heading to Honduras to meet a thirty-three-year-old twice-institutionalized guy from New Jersey who has built an honest-to-god submarine and who could be either batshit crazy or a total genius savant. I have tried my best not to think too much about what I've been told about this man. It's impossible *not* to think about it, though, so I'm at least countering the more disturbing facts with positive thoughts. Inside my head, my positive counter-thought voice sounds, oddly, a lot like Mom's.

Disturbing fact: Somewhere off the coast of Honduras, I'm going to go down a thousand feet in a homemade submarine. The guy who built it has never taken an engineering class in his life. And he was in a psychiatric hospital by the time he was fifteen.

Positive thought I'm countering this with: *Everyone learns differently.*

Fact: He tied a bunch of pig heads and pig hearts and sacks of pig guts to a 140-foot barge, then sunk the barge off of Roatán without telling the coast guard. The idea here was that he would charge tourists to go down in his homemade submarine and watch a bunch of huge deviant sharks chew pig heads from the ropes and tear open burlap sacks of bloody pig hearts. The pig stuff didn't attract the sharks so much, so he shot a horse, paid a fisherman to drag it a couple hundred yards offshore, then chained cinder blocks to it and sank it down to about 1,200 feet. Then he took his mother down in the submarine to watch a freshly shot horse be torn apart by sharks.

Counter: *He is unique.*

It was the highlight of my year, getting to hang out with you. The stuff I left on your kitchen counter is for you—it's all stuff I couldn't fly with back to NYC. So you've got an electric clipper from Longs Drugs, a sixteen-ounce bottle of sunscreen/moisturizer, three diet Red Bulls, and I threw in a book about a dog that some old lady wrote and self-published. I bought it at the library sale when I was visiting Mom and Dad. It's written from the dog's point of view. Anyway, as my older sibling I expect you to use these items to achieve greatness. Electric clippers, hand lotion, diet energy drinks, and a dog's autobiography are more than I had when I was starting out, Trish. And look at the glorious kingdom I've built for myself.

Love—

DAN KENNEDY
NEW YORK, NY

DEAR McSWEENEY'S,

One question I get a lot is, *Ellie, how the hell are you such a genius at giving maid-of-honor wedding toasts?* Another question I get a lot is how to spell *Ellie*. To the first group I answer, *Well, I've had a lot of practice—and a lifetime of best friends.* To the second group I say, *Here's an idea: why don't you just start spelling and see what you come up with, Buddy?* I get pretty fed up with people pretty fast.

Was I born amazing at giving maid-of-honor toasts? Of course not. Was Mozart born amazing at composing symphonies? Yes. One thing you can say about both Mozart and me, however, is that both of us wore ponytails well into our twenties. Another thing about both Mozart and me? We both practiced the hell out of our respective crafts. You'd give Mozart a spare five minutes and you'd find him down in the palace basement, furiously scribbling some song or another. You

give me a spare five minutes, and I will think about how many calories were probably in the portion of LUNA bar I just ate. Then, if I have any time left, I will try to remember whose wedding I am attending this upcoming weekend.

The formula for a solid maid-of-honor wedding toast does not exist. Not unlike snowflakes, every one of my brides is unique, and—for the most part—white. Accordingly, every bride requires her own unique toast. Nevertheless, there are a few extremely general rules that I follow.

About four months before or on the airplane flight to the wedding, I will hunker down and reflect on the friend I'm writing about. The first thing I'll do is write down her name. Then I'll make a note in the corner reminding myself to find out her middle name. Next, I put on those big Bose noise-canceling headphones and close my eyes. I usually wake up about an hour or so later, feeling pretty refreshed and ready to hunker down and reflect on the friend I'm writing about.

At that point I try to think of some of the phenomenal times we've had together. This is the part of the process where my brow really furrows, and I ask the stewardess for a ginger ale, no ice. If any unforgettable moments spring to mind, I immediately write those down. I've never claimed to have the best memory in the world (at least, I don't think that I have), so often I have to furrow my brow for quite some time. Slowly but surely, though, some pretty amazing and unforgettable memories begin to saunter in: amazing times in Cabo San Lucas; phenomenal nights in Las Vegas; unbelievable conversations at the Theta dinner table; unforgettable lemon bomb shots at the Are You Out Or Inn; priceless hangovers in Palm Springs; insane nights in Miami; unforgettable evenings at the beer garden in Queens; phenomenal tofu we've ordered. By the time I've finished, I'm sitting in a pool of my own damn tears, and I have some pretty heavy explaining to do to the rest of the passengers in my row.

Following the delivery of my toast at the wedding reception, there is anywhere from one to fifteen minutes of silence. The fifteen-minute silence usually only occurs when the person who is supposed to give the next toast is in the bathroom (which happens more often than you'd think). As my audience slowly shakes itself out of its collective awe, one guest begins to clap. Then, his or her significant other begins to clap. Then the rest of that particular table begins to clap, followed by the table next to that table, and then the band or DJ, and then the table next

to the band or DJ, and so on and so forth until the entire reception hall is nothing more than a big sloppy mess of applause. *I wish I could do what she does*, I can hear their silent thoughts thinking. *I'm going to go home and practice my speech in front of my mirror, like I used to do after Miss America, or* Cross-Fire. *I hope she can't hear me right now.*

But they can't do what I do. And, news flash, I *can* hear you right now. So hear me right back: Maybe in no fewer than ten thousand hours you could do what I do. However, that is a hell of a lot of hours, and you will probably be dead by then. Unfortunately for you, Ellie Kemper doesn't know the first thing about giving a eulogy.

Let us raise a glass!

ELLIE KEMPER
LOS ANGELES, CA

TRISH KENNEDY!
It is little Danny Kennedy, out on his big magazine adventure. Okay, so, leaving the airport after landing in Roatán this afternoon—after an all-night flight, no sleep before, and then, like, a five-hour layover in San Pedro Sula—the cab driver is speeding along the narrow two-lane road that leads all the way out to West End, where I'm to be holed up in a beach house waiting for this submarine thing to happen. We're driving along when, out

of nowhere, suddenly, a roadblock; the two men at the head of it are in camouflage and waving machine guns.

My first impression is that they're not superfriendly men, Trish. Their eyes track us, we roll slowly up, we stop. They gesture with their guns at the driver and then to me in the backseat, saying a ton of shit I can't understand. It's weird having machine guns waved at you after waking up only minutes earlier. I've seriously been off the plane twenty minutes at this point. I'm still in that mode where you're trying to do the math on how much sleep you got on the flight. I remember thinking: I really want an iced coffee and an oatmeal raisin cookie from the Starbucks by my apartment. And then immediately thinking: That is the last thing I would've predicted thinking when a machine gun was being waved in my face in Honduras.

I catch the driver's eyes in the mirror. He looks nervous/scared. He's an older guy, and it looks like he knows the hassle is heavy and we're about to get a helping of it. The men gesture at the driver's window again with their machine guns. He rolls it down and they speak to him. I still can't understand a word they're saying—as you know, if they would've ordered two Diet Cokes and a ham sandwich in

French, I could have handled myself. But in my head the conversation goes like this:

THEM: Hi, there, driver. We might enjoy shooting you or arresting you.

HIM: Why kill me? Look at what I have in the backseat.

THEM: Good point, sport. It would be more fun to shoot a white freelance-writer type in his little pussy-boy khaki pants and black T-shirt.

HIM: Exactly! Take him. For free.

THEM: You know what, we could even maybe make him do sex things in a fucked-up black-magic island ceremony or something.

After all this the men seem to regard the driver for a moment, then look at each other, then reluctantly wave our cab through. The driver rolls his window back up. When we're driving along again I catch his eyes in the mirror, and he explains: "Snow. Cocaine. They will kill people. They would shoot me to stop the snow from coming in."

At most, a ten-second pause, and then he says:

"You want, my friend? Cocaine? I have. I sell."

ME: What? No! No, thank you. No.

[*Five-second pause*]

ME: Like, I mean, good cocaine, or?

DAN KENNEDY
NEW YORK, NY

DEAR MCSWEENEY'S,

San Francisco, New Orleans, New York, Baltimore, Boston, and Los Angeles: what do these cities have in common? If you guessed "They have all been mentioned in songs by the Counting Crows," you would be correct. If you guessed "All have previously been host to a *McSweeney's*-related event," you would be correct again, and closer to the point.

With your background in systematic logic, I'm sure you have by now divined the thesis of my letter: none of the aforementioned cities is Temecula, California.

As a resident of Temecula, reader of *McSweeney's*, and supporter of public displays of literacy, I have long desired to attend one of the many events that I see advertised on your website. Sadly, distance and the rising cost of bus travel have thus far prevented me from doing so. Other factors contributing to my absence from every *McSweeney's* event ever held include: a temporary injunction against leaving the state of New Mexico, a fear of odd-numbered interstates, and conflicting Lilith Fair tour dates.

I'm sure at this point you're thinking something like, Wait. Isn't Temecula only one hour and thirty-two minutes from Los Angeles (up to two hours and fifty minutes with traffic)? And isn't Los Angeles a frequent host to *McSweeney's*-sponsored readings, release parties, and various other events ending in *-fest* or *-palooza*?

While you are technically correct, what you have perhaps failed to notice is that the prescribed route to Los Angeles traverses Chino Hills State Park. What's wrong with Chino Hills State Park, you ask? Chino Hills State Park is cougar country. And I don't trust my car or my legs enough to risk a trip through cougar country.

Look: we could spend all afternoon brainstorming creative ways to get me to a *McSweeney's* event without forcing me to miss work or aggravating my peanut allergy, but why bother? I have already come up with a solution that is both convenient and tax-deductible (for me, I mean): you should come to Temecula.

If you're like most people, you probably don't know much about Temecula beyond its nickname, "The city where the 2009 comedy *The Goods*, starring Jeremy Piven, was set." While we are proud of our cinematic heritage, it is but one aspect of who we are as a city.

For example, did you know that Temecula (incorporated 1989) is one of two California cities to retain its original Indian name? Did you know that Beverly Hills is the other? My guess is you did not. Temecula has a way of surprising you like that.

Plus, since Temecula is only a few years older than *McSweeney's*, I bet you guys are into a lot of the same activities and actresses and stuff. Like, for example, do you love Maggie Gyllenhaal and commuting to San Diego for work? No way! Us too!

In addition to shared interests, there are many locations in Temecula which are ideally suited for a *McSweeney's* event. What we lack in independent bookstores and student centers at liberal-arts colleges, we make up for in wineries (more than thirty!), Coffee Beans (three), and foreclosed homes (several thousand). These venues become problematic if you're expecting more than a dozen attendees, but that's okay. The nearby Pechanga Resort and Casino has a showroom with seating for twelve hundred, not to mention some of the loosest slots in the state and a better-than-decent lobster dinner.

If it's a more rustic evening you're after, you could rent out one of the antique boutiques or beer gardens in Temecula's historic Old Town district. And should you arrive early, whether to prep the venue or as part of the advance security detail, you must make time to visit a few of my favorite Old Town shoppes [sic], like The Back Porch, The Farmer's Wife, and Jack's Nuts. These delightful stores are guaranteed to satisfy any and all of your cravings for hand-carved furniture, kitchenware, and nuts, respectively.

Temecula may not have the name recognition or season of *The Real World* to compete with your traditional host cities, but there is much about "The Milwaukee of Riverside County" that you will fall in love with. Jazz festivals, hot-air balloons, and Splash Canyon Waterpark (opening summer 2010) are a few examples.

Am I saying the *McSweeney's* book signing, singles mixer, or three-on-three basketball tournament held in Temecula will be the best one ever? Not necessarily. But I am saying if we advertise in the *North County Times* and get a decent hype man, there's a chance that former Denver Broncos running back and current Temecula resident Terrell Davis will attend.

All I'm saying is, think about it.

Sincerely,

KENT WOODYARD
TEMECULA, CA

DEAR MCSWEENEY'S,

The guy across the street is an insurance salesman. He cornered me in my driveway soon after we moved in and asked if I had term or life. He's an affable if fearful person. His six-year-old son was at our house one time and explained that we should never go to New York. "Why's that,

J—?" "Because you'd get robbed," he said. "But why's that?" "Because they ban guns. You can't bring your gun." That was a cinematic moment; a lens telescoped out my window, across the street, through their brick walls, into the dinnertime kitchen, to see the conversations between father and son. I didn't begrudge the kid, since I could see where he got it from. Fear must have some basis. This was after his father, the insurance seller, firmly and without prompting advised me not to swerve my car to avoid squirrels or groundhogs or whatever, especially, especially if the family's with me. He barrels down on them. There's no way you prioritize that squirrel over your family's health. I took note. I should also park my car facing out, as he does. He's always got the car facing the street for an efficient getaway, should it be necessary. When I'm reading on the front porch and he comes home, I see his car pass their driveway, gently brake, and then slowly back in.

I haven't talked much to my neighbors on the other side and up a few houses, but I know the husband is being treated for prostate cancer. He waves from his tool-stocked garage sometimes when I drive by. The neighbor behind us, the one with the trampoline, has been dying of brain cancer for two years. When her husband is walking their dog and I come home to find him at the end of my drive, dog on leash two feet ahead of him, a steaming pile of dog shit two feet behind, and he says, "Oh, that, that was someone else's..." I can only shrug and say "Hi, Billy," because what do you do?

A girl from the bus stop had been missing for a few days before we all learned her appendix had burst. The doctors didn't catch it upon her first hospital visit, and she had to go back late that night sallow, pale, limp, and pretty damn close to death's door. She was in intensive care for weeks, her internal organs undermined. All reports were that they didn't expect her to make it. They used those words. But she made it, and when I hear her grandfather ranting at the bus stop about liberals and his guns and who's out to get him, I don't engage. Her mother committed suicide after she was born. Her grandparents take care of her. I don't know why he's so hate-filled, but I know there's more going on than I see.

The latest self-improvement efforts being made by my wife and me involve trying to understand other people better. That, we suspect, will make us less frustrated. We've tried a number of things, not too successfully, so this is the newest plan. Our kids are growing up—soon both of them will be in school all day, somehow. Jesus, I don't know how it happens. I'm a historian who's no good at dealing with time's passage in my own life. I don't want my children to have to justify their own fears and anxieties by pointing to us. I don't want them to have any. But they'll get them from us anyway, and someone else will (if they're lucky) or will not (more likely) wonder where they came from. We can't avoid it unless this self-improvement kicks in soon.

So there's that.

I was writing because when I got home last week I saw a new car parked in the driveway across the street. It was, as is customary, parked facing the street, in getaway position. I walked inside. My wife was standing in the living room sorting through mail, the sun angling in across the floor. "I see they got a new car over there. Insurance sales must be booming," I said.

She looked at me, looked out the window, and looked back at me. "No," she said, only barely revealing her smile, just enough so I knew that she'd come to understand some essential truth: "That's his parents' car. They're visiting."

I'll be in touch again soon,

BENJAMIN COHEN
CHARLOTTESVILLE, VA

DEAR SISTER LIVING SAFELY, WISELY, SOMEWHERE NEAR SACRAMENTO—

So today I met Karl, the submarine inventor. He knocks on my door this morning, asks if I'm the writer, I say yes. I try to make some joke about how I'm the writer who still needs coffee, but he sort of motions for me to get ready so we can leave.

We grab some breakfast and head down to his place at the end of the island. I'm trying to look like I know what I'm doing: I have a notebook out, a little digital recorder thing that I bought, a few old copies of the magazine in my backpack with other things I've written... I'm basically just shy of wearing a fedora with a little piece of paper in the hatband that says PRESS.

Out on his dock, next to the submarine, there's a tiny radio pumping out a thin little hissing ribbon of "Running on Empty" by Jackson Browne. Karl looks like he's still asleep: board shorts, and distant eyes—like a soldier gone a little bit sideways. He scratches the back of his head, and then he pours a ton of these little white pellets into a couple of cups and puts them in the sub. And then kind of sleepily/absentmindedly he goes: "Sodasorb granules. Soaks up the carbon dioxide from our breathing so you and I don't suffocate down there."

I ask him if the submarine is in good shape, if it's safe.

HIM: Well, the lower window has a metal flange, and something's wrong with it...

ME: [*thinking*] *Christ. Run away. Now.*

HIM: There's some corrosion around it... gotta... look into that.

[*Corrosion? Corrosion? Fucking corrosion! I should have married my girlfriend.*]

And then I look down off the end of the dock at the submarine and do a double-take when I realize that instead of a five- or six-inch-thick Plexiglas porthole window, there is a gaping hole crudely covered by a folded blue tarp, held on to the submarine with some nylon cord. I don't have a degree in engineering, but, having said that: *HOLE.* So I go, "We can't go down, obviously..." And Karl says, "I've got a steel cover we can just bolt over that lower porthole and it should be good to go. We've still got the other window to see where we are down there."

A dozen or so bolts, one steel cover, one rubber seal, and one thin drizzle of glue that apparently has to dry overnight—and then we go down in this thing tomorrow morning.

Okie-dokie/WTF—

DAN KENNEDY
NEW YORK, NY

DEAR MCSWEENEY'S,

Sometimes writing a letter is simply an exercise in getting your thoughts and feelings out on paper. But you should never send it, because what you've expressed might hurt some people. Maybe even a lot of people. Maybe what you have to say should have been said seven years ago. But is it ever too late to say what you feel? Probably, but not in this case. So here it goes.

I think that *Love Actually* is a terrible movie.

Boom.

Let that sink in.

If you, like everyone I've ever met, love the movie, or acknowledge a certain amount of guilty pleasure in enjoying it, there is little I can do to convince you of its terribleness. That Hugh Grant is so charming, after all. And the kids are so cute. A British kid in a lobster costume? Please. I mean, some might call that pandering, and some would say who cares. That's not my point.

Let me just focus on one of the storylines. It involves Keira Knightley, who plays a newly married woman who has *absolutely* no clue that her husband's best friend is in love with her (because he's just so mean!) until she watches the wedding video he made for them wherein the camera lovingly caresses her face ("I look quite pretty!").

He then visits her at *home*, confident that her husband/his best friend won't answer the door, puts on a tape of carol singers (that would fool anyone—just kidding, it sounds like a professional recording, because that's what it is), and tells her with cue-card signs that he's in love with her. He says (via cue card) that he's telling her this because people tell the truth on Christmas. (Do they? I thought we said whatever we had to in order to avoid a crazy family meltdown.) He then strolls back into the night, after having *kissed* her, satisfied that he can continue his relationship with his *best friend* after declaring his secret love for his best friend's *wife*, who now knows that he's in love with her! Even though he tells himself it's over! (Yeah, *right*, buddy. Good luck with that.)

Ugh.

Thanks for listening.

Sincerely,

SARAH WALKER
NEW YORK, NY

DEAR MCSWEENEY'S,

Suppose, for the sake of argument, that your colleagues at a workplace you're leaving after eight years give you an inflatable female doll as a going-away gag gift. Then you decide you want to get rid of it in a creative way—specifically, take it down to the Outer Banks of North Carolina a month later, when many of your friends (not from this workplace) will be gathered there for Memorial Day weekend. The idea being to let the doll (vaguely Asian, if I remember right, and, I should emphasize, *in mint condition, virtue intact*) sit on the beach with you for a few days and then give it a proper sendoff into the ocean, about fifty yards offshore, leaving it for some other lucky soul to find when the tide comes in.

Here's the thing: when you finally let go of the doll, it's very important that she be face up. You never know when the sea might be unusually calm, and if instead of being tossed around by waves and revealed as an obvious dummy, she floats facedown, barely moving, looking unnervingly like a corpse, the Coast Guard plane patrolling up and down the shoreline will come in to take a closer look and circle for a while before they realize they are looking at plastic. What if someone's ship was sinking, and people died while the Coast Guard was tied up? What if the Russians seized on that opportunity to stage an amphibious assault? Remember: *Face up.* Heads, we win.

Abashed,

JIM STALLARD
NEW YORK, NY

TRISH—

Okay, alive down here for now. I've increased the odds against me by renting a motorcycle to get around. Here's notes from today:

This morning Karl opens the hatch of the sub for me to crawl in. Ideally, the glue is dry. Ideally, the bolts are tight. I lower myself onto my knees, start to shimmy in headfirst, take a breath, and my body rockets back out involuntarily; some weird and fast survival reflex I didn't know I had. I try to get in again and my body is screaming *Get out, get out, get out.* I lie to my brain; tell it there's no reason to worry. I get in again—quickly. Karl crawls in behind me. Electric motors whir. We're heading slowly away from the dock.

Loud thud. Hatch just shut, cutting off all sound and sense of the outside. Thick quiet that's only interrupted by the small whir of our electrical.

A big jerk forward. Ballast tanks are pulled, air that keeps sub on the surface rushing out, water rushing in. You can feel it. Surface tension succumbs. We slip below in a matter of seconds, sunlight through the surface quickly becoming a distant orb way above us. The water below looks so dark blue.

Silence I won't be able to write or describe. Silence richer than sound.

We're falling right into the deep blue below. Shade of blue I've never seen on land—huge, impartial, nature, death. Depth seems infinite. Every ounce of the beauty feels like fair warning. Massive, immense. Anything goes wrong, we're a mislaid speck of sediment in all of this.

One hundred feet. Two hundred feet. Sinking fast. Chest tightens a little, heart races, Karl is calm; try to feed off his resignation like it's a nutrient. I'm like offspring mimicking it. I press my face to the glass and tilt my head to look up toward the surface, far away now; silhouettes of a school of tuna maybe two hundred feet above us fade off as we continue our descent.

Three hundred and seventy-five feet. Karl talking about a diver who came out here to the edge and just went down until he died. Love had gone south; just decided this was best. On the wall of the reef, now at about five hundred feet, we see all that's left of the brokenhearted man: his oxygen tank is still there, too. Belts of weights—he wore them to be sure he'd sink. Continue our descent, spin so we're facing the wall of the reef straight on—inches away from the sediment—millions of years to form these walls. Another color, another layer, another one hundred generations of our kind.

The sunlight is starting to disappear up there. Karl fires up the lights. Pulls a laser pointer out of his pocket and starts using it through the portholes to point out the sea life.

Seven hundred feet—the creatures down here feel like they're mocking us. Bioluminescent, translucent skin, abandoned appendages for fins. Humans should have stayed down here instead of walking.

Nine hundred feet: huge thud against the steel, then the sound of abrasion. We've settled onto the bottom. Just lying here on this ledge, settled in. Karl is silent.

Off this ledge, one thousand feet below us, lurk the giant six-gill sharks. I love lying silently here, with our power off; feels like being held to the bosom of something massive, Amniotic hush and calm that I would've never expected.

Karl looks so calm. I feel sort of high and resigned. I am convinced this place is where we're from.

DAN KENNEDY
NEW YORK, NY

DEAR McSWEENEY'S,

My sisters and I aren't sure, but it's possible that our mum, Sue, is currently stranded in Portugal. Sue is sixty-two years old, plumpish, slightly deaf (so also slightly loud, though in a friendly, chatty way), and of British origin and accent, though she carries a Canadian passport. As mums (and moms) go, Sue's a pretty super specimen, lively and fun and active and engaged with the world, and almost exceedingly kind to us, her three adult children. Sue is so super that a few Christmases ago Cara, Anna, and I got little matching mum-heart tattoos—though when Sue saw our tattoos she screamed, "Ew, barf!" and fled cackling into her bedroom; later we heard her crying a bit, we hoped because of the beauty.

In 2008, Sue retired from her job as a social worker, and one of the things we encouraged her to do with her time was learn how to use a computer. Before buying her "Apple Mac," Mum had never even worked a mouse before, but she's proven to be a dedicated learner, and has been doing really well. She likes "accessing the internet" very much (her favorite websites are Google, Wikipedia, and Al Jazeera), and she's also getting pretty good, or at least frequent, at emailing me and my sisters. The only problem is figuring out what she's trying to say.

See, while Sue is a terrifically lucid handwritten correspondent, the whole brain-to-keyboard thing gives her trouble. It usually requires all three of us working in tandem to decode her messages, which tend to be a mess of excessive punctuation, disconnected narrative fragments, and confusing, aggressive demands to answer questions we'd never understood as questions in previous messages. (Think *Tender Buttons* written blindfolded on a French keyboard + guilt complex + lots and lots of exclamation marks.)

This might seem unrelated, but bear with me. Just over a week ago Sue went to Portugal with her friend Irene. They would be staying for five days at something called an eco-retreat. This sounded to me like a low-budget farm where visitors pay to perform menial chores, but Mum was excited, and so we tried to be, too. Of all the activities at the eco-retreat, she was particularly looking forward to milking a sheep, and promised to email us all about it.

A few days into her eco-retreat, Sue accessed the internet and wrote: *Last night we ate a Lamb that had drowned in a water tank an hour or so beforehand—we saw it being hauled out so were in no doubt that it was fresh!!!!* After some discussion, my sisters and I decided that *someone* had drowned this "Lamb," not that it had accidentally fallen into a water tank, perished, and then, out of ecological responsibility, been served for dinner.

And then, a few days after that, Cara, Anna, and I received a message peppered with twenty-nine exclamation marks. It seemed to suggest several things: (1) The eco-retreat was over; (2) Irene had abandoned our mother in Portugal; and (3) Sue was trapped there for good.

This email included cryptic lines like *If you have to be stuck this is a lot better than many places!!!!!* and *I have spoken by phone with my travel agent & she advises me that I am doing the right thing!!!!* But what "right thing" was Sue doing? Beyond *a 6 hour walk along the estuary in Porto!!!!* we weren't sure. My sisters and I conferred: did anyone have a clear read on what was going on? What were all those exclamation marks meant to convey? Panic? Frustration? Joy? It was impossible to tell.

My sisters and I have lately started feeling a nagging sort of responsibility for our mother. Before she retired (and before she got a computer) I thought I knew exactly what her life was and what defined it: her job and us, her kids. But none of us has lived at home for nearly ten years, and now she's not working, either. Her life has become a mystery. She does things like jet off to Europe to milk and drown barnyard animals, and then, possibly, seek asylum on the Iberian Peninsula.

When I'm online, sometimes she'll pop up on Instant Messenger but ignore my chats; what secrets is she so busy accessing? A whole world has suddenly become her domain, and it's unsettling to have no influence over how she's exploring it.

When our mum went to Portugal, Cara predicted, "Something awesome is going to happen to her over there." This worried me, this vague "something," which for some reason had me imagining her hang-gliding across Europe. And with no word since that baffling, exclamatory email three days ago, Cara, Anna, and I are a little worried, especially since, even if she messaged us, Sue would be incapable of explaining what's going on. But we're trying to be excited for her, too. Something awesome might well be happening—it'd just be nice if there were an internet we could access, somewhere, that could show us exactly what it is.

PASHA MALLA
TORONTO, CANADA

DEAR MCSWEENEY'S,
Last night I had a disturbing dream. In it, a beautiful woman I know was standing next to a dead swan. What does that mean? Also, her mother had a block of something that glowed like amber. There was a letter trapped in it:

not a piece of written correspondence, but a letter from an alphabet, though it was the Hebrew alphabet rather than the English one. The letter was a nun soffit. Does that represent finality? And that other guy we know, Gerry, was halved, as if by scythe. His entire right side was gone and you could see inside of him. There were gears and wires. I woke up screaming.

Yours,

BEN GREENMAN
NEW YORK, NY

DEAR MCSWEENEY'S,
A friend recently tipped me off to the Amazon Associates program. Anyone can receive a small referral fee—four to eight percent of the price—for every purchase made of an Amazon product via your individually identified link. It's a vehicle for getting consumers to advertise Amazon products for them. Thinking this would be a means of making some extra money on the first novel I just published, and rationalizing that I've already sold out to corporate interests in far more pernicious ways in my life, I signed up and posted the link to my website (where an Amazon link would have been anyway, sans referral).

It appears that you also receive a percentage on other items purchased via that link, along with your earnings on the designated product. Amazon, in a breach of privacy, displays what these other items are. It exercises great restraint, however, by not revealing who placed the orders. In the one week my book has been out, I have made a grand total of $5.36. (Chai latte, anyone?) In the same period, nine different Amazon Kindle titles were purchased by someone who also bought my novel. They are:

Adult Erotic Fancies: Forced to Fuck
Adult Rape Fantasies: The Taking of Amanda
Adult Rape Fantasies: Sorority Rape
Adult Erotic Fantasies: Gang Rape of Teen Virgin
Aimee & Chloe: Two Sordid Stories of Sin and Incest
Deb's Horny Dad
Honeymoon Perversion
The Horse Mistress
The Violated Virgin

For reasons I cannot discern—either because they are "third-party" orders or because Kindle sales do not apply—I have not earned any monies from the sales of these e-books. I have very conflicted feelings about this situation.

Best,

TEDDY WAYNE
NEW YORK, NY

DEAR TIM,

Unlike some people around here, I will compost literally anything. Eggshells, banana peels, grass clippings—anyone can compost that stuff. Try chicken bones. Try pork tenderloin en croute or spicy beef short ribs. Try tinfoil, or medical waste, or asbestos. Try a mattress. Try breaking that down and then come talk to me.

On one or two occasions various officials, not to mention members of the Federal Bureau of Alcohol, Tobacco, and Firearms, have done just that. Apparently a neighbor, possibly as an attaché of some community association about which I was completely unaware, complained. She came with them, calling it a trash heap, an illegal dump.

"Not true," I countered. "It's a compost pile. I'm making dirt, like God. I'm giving back. You just have to be patient. It can take ten or twelve years."

She mentioned something about the animals it attracts.

She's right about that. That part I agree with. At night it's like the wild kingdom back there—the wild kingdom after the apocalypse, when only the world's most foul, indestructible creatures have survived. Coyotes, raccoons, vultures, possums, jungle crows, rats, wild dogs, skunks, cane toads, at least one very thick snake.

I tried to explain. "Don't you see?"

I said, speaking slowly, as if to a child. "It's all part of it. The animals fight and eat each other. The carcasses rot and get all composted up. More dirt is formed. Gardens grow. The cycle of life is renewed. It's beautiful, when you stop and think about it."

Nevertheless, I am anticipating a long legal battle. My mother wanted them to arrest or at least fine me right there on the spot.

"Just to be safe," she said.

Historically at times like these I like to take her freshly cooked dinner, all neatly (but insanely) arranged on the plate, and donate it en masse directly to the compost pile. And I mean right on top, in full view, so she can see it, still steaming. It always drives her absolutely mental, too—really, beyond description.

"This house is going green, Mother, whether you like it or not," I inform her. She prefers to sleep with the lights on, the showers running, and the thermostat at ninety-one. "It's called sacrificing for something bigger than yourself. You should try it sometime."

No charges yet, but I'll keep you posted.

Yours in the Long Decline,
LEON SANDERS
KNIGHT OF THE SAD COUNTENANCE,
BREAKER OF HORSES
CAMBRIDGE, MA

DEAR McSWEENEY'S,
I would've written sooner, but I "celebrated" my fortieth this year. Birthdays never bothered me much, but the big four-oh has turned things upside down. Since January all I've done is brew sun tea and work on my own personal line of greeting cards. Seriously. That's it.

I've finished a handful of cards so far. My favorite card says, "Hello." Another card says, "Hi." Obviously, that one's for less-formal occasions. I've also written a card that says, "Hola." It's never mentioned during heated immigration debates, but Hispanic folks greet each other, too.

My most recent card is for fans of greeting their loved ones with traditional rhyming poetry. It says, "Screw you." If your friends and family are anything like mine, that will be the perfect card for every holiday.
BRIAN BEATTY
MINNEAPOLIS, MN

HEY McSWEENEY'S,
Remember that guy I was telling you about a few years ago? The one who lived across the street and was able to shoot lasers out of his eyes? The one who could make lightning flash out of his fingers? He died yesterday.
MIKE SACKS
POOLESVILLE, MD

LOCAL

by RODDY DOYLE

CHAPTER ONE
THE CANDIDATE

GOOD EVENING, she said. —Am I speaking to Mr. Kavanagh?
    —Yeah.
    —Mr. Bernard Kavanagh?

—That's me.

—Good evening, Mr. Kavanagh, she said. —I am your Fianna Fáil candidate in the forthcoming local elections.

—You can't be.

—But I am.

—But you *can't* be.

—I can assure you, she said. —I am.

—But you're black.

—Yes, she said.

—And you're running for Fianna Fáil?

—Yes.

—Are you mad?

She smiled.

—Perhaps.

Her name was Chidimma Agu, and not for the first time that night she wondered why she was doing this. Stomping from door to door in the rain, the Irish rain, pretending she loved it. She continued to smile—she had to smile. But behind the smile she cursed her vanity. Why had she listened to that woman?

It would be wise to go back six months or so to help explain why a Nigerian woman was standing on that doorstep, representing a political party that had recently come first in an online poll entitled "The Worst Thing Ever to Happen in the History of Civilization." (The Holocaust had come second, narrowly beating The Priests.) So, we'll go back those months or so.

Chidimma Agu looked out at the rain and thanked God. She had decided to walk to the Blanchardstown Centre, but now she could drive. The exercise and fresh air could wait until the next day, or whenever the rain decided to stop. She grabbed her keys and opened the front door— and saw a woman getting out of a large black car. There was a man in a black suit with her, holding the passenger door. He held an umbrella. Chidimma could hear the soft thump of the raindrops on its canopy. She hurried on to her own car, hoping that it would start the first time. She had just reached the door when she saw that the woman and the man with the umbrella were walking toward her.

—Ms. Agu? said the woman. —Is it Agu? Am I saying it right?

—Yes, said Chidimma. —That is right.

The woman stopped, and now Chidimma was also under the umbrella, which was nice because it was, after all, raining heavily, but also strange because the man holding the umbrella was looking in the opposite direction, deliberately taking no interest in the conversation.

Chidimma quickly understood: he was the driver, not the husband. She had not seen this in Ireland before. As far as she knew, even the wealthiest people drove their own cars. But here she was now, standing in the rain with a woman who employed a man to drive her car, to open her door, to hold her umbrella. A wealthy woman. Possibly a very important woman.

A smiling woman.

—Great, said the woman. —I wasn't sure how I was pronouncing it.

—You were perfectly correct, said Chidimma, also smiling. —Would you like to come in?

—Into your car?

—My house.

—Great, said the woman. —The rain would break your feckin' heart, wouldn't it?

—Yes, said Chidimma. —It certainly would.

Six months or so later, the rain still broke her heart, but she continued to smile at Mr. Bernard Kavanagh.

—Fianna Fáil are muck, said Bernard Kavanagh.

—I'm sorry you think that, said Chidimma.

—The way they've run this country into the ground.

—But surely, sir, the economic problems are global—

—Jesus, love, said Bernard Kavanagh. —What made you join that gang?

—It's a long story, said Chidimma.

—It would want to be, said Bernard Kavanagh.

The wealthy woman sat at the kitchen table, opposite Chidimma.

—Mary sent me, she said.

—Mary?

—Mary Murphy, said the woman. —Big Mary. You know her.

—I do?

—You do, aye, said the woman. —She swears by you. A bit mad. Red hair.

—My hair is not red, said Chidimma.

—Mary's hair.

—Oh. I see.

—D'you know her?

—Yes, said Chidimma. —Mrs. O'Malley.

—That's right, said the woman. —We went to school together. She was Mary Murphy back then. Mad as a brush. She says you're great.

—I am glad that Mrs. O'Malley's opinion of me is so high.

—Sky high, said the woman. —You're the bee's knees.

She sat up now, as if she'd been pinched.

—I need your help, she said.

Chidimma was a psychic. Or, rather, people thought she was a psychic. She never referred to herself as a psychic. She preferred to call herself a life coach—which her husband and daughters thought hilarious.

—I see, said Chidimma.

—You know who I am, said the woman.

—No, said Chidimma. —I'm afraid I don't.

—You're supposed to be a feckin' psychic.

—You *do* look familiar, said Chidimma.

—I'm the Minister for Trade and Communications, said the woman.

—Oh, said Chidimma. —And, please, how can I be of help to you?

—You can tell me how to get out of this feckin' mess, said the Minister for Trade and Communications.

CHAPTER TWO
THE VOTERS

Chidimma Agu (F.F.) looked at the door. It was shut. In fact, it had just been slammed by its owner, Bernard Kavanagh, who had assured Chidimma that he would not be voting for her. He had never voted for Fianna Fáil, and he never would.

—Listen, love, he'd said. —I wouldn't clean my windows with a Fianna Fáiler. No offense, like.

And he'd shut the door.

Chidimma walked to the next house. Her shoes were new; they felt like someone else's. The rain had started to trickle down her back. She could feel the cold drops poke at her—mocking her. She didn't know who lived here. The voter register was in her bag and she hadn't the energy to take it out. She rang the bell and prepared to smile.

Please, Lord, she said to herself. *Let them be African.*

Six months earlier, in the warmth of her kitchen, she had looked across the table at the Minister for Trade and Communications. The Minister had just placed her open hand in front of her.

—I do not read palms, said Chidimma.

—Oh, said the Minister. —What do you do?

—Well, Chidimma started.

—D'you want a lock of my hair?

—No, thank you, said Chidimma.

—That's for werewolves, is it? said the Minister. —Or vampires.

—I do not know, said Chidimma.

She had never laid claim to occult powers. This was unusual in a Fianna Fáil, or any other, electoral candidate. But bear in mind that Chidimma was not yet a candidate, or even a member of Fianna Fáil.

She depended only on a combination of straightforward observation and common sense.

She looked at the Minister and saw a woman who had recently become quite skinny. Her face was a mix of triumph and desperation; the woman was starving and proud of it.

—You have lost weight, she said.

—Aye.

—Congratulations, said Chidimma. —That is a very great achievement. However—

—What?

—Be kind to yourself, said Chidimma. —You have achieved your goal. Now you can relax.

She knew she was saying the right thing. This was what Chidimma did so well. She had just given the Minister permission to eat.

The Minister smiled, and there was something else that Chidimma noticed: the way the smile took over the Minister's face, as if it had escaped after years of custody and was running away in all directions.

—You seem to be quite drunk, said Chidimma.

—Jesus, said the Minister for Trade and Communications. —You're good.

Now, six months later, Chidimma silently thanked God as she saw a black woman standing before her.

—Good evening, she said.

—Good evening, said the woman.

—It rains tonight on the just and on the unjust, said Chidimma, smiling. *Let me in*, she said to herself.

The woman also smiled. Encouraged, almost happy, Chidimma spoke.

—I am your Fianna Fáil candidate in the forthcoming local elections.

—Fianna Fáil?

—Yes.

—But they are rogues, said the woman, and she clicked her fingers above her head.

She took a step closer and peered at Chidimma.

—You are Igbo, aren't you?

—Yes, said Chidimma.

—For shame, said the woman. —You should be in Fine Gael. Fine Gael is the party of the Igbo.

And she too slammed the door.

My God, said Chidimma, to herself. *What am I doing? I am starting a tribal war in Mulhuddart.*

Back in her kitchen, the same six months earlier, Chidimma looked at her watch.

—It is ten-thirty in the morning, she said. —And you are drunk.

The Minister shrugged, slumped, sat up.

—I suppose I am, she said. —But I'll tell you. I can think better with a few vodkas inside me.

—Nonsense, said Chidimma. —Vodka for breakfast?

—I never eat breakfast, the Minister said, quite proudly.

—Listen to me, said Chidimma. —This must stop.

—What?

—This drinking activity. You are a member of the government.

—Sure, they're all at it, said the Minister. —I'm just after coming from the cabinet meeting. I was the only one still able to stand.

—You are a leader, said Chidimma. —You must lead by example.

—You're right, said the Minister. —You're right. I don't suppose you've a bottle of Smirnoff I could buy off you, do you?

—Look at me, said Chidimma.

Chidimma's kitchen was warm, and the Minister was drunk. Her eyes began to close.

Forward, through the six months, and Chidimma stood at a different door, in the same rain.

—Good evening, I am your Fianna—

—Stop there, said the man who had just opened the door. —You should never go canvassing on a Champions League night. You're Fianna Fáil, are yeh?

—Yes.

—Well, listen. If Arsenal win, I'll vote Sinn Féin. If United win, I'll be killing myself. Seeyeh.

Her mobile rang as the door closed.

—How's it going?

It was Gerald McKeefe, the director of elections.

—Not very well, I'm afraid, said Chidimma.

—Good.

—Good?

—I want you to meet someone.

CHAPTER THREE
THE ANGLE

—Look at me! said Chidimma Agu to the Minister for Trade and Communications.

The Minister's eyes shot open.

—You are wonderful, said Chidimma. —You believe that, don't you?

—Aye.

—You are a beautiful woman.

—I've heard no complaints, said the Minister.

She was wide awake now, smiling a smile that was almost under control.

—You are what age? Chidimma asked.

—Low- to mid-forties.

—No!

—Aye.

—You look significantly younger, said Chidimma.

—Ah, now, said the Minister.

Vanity was powerful medicine: it wobbled the sober, and sobered up the drunk. The Minister had stopped wobbling.

—You have so much to offer, said Chidimma. She almost yawned. She was happy with the way she was directing the session, but she didn't know how many times she'd had to listen to herself recite that line.

The Minister belched.

—Sure, I know, she said. —But—

—Yes?

—This downturn—

This conversation took place, remember, in late 2008, before any government politician would have said *recession*.

—This downtown, said the Minister, —is umpress—

She tried again.

—Umpressed—

—Unprecedented? Chidimma suggested.

—Aye, said the Minister. —Umpresidented. And we're getting the blame for it. Especially poor feckin' me.

Six months later, still wet after her night out canvassing, Chidimma walked into the Sanctuary Bar of the Crowne Plaza Hotel, in Blanchardstown. She was looking for Gerald McKeefe, Fianna Fáil's director of elections. She was curious but also disoriented: she thought she'd walked into an aquarium. It was the strange blue lighting, and the fact that the place was very quiet. It was also the fact that, now that she saw him, Gerald McKeefe resembled a cheerful fish in a blue suit.

He waved.

—Over here!

She swam across—it felt like that—to Gerald and the young man who was sitting with him.

—You survived, said Gerald.

—Yes, said Chidimma.

—Good girl, said Gerald. —I've been busy, myself.

—Good boy, said Chidimma.

And she sat down; she sank deep into her chair. She wanted to take her shoes off—quite literally, they were killing her.

She smiled.

—Chidimma, said Gerald. —This man here is Eric Dove. He's going to help us win this thing.

—How do you do, Mr. Dove, said Chidimma.

—I do well, said Eric Dove.

The answer surprised her, because he didn't look well at all. In fact he looked quite unwell. And young—he could not have been much older than fifteen. Perhaps it was the blue light. Perhaps it was the fact that he was drinking Coke from a bottle, with a straw.

—Eric's an ideas man, said Gerald.

—Michelle, said Eric Dove.

—Michelle?

—Michelle Obama.

—Gentlemen, said Chidimma.

She was tempted to stand up—but she didn't.

—There is perhaps a misunderstanding here. I am not Mrs. Obama.

—She's a black woman, said Eric Dove.

And?

—So are you, said Eric Dove. —Use it.

—But—

—Because they'll never vote for a white man. Not if he's running for Fianna Fáil.

Six months back, the Minister for Trade and Communications sighed.

—I liked Agriculture, she said. —I miss the farmers. I could tell them to feck off. They loved it.

—You charmed them.

—You betcha. Did you ever try to charm an economist?

—No, said Chidimma.

—Can't be done, said the Minister. —You might as well be flirting with a feckin' calculator.

—I see.

The Minister sighed again.

—This must stop, said Chidimma.

—What?

—This sighing business, said Chidimma. —We cannot have it.

She stood up.

—Please, stand up.

The Minister stood—it took a while. The alcohol had gone from her head to her knees.

—Say after me, said Chidimma. —I am wonderful.

—I'm wonderful.

—I *am* wonderful, said Chidimma.

—I am wonderful, said the Minister.

And she started to cry.

—Don't stop, said Chidimma.

—I am wonderful, I am wonderful. I am wonderful.

She smacked the table.

—Bastards! she shouted. —I'm wonderful.

—That is right.

—Ask the farmers. Ask any of them.

—You may sit down now, said Chidimma.

—I am wonderful.

—Yes, you are.

—It isn't my fault.

—Sit down, said Chidimma.

She watched as the Minister found the chair and sat.

—I'm wonderful.

—Yes, said Chidimma. —We are making good progress.

—Big Mary said you were great.

—That was very kind of her.

—She said your fortune-telling was spot-on, said the Minister.

—Look at me, please, said Chidimma.

She waited.

—I do not perform magic tricks, she said. —I offer advice.

—Give me some of that, so.

—Advice?

—Anything, said the Minister.

Six months later, Chidimma hung her coat in the hall and walked into the kitchen.

—The girls are asleep?

—Yes, said her husband. —How did it go?

—It was a bit strange, said Chidimma. —Apparently, I have become Michelle Obama.

CHAPTER FOUR

THE HOUND

Chidimma Agu was that strange thing in May 2009: a visible Fianna Fáil candidate. The local elections were less than three weeks away, but Chidimma seemed to be the only politician of any party knocking on the doors of Mulhuddart, in west Dublin. There wasn't a day when she didn't regret her visibility. All her party's mistakes, all the world's many woes—she was the only one there to blame. She had become the locality's scapegoat. Every slammed door, every sneer—she was tempted to quit, several times every day.

It wasn't as if she was a lifetime member of Fianna Fáil. She had joined formally only three months before. She'd been persuaded to do so—to join and to run—by the Minister for Trade and Communications. This had occurred after a particularly satisfactory consultation.

—Your people love you, Chidimma had said. —You have served them well.

—I think they've forgotten.

—Defeatism is not welcome under my roof, said Chidimma. —Say after me: My people love me.

—My people—

—Go on.

—Love me.

—Again.

—My people love me.

—Smile as you say it, please.

The Minister smiled, and Chidimma felt—despite her doubts—that what she did was valuable.

—My God, she said. —Your people *must* love you. Please, come.

She took the Minister to the mirror, which hung by the front door.

—Look, she said.

—Christ, said the Minister. —I'm lovely.

—Yes.

They were looking at a clear-eyed, confident woman.

—I'm the way I was when I had the farmers yapping at my feet, said the Minister.

—They will yap again, said Chidimma.

—You're a miracle worker, Chidimma, said the Minister. —D'you know what? You should run for us.

—Run? Chidimma said.

In an emergency, in any matter of life and death, Chidimma was prepared to walk very fast. But she never ran. If she was asked what she liked most about living in Ireland, she would have answered without hesitation, Tayto crisps followed by the education system.

In many ways, she was an unlikely life coach. This was why so many of her clients concluded that she had psychic powers.

—In the local elections, said the Minister. —You'd be great.

Chidimma was stunned. She looked at herself in the mirror, standing beside the Minister—and she fell for it.

—I was such a fool, she told her husband, Ike.

—Cheer up, Michelle, said Ike.

—Please stop calling me Michelle.

—Okay, he said. —But I like being Barack.

He turned to their daughters, Anuli and Kelechi.

—Can we complain when dinner is late?

—Yes we can!

Chidimma smiled, but she had to coach herself to do so.

—Don't quit, Chichi, said Ike.

—No, she said. —I won't.

—It is why we came here, after all is said and done.

—Yes.

—I am proud of you, he said. —But also hungry.

This time her smile came naturally. And she laughed.

She was tempted to quit again when Eric Dove arrived at her house with the dog. In fact, the dog arrived first, dragging Eric Dove.

—Eric, she said. —I didn't know you had a dog.

—I don't, said Eric.

Eric was Chidimma's campaign strategist. They watched the dog as it started to chew the banister.

—It's yours, said Eric.

—Thank you, said Chidimma. —But I don't want it.

Anuli and Kelechi had slammed the kitchen door when they'd seen the beast. Chidimma could hear them whimpering.

—It's like the Obamas', said Eric. —It's a Portuguese Water Dog.

—It certainly is not, said Chidimma. —It's a bear.

—Google "Obama's dog," said Eric. —You'll see seventy-eight million hits.

—And if I Google "Fianna Fáil candidate and family eaten by bear," how many hits will I see?

The dog—the bear—gave up on the banister, and sat. The kitchen door opened. The bear wagged its tail.

—He's cute, said a sister.

—Yes, another sister agreed.

—Oh, no, said Chidimma.

That evening, advised by Eric, she brought the bear canvassing. Anuli and Kelechi came, too. It took the three of them to hold the lead. It was exactly as Eric Dove had wanted—the candidate walking with her two daughters and their dog. Mulhuddart's Michelle.

She rang the first bell, and waited. Anuli and Kelechi sat on the dog.

The door opened.

—Good evening, said Chidimma. —I am your Fianna Fáil candidate—

The woman who had opened the door screamed. And slammed the door.

The letter flap opened. They heard the woman.

—I'll vote for you if you get that thing out of my garden.

—Promise? said Anuli, the older sister. (She was ten.)

—Promise.

CHAPTER FIVE

THE DEBATE

The dog was sweet; they named him Biffo. But he was not an asset when it came to persuading the people of Mulhuddart to vote for Chidimma Agu (F.F.). So he stayed in the back garden, barking at the grass, when Chidimma went out canvassing.

Her strategist, Eric Dove, was not happy.

—Mistake, he said.

—Eric, said Chidimma. —I am not Michelle Obama.

—Connectivity, said Eric.

—Someone—actually, his mother—had once told Eric that he could, and should, say more with one word than most people could say with a hundred. She'd said this to shut him up, so she could hear what Deirdre was saying to Ken on *Coronation Street*. But Eric had believed her.

—Connectivity, said Eric again.

Chidimma was a polite woman. But—

—What in the name of God do you mean? she asked.

—You, Michelle, black, women, connected. A vote for you is a vote for Obama.

—Enough, said Chidimma. —Please. Enough of this racism.

—Racism? said Eric. —But you *are* black.

—And so is Biffo!

—No, he isn't. He's from Offaly.

—Eric, said Chidimma, —I wish you well. Good-bye.

—I need the dog, said Eric. —It's my brother's.

—He lent it to you?

—Not really, said Eric.

—Your problem, Eric. Good-bye.

The evenings were bright and, occasionally, dry. The plod from door to door was not as dreadful as it had been. The girls, Kelechi and Anuli, no longer went with their mother.

—Politics is not very entertaining, said Kelechi (eight).

Chidimma marveled at her younger daughter's mind, and nodded her agreement before kissing Kelechi's nose. But—secretly—she had begun to disagree. Like Sinn Féin, Chidimma analyzed everything carefully, and she was able to point at four reasons for her growing enthusiasm. (1) Her new shoes were less new now and less uncomfortable; (2) She no longer had to pretend that she was married to the president of the United States; (3) She took great pleasure in seeing her posters on the poles and railings. A great many Chidimmas now smiled warmly on the people of Mulhuddart. Her husband, Ike, had put the posters up and by God they stayed up. Not one of Chidimma's posters had slid down a pole or blown across the N3. The Fianna Fáil harp was clear and easily seen; Chidimma was hiding nothing.

The fourth reason was the last only because it was the most recent.

She had turned a corner, onto a cul-de-sac that had eight houses and seventeen votes, when she saw a man standing on a ladder. He was holding a poster. It was clear that the man holding the poster and the man on the poster were one and the same man.

It was Chidi Adebisi, of the Igbo nation and Fine Gael. He was smiling, both in reality and in print, and he was being photographed by another man. A small crowd—two adults, a child, and a sleeping baby—had stopped to witness this.

—Ah, said Chidi Adebisi. —My worthy opponent, I think.

—Good evening, Mr. Adebisi, said Chidimma.

—It *is* a good evening, said Chidi Adebisi, —as I now have the opportunity to point out to the world at large the lunacy of voting for Fianna Fáil.

The world at large suddenly got larger. Sniffing a scrap, most of the cul-de-sac's residents came out for some fresh air.

—Fianna Fáil, said Chidi Adebisi, —has led us, yes. To the very edge of the abyss.

He climbed farther up the ladder.

—I mean no personal disrespect to my opponent. A wonderful mother, I am certain. But her party! They are criminals and fools.

—They're a disgrace, said someone.

—Disgrace? said Chidimma. —Look at this man here on his podium.

—It's only a ladder.

—He represents a party which proposes to return immigrants to their country of origin.

—That is not true, said Chidi Adebisi.

—You should listen to your party colleague, Leo Varadkar, said Chidimma. —That is exactly what he proposes. At a time when we should unite, to prepare for the strong winds of this *global* recession, Mr. Adebisi's party would tear us apart.

—That's right, love. Give him the slaps.

—The government, said Chidimma, —I can assure you, is in control.

—Nonsense, said Chidi Adebisi.

—Nonsense? said Chidimma. —What nonsense? Look at the government's handling of the swine-flu crisis. A spectacular success, I am proud to say. You have all received your leaflets, yes?

People nodded.

—Believe me, said Chidimma, —whether a pandemic or a pothole, Fianna Fáil is the party that can best look after the people of Mulhuddart. Let this man have his ladder. But vote for me.

She handed her card to hands that accepted it. She patted the baby's head. She waved and walked away. So the fourth reason was this: Chidimma had become a politician, in a desperate fight for votes—and she loved it.

CHAPTER SIX
THE PRESSURE

—Green shoots? said the man outside the SPAR.

He stood right beside Chidimma Agu (F.F.) and looked down at the footpath.

—I don't see any green shoots, he said. —Not here or anywhere else.

—But, said Chidimma. —I am sure you heard our taoiseach, Mr. Brian Cowan's announcement yesterday that there will be rapid growth, starting next year.

—Listen, said the man. —Cowan's a chancer. All I want is a job. Can you give me one?

—No, said Chidimma. —I'm afraid not.

—You're honest.

—Thank you, said Chidimma. —So you will vote for me?

—No.

This was a bad night, at the end of a very bad day. Euphoria to despair, euphoria to despair—she'd been swinging between the two extremes, battered against their solid walls. One woman had spat at her feet; another had hugged her. One man had told her it was great to see black faces on election posters. Another had told her to go back to Brazil.

—I have never been to Brazil, sir, said Chidimma.

—Typical Fianna Fáil. Lying before you even get elected.

The list of things that frightened Chidimma was not extensive. Snakes, machetes, women in pajamas. Snakes had always terrified her, but the women in pajamas were a recent addition.

—Ah, they're harmless, said Gerald McKeefe, Fianna Fáil's director of elections.

—One of these ladies threatened to pour the contents of her kettle over me, said Chidimma.

—Just words, said Gerald. —They mean nothing.

—She followed me halfway down the street, said Chidimma. —With the kettle.

—That's politics, said Gerald. —She's a vote.

—She is a thug.

—She's a thug with a vote, said Gerald. —I hope you smiled back at her while you were running away.

It was impossible not to laugh—but Chidimma achieved the impossible.

—I've been in this game for years, Chidimma, said Gerald. —The Bertie years, the Charlie years. Right back to 1977.

—A long time, said Chidimma.

—It is, said Gerald. —If someone had told me in '77 that I'd end up canvassing for a black woman—

Now Chidimma laughed.

—You're one of the best, said Gerald. —But you mightn't win this time. We're going to be slaughtered, to be honest. But there's the next time.

—Perhaps.

—Think about it.

She hadn't a hope. She knew that now. But there they were, her posters, hanging proud. There was always hope.

—What you're doing is very important, a man had told her earlier, outside the Lidl in Tyrrelstown. —Putting your face on the posters. Making it normal. D'you understand?

—Yes, she said.

—I admire you for it.

—Thank you.

—Do you want to come for a drink?

Chidimma smiled, and started to walk away.

—I am married, she said.

—So am I, said the man.

—Remember me on the fifth of June, said Chidimma.

—And every day in between, said the man—quite a handsome man, but clearly insane.

The days were still exhilarating. But, really, Chidimma didn't know why she was doing this.

She'd called to a house that evening and watched as a woman opened the door and immediately started to cry. Her work permit was due to expire at the end of the month; a new permit would not be issued until her job had been advertised for *two* months, and only if no Irish or EU citizen applied for the job.

—*My* job, she said.

—But you knew the rules, said Chidimma.

—The rules have been changed, said the woman. —By *your* party. I will be deported.

—I am sorry.

—I pay tax, said the woman. —I work hard. Can you help me?

—I am sorry, said Chidimma.

She didn't bother asking the woman for her vote. She just wanted to get away. She felt stupid and brutish. She felt like one of the people who were putting this woman through her hell.

The children were asleep. Ike was asleep. Chidimma sat back—she *lay* back—on the sofa. She found the remote control under a cushion. She pointed it at the TV.

The bell rang—someone was leaning on it.

The Minister for Trade and Communications fell into the hall.

—I'm all right, she said.

She made several attempts to stand up; she seemed to be singing to the carpet. Chidimma was in no mood to help her—and in no mood to join her.

—What is wrong? she asked the Minister's back.

—Everything, said the Minister.

—Oh, for the love of God, said Chidimma.

She was tempted to stand on the woman.

Biffo the dog charged into the hall. He barked and sniffed the Minister's neck.

—Not now, said the Minister. —I'm too tired.

Kelechi and Anuli were at the top of the stairs, rubbing their eyes.

—Who is that? Anuli asked.

—It is one of our country's leaders, said Chidimma. —Go back to bed.

—Is she dead?

—Not yet, said Chidimma.

CHAPTER SEVEN
THE COUP

Chidimma Agu (F.F.) managed to prop the Minister for Trade and Communications against the wall, beside the mirror. She opened the front door, but there was no sign of the state car out on the street.

—Why are you here? she asked the Minister.

—Dess, said the Minister.

She was sliding back to the carpet. Chidimma caught and held her.

—Dess?

—Decimated, said the Minister.

She seemed pleased, and surprised, that she had managed to deliver all four syllables.

—We're going to be dess—

—Decimated.

—Aye.

The children were still on the landing.

—You want popcorn? said Chidimma. —Go back to bed. At once.

They disappeared, but Chidimma knew they were still there, lurking. She could not blame them. Their mother trying to carry a hopelessly drunk woman—the situation did not lack drama.

She got the Minister into the kitchen and sat her down. Then she rushed up the stairs and heard the girls scurrying into their bedroom. She followed them, and heard the noisy exhalations of two bad actors pretending to be asleep. Then she checked on Ike. He was not pretending—he had no need to. The Minister's invasion had not disturbed him. Chidimma cursed and admired him in equal measure. And envied him, too.

She went back downstairs. The Minister's head was on the table.

—You cannot stay here, said Chidimma.

—Where?

—Here.

—Where am I?

Half an hour later, after much coffee and coaxing, the Minister was not exactly sober, but she knew where and who she was. It was Chidimma, so tired, so very tired, who had begun to wonder where and who *she* was.

The Minister had a new word.

—Freefall, she said. —We're in feckin' freefall.

—What do you mean?

—The latest poll, said the Minister. —Labour have passed us. We're nearly neck and neck with the Provos.

She thumped the table.

—Feckin' Mary Lou!

—Please, calm down.

—With her big smile and her maternity leave!

—You must go home, said Chidimma.

The Minister sat up.

—There's no point in trying to orchestrate a coup.

—A coup d'etat? said Chidimma, appalled.

—Aye, said the Minister. —We had a chat about it.

Chidimma was almost afraid to ask—to hear.

—The government? The cabinet?

—Aye, said the Minister. —Not all of us. Just the ones who don't rush home after the meetings. The drinkers, like.

—You planned a coup d'etat? said Chidimma. —Over drinks?

—Ach, there'd be no point in planning, said the Minister. —We just had a chat. Pushed the envelope, like. But the top brass are all Blueshirts. And they'd never take the order from Blind Willie O'Dea. I mean, would you?

Chidimma shook her head.

—And the rank and file are useless, said the Minister. —Fat sissies with earmuffs.

She sighed.

—We're finished.

She sat up again.

—I'm too close to Brian, she said. —What do you think?

—I have no idea, said Chidimma.

There was a new day starting outside. The birds were fighting. The sun wasn't far away.

—I'll have to put some distance between myself and poor Brian, said the Minister.

—I am very tired, said Chidimma.

—A woman leading Fianna Fáil, said the Minister. —How about that?

—I am not yet ready, said Chidimma. —First I must get elected to Fingal County Council.

The Minister stared at her—*stared* at her.

—Seriously, she said. —What do you think?

Chidimma thought about going upstairs, packing her bags, waking her family, and moving to Baghdad.

—It is a very good idea, she said.

—Grand, said the Minister.

She flipped open her mobile phone. The transformation was clear and amazing: the eyes of the world were already on her.

—Come and get me, she said into the phone.

Three days to polling day. The previous week had been the hottest that Chidimma could remember in this city. But she had made it through the bank-holiday weekend—sun, ice cream, abuse, and swollen feet.

—Vote Fianna Fáil, the intercultural party.

—No, I won't.

—Yes, I will.

—Ask me arse.

Three days to go.

Two days.

One.

Chidimma woke on Friday morning. She was immediately aware of two things: it was polling day, and there was a dog going berserk in the back garden. She looked out the bedroom window and saw Biffo attempting sexual congress with Eric Dove, her former strategist. On closer inspection, she realized that the strategist was trying to climb over the back wall with the hound on his back.

She got the window open.

—What in the name of God are you doing?

—My brother wants him back!

—Biffo! she shouted. —Eat that fool!

By the time she got downstairs, Biffo was alone in the garden. Eric Dove was either in the dog's stomach or had escaped over the wall.

Ike followed her into the kitchen.

—The big day, he said.

—Yes.

—Any regrets?

The answer was quick—and honest.

—No, she said. —No big ones.

CHAPTER EIGHT
THE COUNT

Chidimma Agu (F.F.) took real pleasure in the sight of her face at the top of the ballot paper. She showed it to Kelechi and Anuli.

—Look at your mother.

They were with her in the booth because they had no school—the school was the local polling station.

—You look pretty, said Kelechi.

—Thank you.

—You should smile more often, said Anuli.

Chidimma smiled.

—Like this?

—No.

Anuli pointed at the ballot paper.

—Like that. It's funnier.

This day—the day of the election—was actually a quiet day, an anticlimax, but pleasant. Chidimma could do nothing but vote and wait, and wait and eat, and wait and wait, until the next day, when the counting of votes would begin—and end.

She woke up on Saturday morning surprised that she had slept. She heard rain battering the window. She'd get up when it stopped. But it didn't stop. It was even heavier when she arrived at the Fingal count center. Ike was with her; they'd left the girls with Ike's cousin.

The atmosphere in the center was strange. It was full but quiet. Lines of tallymen leaned over barriers, examining the ballots, shouting news and predictions over their shoulders—but there was no real excitement. Mid-morning and, already, some pockets of people looked defeated.

—Ah, my worthy opponent, Mrs. Agu.

It was Chidi Adebisi (F.G.). He wore a suit that shone like dark steel, and a silver tie dotted with discreet green shamrocks.

—Good morning, Mr. Adebisi, said Chidimma. —Any news?

—Your party is being thrashed.

—And me personally?

—You are polling quite well.

—Better than you?

—Marginally.

—As I expected, said Chidimma. —Have you met my husband?

She walked toward the barriers behind which the Mulhuddart votes were being counted. As she drew nearer, a thought struck her, very forcefully: she knew hardly any of the men and women gathered here wearing Fianna Fáil stickers. She had met her running mates, Paddy McManus and Niamh Duffy, before. It had been agreed that they would concentrate on different areas of the ward—and that was fine. But all these others? Her party colleagues—who were they? She felt her anger rise—but blocked it.

—Here she is now.

It was the director of elections, Gerald McKeefe. He usually resembled a cheerful fish. But today he looked anything but cheerful. Chidimma had never seen such misery on a white face.

—It's not looking good, he said.

—Oh, dear.

–Desperate, said Gerald. —But you're in with an outside chance. If the other fella's transfers go to you.

—The other fellow?

—The African lad.

—Chidi Adebisi?

—Exactly.

—What about Paddy and Niamh's transfers? Chidimma asked. —Are none going to me?

—Not many, said Gerald. —Look. This time around you're the black candidate. Next time, you'll be *the* candidate. Do you understand?

—Perfectly.

—You're a pioneer, Chidimma, said Gerald. —I'm proud of you. And, actually, I'm a bit proud of myself. But, Jaysis, we're being hammered. Come and have a look.

She smiled at faces she'd never seen before, shook hands, and realized something very clearly: this was the start of the next campaign—if she wanted it to be.

—Well done.

—Thank you very much.

—You've done brilliant.

—Thank you.

She wasn't going to win, but she wouldn't let herself be disappointed—not *too* disappointed.

A smiling woman pointed to a column of ballot papers on a table near the barrier.

—That's your pile there, she said.

Two papers were added to the pile as they watched.

—A few more of them, please, said the woman.

—More than a few, I think, said Chidimma.

They both laughed.

Chidimma strolled through the crowds with Ike.

—Do all men with ponytails support the Labour Party?

—It would appear so.

—I'm not going to win.

—Chichi, said Ike. —You already have won.

Chidimma stopped walking. And she cried. It wasn't disappointment—not really. It was pride—immense, satisfying pride—that pulled the tears to her eyes. She let them out.

Later that day, in a quiet corner of a quiet—almost deserted—city-center restaurant, the Minister for Trade and Communications smiled at the straight-backed man.

—So, she said. —That's a plan, is it, Major General?

—Call me Liam.

—No, said the Minister. —I'm happier calling you Major General. It's more—I don't know.

She smiled again.

—So, she said, —when I get to the end of my speech and say, "I have great faith in the Irish people," that's the signal. You'll put the tanks onto the streets.

—We've no tanks.

—No tanks? said the Minister. —We can't have that. We'll have to get you a few tanks. Would you like that, Major General?

—Yes, thank you.

—Proper order.

She lifted her glass.

—The farmers are with us.

—That's good.

—We can make do with the tractors till we get you some tanks.

HIS SISTER, HER MONOLOGUE

by HILTON ALS

SOME FAMOUS PEOPLE get cancer. That's a look. Other famous people—my brother, for one—get MS, and that's a look, too. But the attitude I can't take is the one that says you *better* sympathize. Like when a famous acting bitch gets pregnant. Bitch plays her condition up like it's Mother Superior time. You've seen it on *Access Hollywood*, on the TV: Bitch pushes that baby out and Hollywood acts like she ain't ever laid down with dogs, gotten up with fleas, and bitten their heads off. In the press, she's pressed, correct, done, 'cause she's living the right way: Mrs. Morality.

Acting has come to this: engaging less in make-believe than in making a bad carbon copy of reality. All an actress needs to do to get a little juice these days is give up on being an actress and take on the real-life role of wife. Or mother. I never got to that. I always preferred playing myself.

Famous Bitch says in an interview (*simpering voice*): "Well, even though I done sucked off every piece of trade from Hollywood to wherever to get what I wanted, I'm pure now—I have a child." I say, is this a woman? She goes on: "Oh, no, I could never do that now"—be it drugs, going down on a girl producer, whatever—ever since she's given birth to innocence. Breasts leaking, she could feed a nation. I say, is this a woman?

Uh huh, especially when she's a so-called actress. For them, the world is a photo op too great to give up once it's been gotten. There she is, working the phone lines on TV telethons, raising funds for the surviving family members of this or that whatever. Fuck *Medea*. Fuck doing rep. Tell today's acting bitch where America's axis of sentiment is turning, and she'll turn that way as well.

I won't live long enough to learn how to play that part. I'm sixty-four. And look what I got. A half-assed career. Laughter. Many faggots on my phone: *That's hysterical.*

Aren't the queens fabulous? They don't want much: an orgasm and a cocktail. And all they want from an always-looking-for-a-job acting bitch like me is that I be fierce, go to premieres, *be*. And I love it. Love their demands. Helps keep my shit rigorous. Don't get it twisted, though—a queen *will* find the holes in a bitch's fishnets. They just won't try to kill you for being different.

Sometimes, at the video store, in the rock-and-cock section, I rent what the boys are doing, just to stay in touch. I love those dolls. I take those tapes home and watch assholes puckering. Leather straps. The pizza boy, the pool boy. Drama and attitude and then the cock shot.

I'm in a similar business. I do voice-overs for porn films. I'm an artist of sorts—a foley artist for rock-and-cock movies. Split snatch, too. My voice goes both ways—male and female. My mind goes both ways, too. I've been at it for nearly twenty years now, ever since Richard failed me for the last time. In a sense, he and I are in the same business: talking dirty. But that was his choice. This is my survival.

I have appeared—if voices appear, and they do—in everything from *Fags in Love, Fags on Vacation* (1992) to *Mystic's Pizza* (2001). You've felt yourself while you've felt me doing Polish accents. Or anal discomfort. The old gag and sputter when it comes to oral. I do it all.

No one does it better, either. (I've twice won the porn industry's highest honor, the Hot D'Or, for Best Sound, Oral Division.) No one does it better because no one in the business I'm in believes what we do has anything to do with acting. But it does, because acting is convincing folks to feel something. And you've felt yourself while I made the sounds that made you feel something.

Just recently I did a scene where the woman—a skinny white girl who looked like she'd just been shipped in from Estonia—was getting spanked and rimmed by a trannie who may or may not have also (at least in the movie) been her uncle. The director couldn't get the money shot right. Not the close-up or the cum, but the sound of joy and pain that the girl onscreen needed to make while her uncle ate her ass, her face buried in a pillow, a few sparkles from out of nowhere on the small of her back.

So I searched what I had been once and when I could have made a sound like that, just to add a little reality to the scene. Background. I went looking for it blindly, like a mole distressed by hunger. I tapped into a little memory of pain and confusion, the high drama of it. I'm in the kitchen with my mother and some of her friends. We are in Peoria, Illinois. The time: the late nineteen-forties. I may have been four or five, I can't remember. I may have been standing in between my mother's legs. If I am, she has just washed my hair and is greasing it. She had to be doing something. She didn't just sit down and hold you. This was back in the day when grooming a child was as sincere a form of attention as a black mother could muster, mammy myths to the contrary. I am bearing the weight and sound of her circling hands working and working the grease into my scalp, the warmth, the grease, the murmur of voices rising and falling, fighting the need for sleep. The two or three other women in the kitchen are doing what women do: creating an atmosphere of domesticity that could shift, at any moment, into an atmosphere of violence. Snapping peas and then threatening to break some errant child's neck. The story they tell—it sounds like a round—is a story they like telling and elaborating on, when they can. It reminds them of when they were young and nothing had run out, least of all time. The story goes: Once, long ago, they knew a girl, very beautiful, who had a great love. He was handsome and had sworn his heart to this young beauty early on. Before they could marry, though, he was drafted into the service. World War II. He made it through, four years, and he came back home afterward, after saving all those Jews. He had a part in his hair. He was with his girl in her mother's kitchen, a celebratory dinner. His girl had curlers on; she was wearing a pair of pedal push-ers. She was sitting on her mother's blue-and-white-enamel-topped table. To impress his love, the young man showed her a gun, something called a Luger; he had smuggled it out of Germany. The young man had assumed the safety was on, but it wasn't.

I remember thinking back then: So this is love: happiness burning on the stove while a section of the dead girl's flesh smoked, too. I won-dered, then, where the fatal wound had been inflicted. Her chest? Her stomach? None of the women ever said. But as they talked, they pro-vided the voice-over and the laugh track to my imagining the dazed and inconsolable lover being led away in handcuffs, the great outpouring of Negress sympathy that met him as his part grew in, behind bars. The girls who had known the accidental murderer and his dead lover grew into women, visiting him in jail, taking him fresh-baked pies with no files in them. They carried those pies and new gossip, tightly wrapped in their white scented handkerchiefs, right up to the grille, all in love.

Of course, underneath their sympathy, they visited him out of envy. By not shooting them all, he had indirectly denied them their tragic heroism; no one would ever talk about those women in the way he remembered and talked about that dead girl. All they'd been left to was cooking and eventual bitterness. They didn't even keep up with that man when he was released from prison; they couldn't put their fantasies on him in the free world, so they weren't interested.

I thought about all that. And then I went into the booth and did my part. And I nailed it.

There's this trend—have you noticed?—of boys who are into barebacking. Fucking without a condom. Cum dripping out of that pink-brown hole, cum dumped there with no thought of the scum bucket dying. People tell me there are clubs devoted to this activity, people taking cum, others giving it. Most of the movies I've seen featuring this practice are set in Palm Springs, for some reason.

When I watch those films I look less at the men shooting shit into gaping holes than I do at the boys on the other end—something else to identify with. The men shooting shit—that's what men do. But what about the queens who walk away with The Condition because of the shit so to speak that's shot into them? It's the doll lying on her back, maybe acting, but I don't think so, saying "Give it to me, Daddy, Daddy give it to me," that has me upset. Does that make them more fabulous? Their gayness more real? I say, are they actresses?

Maybe those barebacking queens are saying they literally put their ass on the line for a part. Acting is acting and I'm using what I've got and I needed to play the part of bottom bitch for whatever reason. Maybe they're saying, opening their assholes up: AIDS is my Oscar.

Those bitches dripping cum, eyes dead, but still looking for the cameraman's key light: that's what happens when you're an actress. All an actress is ever saying: Look at me, even as I'm dying.

Love is complicated, if it exists.

*　　*　　*

Stanislavsky wrote that acting was an "if." And that "if" was synonymous with intention. Let's say you're playing X. X must want something from Y. Trying to convince your stage or film lover that they
must run off with you in order to prove that they do indeed love you,
for example. That's the part about acting that has always confused me:
my intention. I have never had one, other than to be an actress. I could
never imagine wanting anything except the praise of the queens who
loved me when I first started out, and who love me still. Me: a black,
uninhabitable rock with maybe a couple of talking birds pausing on it
in the middle of the sea.

Aren't the tech boys fabulous?

When I go to work I'm treated like the star they know I am. They
get me a glass of water or anything else I need before setting me up
in the booth, facing the screen. I put my script on a stand. The tech
boys make sure my headphones are clear, free of earwax. I'm the Marni
Nixon of the gash-and-gnash set.

There in the booth, I stand in front of the microphone until I feel
I've found the voice I need. And when I do feel it, I give the cue to roll
tape. A director is rarely, if ever, present nowadays. No need, no need.
I've been doing this so long, no one can tell me how to do it more real
than it needs to be. I'm an actress.

My friend Charles got me into all of this. There we were in LA,
in the mid-seventies, broke and brotherless, and Charles got me work
doing some looping for a B movie he was in. Something by Roger
Corman. They needed a girl to approximate the offscreen sound of
Charles fucking a girl in a motel room. One thing led to another,
I met one person and then another; I established a reputation. So far,

I've survived. Porn shot on film and then on video; nice seventies pussy hair and then shaved, babylike snatch; Tom Selleck lookalike mustaches and butt-fucking against a black velvet scrim followed by what we've got now: barebacking in Palm Springs. I stick to what the audience needs, which doesn't really change all that much.

I like to mix it up, though. Throw in portions of myself—my thinking—into my characters' voices, when I can. The other day, I came across a tape I did some work on: *Mandingo Makes Manhattan* (1983). The film is a little riff on *Roots*. The protagonist is Kunta Kinte Johnson. He's black, naturally, and does a number of white or mulatto-looking women. The director asked me to supply a few of the requisite *oohs* and *aahs* for Kunta and the colored women. He wanted those *oohs* and *aahs* performed in the Negro style—all guttural, like a funky urban chorus. As it happens, I find Negro and Puerto Rican voices difficult to perform. *Their* performances—if that's the word—are so stilted. Not to get all Mary McCleod Bethune about it, but since those people are looked at in the wrong way most of the time, they can't fuck in a way that lends itself to the viewer's imagination. They're too self-conscious, too mindful of the camera. They act like people in a documentary.

Maybe they're too vulnerable to the whole enterprise. When you watch fucking, you want to be the one to take off the girl's (or boy's) clothes with your eyes, your imagination. What you don't want is for the fuckers to make you feel as if not only shouldn't you be stroking, but you should be in church, or contributing a little something to Planned Parenthood.

Rarely do the visuals in my work bother me, but something—a pile of sick—wells up in my stomach when I watch all those black and Latin people fucking. Maybe they remind me of my brother. Maybe they're not my type.

* * *

Of course, there are certain tonal facts about my voice that I can't ignore. I am a Negress. As such, I have a great deal of bass in my speech that cuts girlishness off at the pass. In addition, being a black American, I make of English what I will, since it's not, historically speaking, my first language. Or, to put it another way, I have made of English a form of American that other Americans don't speak, because they don't have the confluence of history and genetics that I do. It's interesting. I think the best vocal interpreters of Gertrude Stein's work, for instance, are people like me, since we get her form and her brilliant, protracted insight that American makes no sense to begin with. It lies too much, just like her bastard son—artistically speaking, anyway—Richard Pryor.

I was able to infuse some of my disgust—similar to the disgust I feel about today's acting bitches, marriage, my brother—into *Mandingo Makes Manhattan*. In the film you see two blacks—a man and a woman, named Kunta and Re-Re—fucking. Re-Re is called Micro-Pussy behind her back, because she can't take all of Kunta's quite considerable dick. So: white sheets. Lube and pussy juice shining in the key light. Then you hear me. I say, as Kunta, pushing my dick into Re-Re, panting: "Can I go deep?" And then I say, as Re-Re: "No." But as Kunta you can hear me go deeper anyway. Playing Re-Re, I object: "I told you *no*. Hey!" They fuck some more. And then a kind of haiku laid out, as it were, in philosophical terms:

KUNTA: Nigger, I ain't going deep.
RE-RE: Nigger, how in the fuck you gonna tell me?
KUNTA: 'Cause I'm looking at my dick, all right?
RE-RE: You ain't in my pussy, either.
KUNTA: I *am* in your pussy.
RE-RE: No, *I'm* in my pussy. I can feel how deep you going, nigger.

KUNTA: No, your pussy is *yours*. *I'm* in your pussy.

RE-RE: So, I know how deep you're going, so back up. I'm serious.

KUNTA: Look, Re-Re.

RE-RE: Nigger.

They fuck. Then:

RE-RE: Come on, nigger, hurry up.

He comes.

It wasn't until I'd listened to this again recently that I thought how many of the feelings you'd like me to express about my brother are expressed there, depending on how you listen.

I love my work.

It provides me with certain necessities. This so-so apartment in West Hollywood (the walls are too pink, though; I'm not thrilled about the constant sunlight). The requisite car. Stamps to put on the envelopes to mail the bills.

On the job, technical problems arise from time to time—a glitch in the projection, audio wires crossed—but that interests me, too. The downtime provides me with more time to read. I am an actress, and, as such, much of life is made up of waiting, reading, looking for characters to imagine playing in the books I read while waiting to be told whom to be.

An actress's job description is this: the search for self through words, characters, and situations that are not your own. Another reason I could never be a star: I lack a fundamental interest in finding the phrases that fit my personality. Because that's what stars do: find the parts that define their personality further. Kate Hepburn *is* Jo in *Little Women*, that kind of thing. Had I been young enough in the eighties, or interested enough, when women were shoving yams up their twats while talking about the patriarchy or what have you—well, maybe I would have gotten somewhere, talking about a brother. But all of that was as distasteful to me then as my need for you to listen to all this is now.

I like metaphors. I like history. It plays tricks on my mind as I stand in the recording booth, watching whatever. Faces grimacing in some hotel room in Cleveland or wherever with no sound or the wrong sound coming out, waiting for me to correct them—those faces are bracketed in my mind with soldiers in the trenches in World War I, men dressed in green woolen coats, pith helmets, bandages tied around their calves, the gas about to disfigure their enemy's eyes, his mouth, melt the skin.

I don't know what makes my mind work that way, makes my eyes see the things it sees. I grew up with books—there were so many people, all of them talking, that reading was my only way out then.

You know the facts: me and my brother, Richard Pryor, were raised in Peoria, Illinois. I was born in 1938, a little bit before the war started, Richard in 1940, a year before Pearl Harbor. Our mother was a whore. Our grandmother ran a whorehouse. Our father loved them both. Pussy was the family business. There was so much pussy around, I used to wonder: Do I have a pussy, too? And: If I have a pussy, will that make me a whore? I used to sit in the corner of our grandmama's living room, playing with my titty and eating a honeybun, waiting for somebody to love me the right way, like anybody knew what that was.

I'm reluctant to talk to people like you, a reporter, because Richard talked to you all all the time. And the shit he didn't tell you he talked about in his act. Maybe that's one reason I became an actress: to be free in a different way than my brother was free, spewing his guts that way. My freedom comes when I have another name, a different voice. Same as when I was a kid. Everybody was involved in the real-life drama of living in that house; everybody talked and talked. Living there, I could barely hear myself feel. Books were my release.

Everybody said how white I was, reading the world. But after I was *in* the world, white people didn't believe how much I'd read; that's not what a black bitch is supposed to do. Heh. The stories, the characters I found when I was a little girl—they told me how I could live if I busted out of all that pussy and death.

I've decided to close the book on a real white woman, though. She's the enemy of sisters like myself. You know her. There are enough famous photographs of *that writer* dressed in linens and hats, that long face a kind of weeping willow of thought—Virginia Woolf, also known as Suicide Bitch.

In some of the pictures I've seen, she's surrounded by homos. I hear that. But what I can no longer hear is people in your line of work going on about her meaning. Her feminism. Her process of intellection. Her mean-spiritedness, which passes as a kind of high literary style. To me, her life and work taste as insulting as the toe jam not looked after before the foot is shoved in some unsuspecting lover's mouth. As a woman, I've tasted it. As a woman saddled with a famous brother, I know more about what she thinks she's writing about than she'll ever understand. Her name—don't make me say it again—sounds as ugly to me as you asking after Richard.

In *A Room of One's Own*, she writes a kind of fairy tale. She says, What if Shakespeare had a sister named Judith and the sister's brilliance went unrecognized because she had to take care of everyone else? Had to mother a father and look after the cutlery? Suicide Bitch probably made Shakespeare's sister up because she never knew a bitch—including herself—whose gifts were obscured by any living man. But

I have. I've tasted nothing but what she thinks she's talking about. I *am* the contemporary Shakespeare's sister. Except instead of saying "Fear it, Ophelia, fear it my dear sister / And keep you in the rear of your affection / Out of the shot and danger of desire," Richard said something like "My daddy told me once, 'Boy, whatever you do, don't eat no pussy.' I couldn't wait to eat a pussy." Did that destroy me? I survived. Suicide Bitch would never have the slightest interest in women like me, women who endure a brother's fame and emerge from its jaws, mangled but intact. That would be too complicated for her reason.

But to continue. Buried in *A Room of One's Own* is this line: "It is one of the great advantages of being a woman that one can pass even a very fine Negress without wishing to make an Englishwoman of her." I took this to mean: who gives a shit about a colored bitch; your invisibility is your freedom. I agree. I do voice-overs in front of actors who don't even know I'm there. But why does Suicide Bitch have to drag a Negress into it? Because that black bitch by definition tells a white bitch who she is.

Listen, my job depends on my physical invisibility but never my absence. My voices are real because I believe in them enough to apply my interior voice to their reason. I resent Suicide Bitch. I resent her talking about me as though I wasn't in the room.

In something else, about *Middlemarch* and *Jane Eyre*, Suicide Bitch wrote, "We are conscious not merely of the writer's character... we are conscious of a woman's presence—of someone resenting the treatment of her sex and pleading for its rights." She goes on:

> This brings into women's writing an element which is entirely absent from a man's, unless, indeed, he happens to be a working man, a Negro, or one who for some other reason is conscious of disability. It introduces a distortion and is frequently the cause of weakness. The desire to plead some personal cause

or to make a character a mouthpiece of some personal discontent or griev-
ance always has a distressing effect, as if the spot at which the reader's attention is directed were suddenly twofold instead of single.

Looking at the kettle calling the snatch black, I blanch. If there's
anyone we can hold at least partially responsible for the mealy-mouthed
non-think that permeates contemporary women's writing, let alone
their lives—all of us Negroes!—it's her. Everything she ever wrote was
infused with special pleading for her genius, her madness, her Leonard.

And anyway, what's an artist but a mouthpiece for his or her sen-
sibility? Look at Richard. And actually, Suicide Bitch is just the kind
of girl Richard would like—imagine Richard fucking Suicide Bitch!
Talk about riding Miss Daisy! Talk about a joke that would play well
under layers of voice-overs. I saw him with someone like her so many
times: a homely white girl who grew even more smug under his hetero
heaving. I hated the black girls who became enamored of Richard even
more. They all had terrible voices, the kind of voices that made my ear
ache with their flat whininess, their mean, competitive, cunty feminin-
ity. Those black girls, their talk was imitation talk. And the sound they
were imitating—are imitating still, for all I know—was the sound of
white girls whose hair and career they envied.

You see a lot of those types of black girls in Hollywood now.
They're jumping out of airplanes every other second and then heading
straight for the hills, looking for a male star who'll make them a star,
too, while keeping their eye out for that white girl to hate.

Maybe Suicide Bitch would be too much for Richard. They were too
much alike: one big "I" insisting on their reality. I'd like to fuck some
truth into Suicide Bitch, if I could get it up. I could tell her a thing or
two, while I humped her, about what Shakespeare's sister really felt like,
my hot breath on her dead white face, saying: I lived, this is what happened, all of life is imagined and made into art so that I can bear it.

* * *

Aren't the old songs the best?

When we were little, Richard and I used to sit in Mama's yard and sing:

Salty dog, salty dog
I don't wanna be your Annie doll
Honey, let me be your salty dog
Candyman

Two old maids
Sittin' in the sand
One were a she
The other were a man
Salty dog
Candyman

Worst day I ever had in my life
My best friend caught him kissin' his wife
Salty dog
Candyman

The lyrics tickled our noses like sand. We laughed so hard when we came to "Two old maids... One were a she / The other were a man," because back then, when we were certain that time would never use us and spit us out, we knew we'd never end up being anybody's old maid.

We were sitting in the grass when we sang, and Mama wasn't technically our mother; she was our grandmother, our father's mother. Our Daddy never had a chance with a mother like that. Even though she was a whoremonger, Mama was a woman of such enormous efficiency that she swept any ambition our parents might have had under the rug, like dust.

As I started to tell you before, in the nineteen-thirties Mama—me and Richard's grandmother—owned one of the most popular cathouses

in town. (She didn't close up shop until forty years later, when Richard
hit.) She absorbed her children into the business. First she had Daddy
working for her, running errands: picking up Kotex for the whores
(there were about five girls who lived with us, aside from our mother
and grandmother), finding doctors who would kill babies. By the time
he was sixteen, my Daddy was a baby pimp.

When he met our mother, he was in his early twenties. She was sixteen, a pretty girl he knew from around. He didn't even have to seduce
her into giving her pussy up. The promise of his love made her do it.
But Daddy didn't love her anymore afterward. She was always looking
for the right wrong person to do that.

It was like growing up in show business. I never knew anything
else. Daddy was the kind of man who was so stunned by his mother's
formidable presence that he used to grind his teeth as she shaped dough
into ovals on a Sunday. Other times she carried a knife around and he
lived in fear of his own face. Often he looked like the fear you hear
in Richard's voice, in one of his routines. Skittish, like he's telling a
joke—on Mama. And she's waiting offstage to give him the back of her
hand, by way of a little colored criticism.

Richard loved Mama. Her control. She was a star who dominated
everything around her. I think he was hell-bent on becoming a star in
order to duplicate her power, but he never had her inside strength. He
thought that by imitating her image, he'd be a Mama, too, but he was
always too lovesick for that, and not nearly as ruthless. He was much
more like our real mother.

Richard went off to the Army when he was eighteen, right after he
found out that Daddy had been fucking some girl Richard loved. Daddy
got that girl pregnant, but the girl lied and told Richard it was his.
As I've said before, the business I'm in now—nasty talk—it's a family
tradition. Lies, too. Daddy hated Richard as much as he hated his own
mother. To him, his son was just another woman: charismatic and awful.

Eventually my brother came to stay with me in New York for a while, after I moved there looking for work as an actress. Did anyone tell you that? That was in the sixties. He got a few TV spots; he wore black pencil suits; he was a less-menacing-for-all-his-jocularity Bill Cosby. In the late sixties, right before he found his voice and blew up, he moved to California. And in the hope that his star would confer some star status on me, I followed him out there. For the record: he let me into his house for a bit, but not his career. I haven't seen him in more than thirty years. When we were kids, it was like we were married. Now I call him my wuzband.

As it happens, she wasn't wedded to anything. As it happens, she lived in a way that suggested she could pull up stakes at any moment and hit the road—to join a traveling circus, say, or do a little summer stock somewhere in America, dressed in spangled tights and a red tiara. In her sitting room—which is where the reporter conducted the interview—there were books, VHS tapes, a video player, a DVD machine, two chairs, and a sofa. The reporter sat on one of the chairs facing her. She sat on the sofa, his tape recorder between them. The furniture was of a type peculiar to Los Angeles, irrespective of class: white linen with a fine dusting of cat hair, even though there was no cat in evidence. It all looked as if it could be folded up and put in a box in an afternoon.

That was always the dream of the girl performer, no matter what her age: packing up and heading off to illuminate the darkness, a sparkler in each hand eclipsed by the brilliance of her smile. As it happens, Richard Pryor's sister did not smile. She sat with her feet arched, balancing the lower half of her plumpish body on her prettily painted toes, ready to spring for her suitcase.

As Richard Pryor's sister spoke, the reporter was aware of a peculiar sensation rising up in him. When Richard Pryor's sister said "Peoria," "house," or "when

Richard and I were children," he stopped listening. He stopped doing the work of the reporter and instead ran with his preferred translation of Peoria: a green and brown landscape. Richard Pryor as a child, his nose bigger than his head, his sister's white cotton socks slipping down into her patent leather Mary Janes. There they were, Richard's older sister pulling their shared red wagon, Richard sitting in it, his little baby tits jiggling, a somewhat somnolent breeze wafting over their sweaty little bodies performing the perfect relationship of love: one being carted and the other carting. Thank God for the tape recorder. Otherwise, the reporter would have had no idea, after a while, what Richard Pryor's sister had to say.

He had been interviewing her for three days now. He'd been with Richard for much longer, two years or more. When he began his work, the reporter had approached his subject with the best intentions in the world. Acquaintances and friends of friends of Pryor's called to set up meetings, clamoring to be heard. They showed up for their interviews with eyes narrowed against the past, but dressed well enough for the mirror and an expense-account lunch. The interview "process"—strange word— was always the same for the reporter, no matter whom his subject was. But what made Richard Pryor different—and one of the reasons for the reporter's continued interest in him—was this: Richard Pryor had all but stopped speaking.

In the early days, people on both sides of the fence—family members and film producers alike—were "intrigued" by the project. There was much back-and-forth between the two camps. Each used the reporter as an intermediary, not least because he had read all the material and knew the players involved. He had many lunches with screenwriters who wanted to soak up his "insight" before they went in for a pitch meeting. But invariably those screenwriters were vetoed by one or another of Richard's kin—his wives or children or former schoolteachers—because they felt, for one reason or another, that the writer didn't have the right to take on their Richard, whoever that was. Richard Pryor's life story was not his own but theirs, and since he rarely spoke now, what objections was he going to raise about how his family saw him, or saw themselves through him, in the refracted light of his fame? The

two or three—and then ten—producers who were attached to the untitled Richard
Pryor project would individually take the reporter out to discuss the nonexistent
deal, and to talk about the ways in which his behavior was or was not helping the
project move along. Perhaps he should consider, they said, being a little more rock n'
roll, or rather gangster-ish, when he met with potential screenwriters? To give them
a feel for what the material could be, as opposed to just the facts, ma'am?

In the end, the producers went away. If only, they said, the conditions his
heirs attached to the project were not so risky, and—in the Hollywood parlance—
Richard Pryor not so "dark" a subject. Still, it had been interesting for the
reporter not to write, for a while, and just have lunch.

When I first began doing this kind of work, I looked into its his-
tory. There's a link between the foley artist and what came before: the
Japanese *benji*. I love shit like this. History no journalist can fuck with.
In the nineteen-twenties, before sound came in, Japanese movie-theater
owners hired live orators to recite the dialogue through megaphones.
Some of those orators became as famous as the stars on the screen.
Listen to this bit of beauty from a book I cherish: *The Talkies*, by Arthur
Edwin Krows. It's from 1930.

> The prime point here is that too much stress should not be placed upon
> what is sound and what is picture. As soon as talking films became a theat-
> rical actuality, critics sought their standards in distinctions between these;
> but the artistic differences are not between sight and hearing as such. The
> truest, most genuine appreciation of art takes no cognizance of eye or ear.
> In admiring a fine statue no one thinks importantly about the physical fact
> that he *sees* it, or, in listening uninterruptedly to a beautiful symphony, is
> for a time aware that he *hears* it. The instant he is conscious of either, then
> his enjoyment ends.

That's what I'm talking about. My voice is equal to what you see.

For some, what's heard during fucking is more powerful than watching the act itself. When I first started off, I had to do much more than voices; I had to put on rubber gloves and submerge my hand in a jar of lube while rimming a carrot in order to get the sound of penetration right. As my voice earned some demand, I didn't have to do so much incidental stuff. But in a sense, doing foley for stroke flicks is the greater challenge, since the sound makes the surreality richer. The films you hear me in are about people pulling out at the deepest moment of connection. I define that as the sound of love. It's also the sound of me loving and being abandoned by Richard.

On January 18, 2001, *Adult Video News* reported this: the institution, in the porn industry, of the Cambria List. The list is named after Paul Cambria, a lawyer specializing in the First Amendment. He represented Larry Flynt; the list was supposed to help the rest of the industry stay out of trouble during the Bush Administration. Here's what it said, under the heading BOXCOVER GUIDELINES/MOVIE PRODUCTION GUIDELINES:

Do not include any of the following:
No shots with appearance of pain or degradation
No facials (bodyshots are OK if shot is not nasty)
No bukakke
No spitting or saliva mouth to mouth
No food used as sex object
No peeing unless in a natural setting, e.g., field, roadside
No coffins
No blindfolds
No wax dripping
No two dicks in/near one mouth

No shot of stretching pussy

No fisting

No squirting

No bondage-type toys or gear unless very light

No girls sharing same dildo (in mouth or pussy)

Toys are OK if shot is not nasty

No hands from two different people fingering same girl

No male–male penetration

No transsexuals

No bi-sex

No degrading dialogue, e.g., "Suck this cock, bitch," while slapping her face
  with a penis

No menstruation topics

No incest topics

No forced sex, rape themes, etc.

No black men–white women themes

Notice that nowhere on the list is there an edict against the voice—
that is, there are no directives against the way the voice can and should
be used. Of course, there's that reference to so-called "degrading
dialogue"—e.g., "Suck this cock, bitch"—but when isn't need degrading? In any case, I get around that particular mandate by making it
sound more like a question—"Suck this cock, bitch?"—or punk-ass
pleading, and therefore more like love.

Sometimes it's fun to make shit up. Maybe as a way of getting at
myself without having to go through all the boring pedestrian shit
you want to hear, like where I was born and what it was like, having a
brother. Cancer Bitch made shit up all the time. Acted in plays, acted
in movies. I was her paid companion and half-assed dresser from 1961

to 1964, beginning the year I moved to Manhattan from Peoria. Cancer Bitch—that would be Diana Sands.

She and I were friends until her death. Who can forget her? She was tiny, with high, high hair that didn't necessarily make her appear taller but gave her a kind of heft she didn't have otherwise. Black hair, shaped like a pineapple; light came through the curls. Bee-stung lips, I guess you could call them. She looked like a light-skinned colored lady of a certain age no matter what age she was. And then there were her eyes—rent one of her movies and see them in close-up. No amount of pain you'd ever experienced could ever eclipse the sadness in them. She was always alive, even when she had cancer. Not just alive to the scene or character or camera she was playing to, but available to the alchemy that was happening right before you as you watched her watching, holding on to her character's life with her hands, a character she made live in her admirers' minds by doing what used to pass as an actress's work: taking the page and running it through her body, her mouth, her brain. And when you went home after watching her onstage, her character went home with you, too. She was that good.

She stole Jimmy Baldwin's man in '64. Most likely he handed his man over to her. Subconsciously. He was that way. I knew all about it. She had a role in one of his plays, *Blues for Mister Charlie*; Jimmy, he of the pop eyes and sense of duty toward the abstraction known as colored people, hadn't written her much of a part. Or, rather, it was too much of a part: as Yolanda, she was meant to play a slain civil-rights leader's pregnant girlfriend. Yolanda had to deal with a lot of verbal histrionics.

Truth be told, Diana told me, what interested Jimmy more was Cancer Bitch's part in the drama of his relationship with Lucien. Lucien: Baldwin's Swiss piece carried over from Paris, where they met in the early nineteen-fifties, in the days of cafés and such. And as is the case with most relationships in which queens fall in love with someone so pointedly different—which is to say someone who is essentially straight—Lucien loved Jimmy but didn't want him. You know the way: after the first seemingly tender kisses, the nose under the armpit, the shock waves of pleasure, toes curled, temples damp with perspiration and the thrill of the mind turning off, blind to any ambition other than the tactile and the dreams it can lead you to—after the first few times of that, Jimmy perceived—it took him a while, as it takes many writers a while to see that truth has nothing to do with their imaginations—that Lucien really wasn't in it, and could take the romance away from Jimmy. Which he did.

We can not see things on purpose for just so long. Later, Cancer Bitch asked Lucien how he could put his body in a situation that wasn't exactly what he had in mind, meaning how could he separate his body from his mind, what people laughingly refer to as their desire—how could he put his body, which eventually became *her* body, in the way of Jimmy's cock? After all, *she* didn't have a cock, or much of one to speak of. And Lucien said, What makes you think any of those things are separate? Jimmy loved me. But then I opened my eyes and there you were. It's a wonder, the eyes and mind and flesh.

Actually, he didn't "just" open his eyes. Jimmy introduced them. He had brought Lucien back with him from France with the secret hope that his fame, which was significant for a writer, would somehow keep Lucien in his fantasy of shared love. But it didn't work.

Blues for Mister Charlie was the old Jimmy exegesis on white on black—the stage was, in fact, divided into "Blacktown" and "Whitetown"—and Diana Sands, Cancer Bitch, was somewhere in the middle of those towns, bringing to the hackneyed genre Jimmy's play grew out of—a little Archibald Macleish, a lot of Clifford Odets—her weird naturalism, colored at the very core. No other country could have produced her. The head-snapping. The lies you tell to save your children or get out of mothering them. The little laughter that is like a bulwark against laughing outright in ridiculous white people's faces because they might kill you if you did. All this Lucien saw in Diana when he attended rehearsals. He saw it without quite understanding what Cancer Bitch meant, because the only colored person he had known up to that point was Jimmy, and Jimmy had lived in France too long, had prettied his Negroness up, thrown L'Air du Temps over the hogmaws.

Jimmy thought he was directing the play—he shouted instructions at the actors over the (white) director's head, and the director didn't say shit; Black Power was a new and intimidating language—but really he was directing the path his life would take: to become the child to Lucien and Diana's parents. Truth to tell, that was all he wanted— someone in his play and someone watching the play he had written involved with one another. His real story was an old one: the terrible father, or rather stepfather—Jimmy never knew his biological father— and the mother whom he adored but resented because he couldn't save her from Daddy. I say, are all sons born to that? Mother cutting the carrots while Daddy's twisting her nipples in the dark, telling the little Mrs. that she had to ignore her son, the one who wrote so he'd eventually be acknowledged somehow, somewhere? And what did that mean to the little Mrs., especially with a Daddy Baldwin who couldn't provide anything but babies, not even the carrots? What kind of Mrs. is that? One who accepts the babies but no food to nourish them with? A stupid one? I say, is this a woman? Didn't she have any kind of imagination about what a Daddy is supposed to do? Let's not get into the fact that it was the times, her circumstances, she was black and poor, uneducated, blah, blah, blah. She became a Mrs. so she could have a son who would provide her with something. An imagination. Who could move her into her true glory as a woman.

Is a blow to the imagination the same as a blow to the ego? Maybe to someone like Jimmy it is. To not believe, or have other people not believe, in what he had, made him redouble his own efforts to court Cancer Bitch himself, so Lucien could see how close to a girl Jimmy really was. If she was by his side, Jimmy thought, Lucien wouldn't be able to tell the difference between them. And whatever Lucien was willing to give up to Diana would be his, too, even just a little bit, which is never a little bit, not really, to someone like Jimmy, who was all heart and theatrical calculation.

Biography explains nothing, but it's fun to tell these stories.

In an essay titled "Notes on Black Movies," written in 1972, the film critic Pauline Kael observed:

> Peggy Petit, the young heroine of the new film *Black Girl*, doesn't have a white girl's conformation; she's attractive in a different way. That may not seem so special, but after you've seen a lot of black movies, you know how special it is. The action thrillers feature heroes and heroines who are dark-tanned Anglo-Saxons, so to speak—and not to lure whites (who don't go anyway) but to lure blacks whose ideas of beauty are based on white stereotypes. If there is one area in which the cumulative effect of Hollywood films is obvious, it is in what is now considered 'pretty' or 'handsome' or 'cute' *globally*; the mannequins in shop windows the world over have pert, piggy little faces.

When I was starting out, there were even fewer black girls on screen than there are now. In the sixties, there was Gloria Foster, and Abby Lincoln, and Brenda Sykes, and the fabulous Judy Pace, who played the first black villainess on TV—on *Peyton Place*, starring little Miss Mia Farrow. What a voice Judy had! Snide and contemptuous and full of hard, cold luster. All those girls were fabulous, in their way. Glamorous and real, which is one definition of movie acting. Their naturalism didn't exclude their coloredness or femaleness. They didn't treat sex as a big deal, either; it was all integral to the inherent humanism of their behavior.

But by 1972, *globally*, like Ms. Kael says, Gloria, Brenda, Judy,

Diana, and not to mention myself were out; movies shifted away from documenting the realism of human interaction to the by-now-predictable surrealism of black bitch in a head rag putting down whitey or an ineffectual husband.

You hear tell now of these actresses like Halle Berry—globally cute and acknowledged as such by picking up an Oscar for it. What Halle wants—what "actresses" of her ilk want—is to be living molds in a global idea of what men are supposed to want: perky-looking chocolate drops that taste like shit and are therefore naughty because black equals shit. Imagine what a black bitch who can actually act feels like when she sits in the cinema of today, recalling the ghosts of the past— Gloria, maybe, and a little bit of me? Imagine what Gloria—who played nearly two hundred characters in *In White America* onstage, back in the sixties—would have thought sitting through contemporary crap like *Juwanna Mann*. Imagine what I felt like looking at Halle with her tits out in *Monster's Ball*, telling some cracker to "Make me feel good." How could I have played that part without feeling my mama in the background, about to go upside my head because I'm declaring a need to a white man?

Or maybe the only thing separating us is my fat ass. Having Richard's face—or his having mine; remember, I'm older—has been a hindrance in my career; people see his fame in me long before they see what I can do as an actress. When people see me, they see Richard's hilarity. In the old days—the seventies—when there was no black performer bigger than Richard, I'd show up for some movie audition or another and the casting director would ask me to put a "Pryor spin" on whatever part I was up for. So I'd look up from the script and start cursing the room out. Then I'd throw the script down and walk out the door. That got me a few laughs, but fewer jobs.

*   *   *

Maybe some low blue lights here, or red. And many cigarettes leading to other cigarettes. Jimmy and Diana smoking and smoking in a bar in Harlem after a particularly frustrating rehearsal. Maybe a little discussion about the play, mouths sticky with cocktails, and Jimmy's black, black skin—an arm—resting on the table, Diana's light, light skin in a sleeveless shift made blue or red by the overhead lights, lights flickering through the holes in her pineapple hair. She's an actress. She says: Well, I don't know if my believability is up to the play. But what she means to say is she isn't sure if the play is up to her believability, the lyrical naturalism in her work, which made of each prop, each wearing of a costume, the very thing you would have worn yourself and done and said yourself, were you not in the audience yourself.

"Oh, baby," she said, "the part," she said a little tentatively, drawing her audience of Jimmy in, "it's a great part, that's not what worries me, what worries me—"

"Yes?" he inquired, never taking his eyes off her. The famous Negro concern overlaid with an analytical listening quality. "What's wrong, baby?" His mouth split, revealing the famous space between his upper teeth. She had a smile, too, and she used it.

"I'm not at all sure I *get* all of these characters; I mean, I'm not at all sure I'm accessing my character properly. Can we break it down?"

This was the kind of conversation his egotism could bear, since it was not "just" about his work, but about how his work had become her world and thus transformed her into someone he could recognize: a character expressive of his thoughts and feelings. Aren't actresses fabulous? They may know in their minds that they're acting, but their bodies don't show it.

In any case, in that bar, lighting another cigarette in his high faggot style of physical expression—talkative arms and hands that cut the air, leaning forward in his chair to his interlocutor, touching her shoulder with one arm and his heart with another—Jimmy said: Chile,

chile, chile. Did I ever tell you about the time when I was a chile—this was when I was in the church—and I was preaching then, preparing one sermon a week? I stood before the people, a nigger Ezekiel, and I preached not because I had the word—I had many—but because I wanted to escape, and because I was in love.

The church was my escape. That is a convenient phrase. Wait. The church was and wasn't different from home. There was home, there was the church, and there was the street, all filled with black people. And how could you not look at them and see Jesus, his Jesus hair, the thorns in it wound tightly in nigger hair piled correct under a picture hat? Negroes high-stepping into eternity, not even seeing the blood dripping before their very eyes? Flies sticking to the blood, can't wash their face because the Jesus blood has burned a hole in it, Jesus rays of acceptance and sorrow over the acceptance coming out of the hole? You can't see anything else if you stay, and you can't not stay, because you're a child aspiring to be Jesus but yourself, forgiveness gouging out your face. But to say any of that is to be exiled by the very people you love.

Cancer Bitch didn't think about what he was saying much; some of it was bullshit that she could already find the holes in. His whole thing about exile, for instance; only famous people complained about all that, after they'd achieved it.

Cancer Bitch knew that no matter how many plays she appeared in by people like the man sitting in front of her—ugly in a way that made you feel protective of him; ugly in a way that made you think, Damn, could it be that I'm that ugly, too—she would never be famous like that; she didn't want fame bad enough. What she wanted was to *act* bad enough, and when did a bitch ever get famous from love? She had known people like Jimmy throughout her career—they started off as artists with something to say, and they ended up being some cause's voice, living to tell the story of people who needed them as opposed to needing to communicate something themselves. And the love and attention that their work garnered them—that love and attention stood in equal proportion to their insecurity, their feeling that they would be less without being known, that the next black bitch with a typewriter would supplant them. That's what drove them: the fear that they would no longer exist if they were on the level of Cancer Bitch. Or me.

Jimmy drank, I think, Scotch in those days. He had many of them, sitting there talking to Diana. If I played her sitting there, in conversation with him, how would I do it? I'd work from the inside out, in that Harlem bar, uptown from where Jimmy, with his playwright's paranoia, thought Burgess Meredith, the director, was clobbering his play and so undermined Meredith's authority with *You're white, you don't understand my characters; I didn't write this play for you but for my people who are up there on the stage, with their guts and hems showing*, the long moan of the writer who has too much mouth left over after the non-writing is done, so he can't leave others to the interpretation of it, and besides which, what Jimmy was fighting with was not so much his director as the knowledge, never faced, at least in the press, where he lived by now, that the play wasn't any good, that he had lost his way as a writer, producing work he was supposed to produce as opposed to the walk he was the propagator of, mixing cotton fields and crepes, chitlins and coq au vin—this can appeal to a girl, especially if she feels sorry for you because you're ugly. And so I'd listen when he said, lighting another cigarette, a little column of white between his two dark columns of fingers, the same fingers that maybe had been inside of Lucien's mouth—

"And so I learned to perform, because if I didn't I would upset the needs of the people, the people all around me; I'd be called out as a queer, which is to say a living example of someone who didn't believe in them and their Jesus need, because after all there I was, godless, because I'm a queen, and a slave to my queen ways, dirty cuffs dragging in the gutters and bowed down like a dog waiting to be made upright by a word from heaven. Their church was a kind of revenge fantasy—things would turn out better in the next world because Jesus—who was God, too; we didn't make any distinctions between the two—would allow us to step on white heads to get there. We would win the moral war that our very presence in the world, in our slum, in the church, said we would win because we had worked so very hard at suffering.

"So they pushed out everything that was wrong with their world, which is to say people like me, so it wouldn't show up in the next. They didn't want any smart niggers to question how and why they had come to think of themselves as chosen in the first place. They'd bust your ass if you read anything besides the Bible, developed an imagination outside of their imagination, said a thought; because you said a thought, you were white. *You sound white*—that's what Daddy and some of my siblings said after I'd discovered a building of lies: the library. I went to the library and came out white. Only my mother didn't punish me for reading, because I was her imagination waiting to happen."

Cancer Bitch adjusted her brassiere strap. It was maybe a little dirty; sweat from the rehearsal and a little baby powder coming down the inside of her armpits, little crumblings of baby powder like butts of wet chalk or pumice stone. She was a little uncomfortable. I say, is this a woman? Diana couldn't act any of this, but I can.

Women lie. An actress lies even better. I don't mean all of that "let's pretend" shit, either, although that's precisely what I mean, too. An actress will believe anything, including herself. They convince their bodies of something and then it exists.

For instance: it's Dover, 1943. Twelve seagulls circle four American servicemen who sit on a cliff. They are picnicking with four English women wearing flowered print dresses and cardigans made at home in front of an electric fire long before they knew the Americans, knitted by the Philco, a little red dot of music in the gloom.

Maybe one woman has red hair, and she longs for the Negro American soldier, but is too shy to imagine anything but his tongue on the red tongue between her legs. Those are the clues a director or script might give, and a real acting bitch will say: Got it. And then she'll try to represent the foregoing.

I have never been to Dover, but I could play that place. I could also play that white woman. I could have red hair if I dreamed about it long enough. Long, flowing shit.

Despite her fear, the English girl—myself—went for a walk with the Negro American. They—we—went and sat somewhere near the cliffs, and he kissed her. I know that kiss; those were the first fat lips I ever licked. The kiss is a little dry because you're outdoors, and a little salty because you're near the sea. The kiss is not a kiss on the brink of catastrophe, like the beginning of every love story I've ever known, which goes from hope to boredom to disaster in an instant.

Later in the story, my best English girlfriend tries to fuck him, but I find out. I cry. I love to cry. (A producer friend of mine once described an actress as a woman who feels the need to cry in front of three thousand strangers. Too true!) As the red-haired English woman, I trusted too much. I loved the black American too much, and in a fit of anger I say to my former best English girlfriend: you should get cancer, bitch, and die. Maybe that last line isn't in character. You see, I need a director. If I had a director, he could show me where the hair falls on my shoulders and I could take it from there. As much as a bitch needs dick sometimes, she needs a director more, just as she needs a writer's language in order to be someone other than herself. I wish someone would hire me apart from voice-overs.

* * *

Journalism. Bullshit. If it's the "truth" about Richard you're after—haw haw—let me say up front that I'm perfectly aware why Richard is a success and why I am not and why I am not bitter, now, because I am able to understand it: he was able to perform some version of "blackness" and I was not. In the later films—before he got sick—when he was yukking it up in shit like *The Toy* and whatnot, he was a mass of colored buffoonery and feeling sporting a Jheri curl. If you look at him in that film and others, he starts to bear more than a passing resemblance to Flip Wilson crossed with Stepin Fetchit. That was always his thing—a kind of Negro nervousness that white people in particular were able to feel somewhat comfortable with, no matter how "transgressive" or whatever the fuck his humor was considered by journalists and reviewers and the like, since all he did as far as I was concerned was bug out his eyes in a sketch of colored fear. What a caution. I could never do that. So humiliating. How can you want to be loved so much that you make your race some kind of shtick? I am an actress. I could never wear the head rags and look up pleadingly at master as I dusted the doorstep where last the lilacs bloomed, hoping he wouldn't rape me again tonight in some shitty teleplay that becomes a hit on ABC, and what have you.

I'm not a sympathy-getting bitch, I told you from the start. You won't catch me telling a target liberal audience how we done suffered, and how my cunt was raped by America. And no one would believe me if I was cast in that part, anyway! I'm too much myself, too much of a mind that shows its thinking—which is what acting is, too—to be believed as unschooled in life, let alone books. That's hard for white people to accept, I'm sorry to say; they wouldn't know what a colored actress looked like who wasn't playing a slave. Nothing's changed. If a colored girl wants to be seen as an actress, she's gonna have to spread 'em. So what's there for me? Richard and Halle took it all. It's a shitty thought, but I've said it.

* * *

Actresses—they're women in search of a self, like all women. But at least a real actress like Diana or myself will admit it. An actress has her eye on you—an audience—while in her head she's looking for a way to get her proverbial Daddy to pay for a script she can play. No abuse is too great to withstand to make that happen. A black eye as the actress blackens the chicken. An acting bitch can even watch herself as her eye is being blackened, and plan what costume she's going to wear to go with it. An acting bitch can stand outside herself while working on the inside of her character, which is to say herself. I say, isn't that something? Maybe Cancer Bitch didn't think like that after a while, given the cancer. But she never did stop acting. Maybe a better phrase is: She never stopped presenting herself. An acting bitch doesn't stop acting until God yells "Cut!" Toward the end— I saw this myself—Cancer Bitch was up in the hospital bed, shit stuck all up in her, liquid dripping every which way, maybe even out of her asshole, tube stuck up her ass like a plastic Daddy. Her hair was melting against the pillow. Black hair against a white hospital pillow, spreading against a sky of illness. And when she saw me—I had come to visit her—Cancer Bitch pulled the white sheet away from herself, exposing all those tubes, the liquid Daddy in her ass, and said: "Ain't this some shit?"

Metaphors sustain us. To talk about Cancer Bitch as she was—the tubes leaking, her ass—is beside the point. Or beside her point. She was an actress, and as such had a fundamental disrespect for "I." "I" doesn't take into account all the years a bitch spends on becoming something else. Find the character and you find her. That was Cancer Bitch's life work—to be something other than herself, in order to talk about herself in terms beyond the kind of shit that biographers encourage: no metaphors but the thing itself.

I blame Cancer Bitch's acting for making me an actress. To identify me solely as Richard Pryor's sister, to ask me what that's "like," is a question that strikes me as being as pornographic as my mouth. It's as greedy and innocent as a child asking his mother to describe what he was like when he was little. I am an actress. And as an actress I'm interested in Diana Sands and emulating the will she exercised to get over herself and into you, whoever you are. What force! By the time Diana said, "Ain't this some shit?" she knew what she was talking about: acting and dying.

I am an actress. We find truth—human truth—by pretending to be people we're not. That frees us to explore the metaphor of being. Okay, so you'll write that Richard did this, he did that. How will that resonate in the reader's heart beyond the thrill of gossipy revelation? And as to Richard's black celebrity: isn't that an oxymoron? What you want are stories about his black infamy, not a sister. Acting isn't funny, but *being* is. Richard was never an actor. All he did was put his being out there. People responded. He became famous. What he did wasn't as complicated as acting. Diana Sands was an actress. There are no jokes about her.

"I" is a sitcom. "I," at best, is a pratfall in slow motion. I am an actress, which is to say a woman who pretends to be something other than herself. Risking exposure and not. Richard would never do that. He could never be someone else's text. He'd always fight to be Richard instead of trying to inform the part—Hamlet, whatever—with the deepest parts of himself.

That's not what I do. Honor that. Honor the fact that you'll get more of what you want from me by allowing my "I" to speak through other characters, scenes, events. Allow me metaphor even though I'm not supposed to dally there, being colored or whatever. I know, I know, being colored, I'm not supposed to exist in the realm of ideas; my skin would dirty them up. The general audience expects my shit to be black and raw and "real"—like my literal shit. Like Richard's. Fuck you.

In fact, I blame Richard and his popularity for helping to formulate the audience's expectations whenever they see a black face onscreen, or on a book jacket: Aha! the viewer thinks. Here we have more officers in the race-class-gender bores! And with them come whores! Drifters! Pimps! Junkies! Grifters! At one time or another, Richard and I have been all of those things, but why not allow us the flowers, too? You can see them near the footpath I walked past the other day, years ago. This was in 1993. A man is leaning drunkenly against a crooked fence. Flowers at his feet. They call him Gary. Gary's not drunk, he's just on drugs. Sometimes his own existence is too much. But he can hold a job. He works at a crab house in Baltimore, separating the big and little crabs into different crates. Gary works in the crab house even though he's allergic to the things. The money he makes there is just enough for drugs; just enough so that he doesn't get too sick. It's the first selfish thing he's ever done, being a junkie.

Like all junkies, Gary is a baby; he lives in his mother's basement, so he doesn't pay rent. After he gets high, he likes to read his books: books on chemistry, religion, history. Book knowledge has made him feel funny ever since he was a kid, different from everyone else in his neighborhood, most of whom didn't read and grew up on drugs, including his former wife, Fran, who had a junkie's contempt for Gary from the very beginning and, also from the beginning, a distrust, a steady hatred for what he tried to give her before he started getting high: love, a bit of security, a home. Which is what Gary knew growing up, before drugs.

But Fran couldn't deal. Sometimes, when they were married, she'd grab his cock roughly and sit on it. He would have preferred inserting it into her lovingly, but that journey of love always disgusted Fran, especially since she knew that Gary was always worried about whether or not he was hurting her. Sensing his worry, Fran shat on it, and then she shat on his cock. Gary had a sap's heart and didn't know that the worst part of loving those who do not want to be loved is this: denying them the instant intimacy of fucking, leaving, and never seeing them again, so you live on in their imagination without the further burden of touch. Gary never realized that if only he'd thrown Fran onto a pile of empty crab shells from time to time, they'd still be together. Stunned by pain, she'd be too distracted to notice his love, which made her think of piles of sick. In the sick, there were chunks of options. That was the worst.

Gary let Fran have her own life. She had never had that before. Everyone she had ever known growing up—friends, family—lived a kind of predetermined existence: get up and drink and then scramble for the next drink; get up and snort or shoot, and then knock in the head of some old lady with just enough change in her purse so you can have the same day the next day, and the day after.

They got married in 1983, a few years after they graduated from high school. They were married—or rather, they lived together as Mr. and Mrs. McCullough—for eight years. Then Fran left. In the beginning, Gary gave Fran her own pocket change. After that, he gave her any number of other things: a nice house, a little boy, some nice outfits. In those years he worked security; he always had at least two jobs, plus he invested what he made. Gary thought he and Fran were living a love story.

Fran never thought so. By giving her everything he thought she should have and more, he opened up the world to her. She had the luxury of picking and choosing what she might like for herself. But what Gary didn't know was that no one likes living with options. It makes you feel motherless. Everyone looks for someone to tell them what to do. To resist or accept the perfection in that is one way to get through life. That is the work of an actress: No, I will not hold the teacup that way as I walk across the stage. Or should I? Why tilt my head just so to catch that light in this movie scene? But perhaps, dear director, you are right. I am less equivocal than most actors, because I am less interested in the game of approval than most. I never say to the director: If I do X, will you love me? Because I know they won't.

Directors used to hurt me. When I worked in front of the camera, I generally disagreed with any and all interpretations of my body, since their interpretations are just that—some white boy saying that the distribution of my weight on a given mark is wrong. When I was younger, I'd shift my weight from one leg to another, stick my left hip out, try not to be obtrusive, someone with flesh, even though I was being paid to be seen. It wasn't until many years later that I realized my being colored had something to do with my being off the mark; that is, the colored body is a kind of joke, like the kind Richard would tell about black pussy taking a walk in America. He'd say: Say there, labia too plump, clit too long, people drowning in pussy juice, better wrap that shit up and look for Jesus before I throw up. Richard would have said that in any number of his voices—it's the only way he could make a character, through his voices. Most of the voices he became famous for were just imitations of the people we knew while we were growing up; they weren't acting. I guess he used his body some, used it to show how ridiculous coloredness looks in the context of America; sometimes he could look like a coat hanger hanging on an empty clothesline blowing around in someone's front yard and you could see white people looking at the hanger from their living room window all scared and mesmerized. Or sometimes he could look like a hamburger on a griddle with bean sprouts and hairy tendrils sticking out of its burnt surface, assaulting Americans with fat and weirdness—their worst fears. In any case, what Richard was trying to show based on my telling him stories about the unequal distribution of my weight on the set was that by now it doesn't matter what coloredness looks like, or how it presents itself; it stopped belonging to its body a long time ago, after it was co-opted by Jesus, drugs, biographers, audiences who deluge you with their dreams and expectations—which are, in turn, defined by politics, weather, whatever—and whatever directors have to say about it.

To compensate, the colored spirit became bigger, as if that would protect us. We empathize with all bodies, not having one ourselves. We empathize with all audiences, always being one ourselves. That can be the making of an actress—accepting that one is everyone and no one. I've learned from a brother that, in the end, if you're colored, your fame makes not the slightest difference in terms of how you are seen or not seen by the world, let alone yourself.

A friend who edits books told me this story: Once, the music impresario Quincy Jones was running around pitching his life story to a bunch of publishers. His agent, Irving "Swifty" Lazar, was in tow. So, Quincy is pitching his life story to a roomful of editors, and "Swifty" interrupts and says, "Why don't you tell that other story about your life, Sidney?" Meaning Poitier. Nothing's changed much, certainly when it comes to the Negro in Hollywood. If you're colored, you have to handle things for yourself.

That's what I did. I became myself when I began to tell directors that I couldn't agree with what was being made of me, since I knew they didn't know what to make of me. So let's start somewhere else, I'd suggest to these directors, like with the text, a little improvisation, some sense-memory exercises about a brother. As a result of my candor, I worked less in front of the camera, even less onstage, but when I did, I felt my pores open up when I missed my mark. I was alive to myself. Resisting the direction I needed, I became the character I needed to be—for myself.

Maybe it's better as a joke, though: the body dragging itself through experiences directed by a reality not your own. If Richard's life shows you anything, it's how white people can make you crazy by saying what you are: too fat, too lazy, too loving, too dangerous, too close, too political, too silent, too druggy, too talkative, too generous, too loud, too drunk, too strong, too sensitive, too cruel. That's what Richard's success is based on, a little bit if not a great deal: recounting what the body has seen and felt when certain people can't see or feel you at all.

The trouble with Richard, though, is that he became rich and powerful doing what he did, which contradicts the beauty he found in his nothingness. If you become well-known because of an act of invisibility, you're fucked, because your fame makes you part of the quotidian. You can't really make theater out of these contradictions unless you're an actor, which Richard never was. An actor can sort all of that out and make it clear to an audience just where the confusion begins and ends. Richard just lived in it—all colored and crazy. Add to that earning a lot of money for being yourself, which makes no sense to the colored soul at all—money as a reward for being nothing?—and you end up a nasty joke, a jogging matchstick. You know how it goes: What does this lit matchstick look like, standing upright and then moving across the counter? Richard Pryor jogging.

In actual fact, no one can handle vast quantities of power or fame. Richard couldn't. It nearly burned him alive. He was always looking for something bigger than himself to tell him what to do. We all are. Being an actress is one of the few jobs on earth that tells the truth about this need that exists in humans—to be told what to do. When we were little, Richard looked to me for that—I always thought that was because I was his older sister. But that's not it, not entirely. You can see it in children, and their need to be disciplined. Children stamp on flowers to show the blooms who's stronger, and then look to their parents for their punishment. It's the limits we impose on children that help them define who they are.

Sometimes, you can find direction in a marriage. At least, that's what Fran was hoping for. In order to become herself, or rather, *be* herself, Fran wanted to be told what to do so she could hate it. She was like that lyric in the song: "You know I do it better when I'm being opposed." She was my kind of actress.

For Fran, a day was not a day unless there was a little killing in it, some rip-offs of the jack-offs. In the last years of her brief marriage to Gary—1989 to 1991—she worked as an operator for the phone company, but she partied more than she showed up for work. Mostly she liked to stay at home, snorting whatever and spitting invectives at her kid, whom she would sometimes forget to feed.

Sitting in the split-level house Gary had bought for her a few years into their marriage (she had covered nearly all the floors in blue shag carpeting), she wanted something to happen—a firm hand across her face, say. Something more directly cruel than the bullshit Gary gave her, something to make their life together seem more real, beat-up, tangible. Gary did hit her once or twice when she filled the house with drug trash, but what was that to her when she knew his heart wasn't in it? He'd never go out into the world and do a little killing himself. And what kind of husband was that? She would have licked his stank fingers if there were little murders on the tips of them.

The truth of the matter is, Gary was fixed in his dual roles, as a success and as an underdog. He worked hard and did well not only because he wanted to take care of his wife and mother, but because he wanted to wrest from those women all the love they had stored up—the love that he perceived the world didn't want. It never occurred to him that some colored women can be foul, too, being human.

Think back to Richard and our Mama. Not our mother, who barely raised us, but our grandmother, who did. She was as ugly as red mud and as tall as a pile of buffalo dung. Richard attached love to that pile; he kept throwing himself onto it, never mind the filth. Gary was like that with any colored person who came his way, especially women, even though the people who knew him made him feel embarrassed by what his love could yield: not love in return, but competition. Generally speaking, people felt morally diminished by his concern— his goodness—and so, fearing that they could not better it, or even live up to it, were compelled to behave as badly as possible in his presence, borrowing money they could never repay, going after girls Gary found attractive, telling him lies, asking for help they didn't need, telling him he was an ass loaded with books, trashing his secrets. We were a quartet, Gary and Fran and Richard and I.

When Gary got his job at the plant in Baltimore, word spread that he wasn't really black. What black man in his right mind would want to be an overseer at a shitty company in a small town? He reminded his coworkers of the old days in the fields. They said he was just like a house nigger, a spy always asking after his coworkers' wives and children with trouble in mind. He was always lending the new guys money until the company cut their first check, or going to the hospital to visit other guys who got laid up on the job, bending down to smell the flowers he'd sent them on his own dime. What kind of human was that?

The problem with seeing all colored people as a tribe that he, Gary, some ghetto Jesus of infinite heart and thorns, wanted to bundle up, throw on the back of a mule, and take to the promised land with its water sprinklers, shag carpeting, and aboveground pools, was that his love would never make any of them different. Fran was the only one to join him in his promised land, and she hated it there. By being outrageous and foul and dressing her foulness up with perfume and wit, she made him differentiate between herself and the other colored people he wanted to love and save. She was an artist. She could stand outside of her sadness and comment on it with contempt. Hatred was her art. Gary had never known colored people like Fran when he was growing up; at least he didn't want to remember that he had. He kept coming back to his dream of saving her in the way one always comes back to one's desire, which is always riddled by absurdity.

From the first, Gary had been thought absurd, especially by his Daddy, who learned to distrust his son when it became clear he had a heart; that turned Mr. McCullough's stomach. But since his father liked the taste of his own bile—a Daddy taste, or rather, the acid of son-hate that defines Daddy as a smell—Gary thought he was giving his father what he wanted just by existing so he could have someone to hate.

As a boy, Gary thought he could save his mother, who worked so hard for him, by making money, helping her around the house, being different than a Daddy. As the youngest McCullough in spirit if not age (he had two younger siblings), Gary would jump out of bed first, his heart beating fast and his mouth wet with the desire to do good. Daddy always felt little Gary was trying to show him up by making the beds, sweeping up, taking the sour laundry to the wash, but he wasn't; he was just working toward a certain repetition he wanted for the rest of his life: his mother having a look at how he had tidied up (even dusting her alabaster Jesus, and her bust of John F. Kennedy), taking him in her arms, pressing his head into her warm bosom, and then saying those two words of love: "Oh, my!"

Even as a grown-up, so-called, Gary thought: Maybe if women

like my mother are not loved in the world, they can give me more of what they've stored up. Maybe if I make one more bed and some extra cash, they'll put a wedding ring under my pillow. Who's to say that if Gary had been filled with enough *Oh, my!*s as a child, he wouldn't have worked so hard to hear it? But his mother loved him and his father couldn't.

Maybe absence is all we hear. It's the shell we can't pry our ear away from. Gary was human, despite his goodness, and so he fell in love with its lack in others, fell in love with Fran, who, like his father, made him believe what others said about him: that his care was a covert bid for attention, a shitty star turn. Fran made him ashamed of his own nature, and made him feel that all the girls in high school were right for having exclaimed, as he approached: "Here comes the leech!"

Now, at thirty-one years old, he wasn't any different. He was sitting at the kitchen table. It was five o'clock in the morning. He was looking for a clean plate to eat an egg on. He couldn't find one in the pile of filthy dishes Fran had stacked in the kitchen sink. He had no woman to wife him. He saw a roach crawling over the pots filled with Fran's hair chemicals and old macaroni and cheese. In his heart, Gary couldn't believe that that roach wasn't a love bug after all.

Where had the time gone? he wondered. Perhaps, he thought, this wasn't enough for Fran: the sour breath of morning. She didn't even stir when he got out of bed. (He had time to sleep for only three or four hours; just enough time to get the poison of dreams out of his head.) She'd never even made him a lunch, let alone gotten up and fixed him an egg.

There was a certain beauty in that, he reasoned, boiling his own eggs. He toasted some about-to-go-bad bread. Wasn't there a beauty in her bad moods, too? Wasn't that love enough, he thought, seeing love in the bugs feeding on her dirty pots in the way he always wanted to feed on her?

*   *   *

Talk about roaches! Imagine my brother as Kafka. Imagine Richard as Kafka or his roach. Those are the parts he could play. Richard and Franz had the same nose and fears—the Jew and the Negro. At the end of that story, after the roach in fact and at last dies, a bug to martyrdom, the family—the roach's parents, and his sister, Grete—leaves for the countryside. As they travel away from the city, the air grows sweet. Kafka writes:

> It struck both Mr. and Mrs. Samsa, almost at the same moment, as they became aware of their daughter's increasing vivacity, that in spite of all the sorrow of recent times, which had made her cheeks pale, she had bloomed into a pretty young girl with a good figure. They grew quieter and half unconsciously exchanged glances of complete agreement, having come to the conclusion that it would soon be time to find a good husband for her. And it was like a confirmation of their new dreams and excellent intentions that at the end of their journey their daughter sprang to her feet first and stretched her young body.

I could play that sister, if I had a brother who would play Kafka. I could play the horror of her young flesh as it promises to grow old. Her innocence, even in the face of her brother's dead feelers—so stiff and cold—is the real tale. We can survive anything, if we make it up.

Fran shut the door. She took off the trench coat she had thrown over her bra and panties. She threw the coat over the banister. It was a Thursday, around two or four. (This was in 1991, two years before Gary was leaning drunkenly against the drunken fence.) She had just gotten rid of her kid again. He was seven. His birthday had passed days before. September. That month also marked her eighth year of marriage to Gary. This was the longest she had ever been with anyone. She had stayed with Gary largely because he paid for her drugs; now she didn't even care about that.

She had put on her raincoat to go to the door—many afternoons, when she got up, she'd go to the front door half-dressed, looking for someone to take her child away. She'd throw her raincoat on over her bra and panties and wait until a teenager—they were more irresponsible; she liked that; danger lurked wherever they stood—passed by. She'd let the pimply kid see her tits a little bit, like they were the promise of something to come, and then she'd beg the kid to take her little boy up the road for a burger. She'd say there were a few dollars in it for him if he did. She didn't say her tits were his if something happened to her little boy on the way home, but that's what she hoped for.

She couldn't face it again: hitting that bedroom and all that would ensue, crawling back into bed and the chemical migration to some other place. What would be the point in starting all that up again now, when Gary would be home soon? Asking her, again, to crawl out from under Morpheus? He was always bugging her to be a wife. She didn't know how to do that. She stood at the kitchen door. Dull, dull, dull. Dull dirty dishes, dull flies on stiff, dull dirty dishrags. Her failure at domesticity didn't turn her on like it had in the old days, when she began her descent into fucking everything up. That was five years ago now. Then it had been thrilling to watch Gary get mad, or rather, complain, since she thought it would lead to other things—namely her challenging him and not winning. But she could not drive him to bloodlust. So all she was left with was her failure.

What did it matter that she was in a better house, in a better neighborhood? It was like she told Gary when they moved in: "What am I supposed to do here? Twirl around baking cookies? It ain't me, Gary." He didn't listen. She knew that the minute his back was turned, she'd be inviting dope fiends in—her sister and brother, Scoogie—to fuck it up and make it more like the kind of home she had grown up in. After a while, she didn't even care when Gary came home to watch her destruction; her siblings and friends went on in front of him, blowing blow in each other's depressed and giddy direction.

She moved toward the sink. If you can't beat 'em, join 'em, she thought, stretching on a pair of yellow rubber gloves. But the congealed grease and dead hair in the burned once-enamel pot she'd used to rinse the relaxer out of her hair turned her stomach, making everything in her bra feel queasy. And anyway, the gloves were cracked, dry from disuse. They made her hands clammy. But she didn't take them off when she returned to the kitchen table, annoyed that the smell of Gary's customary breakfast—hard-boiled eggs and toast—eaten hours before, was, for her, more awful than all the things she had done to foul up the kitchen put together.

She was an actress, fond of props. They gave meaning to the scene. She sat back down and enjoyed the image she had of herself, dressed only in her bra and panties, hair half-done, wearing a pair of cracked yellow gloves. The gloves were a distinctly domestic touch, and therefore useless, which interested her.

You ask about my brother's fame—what that was "like." It's the same for all of them, the ones who eventually make it. They have the same generator. It's fueled by hysteria and self-interest. Their hysteria is based on a kind of screaming insecurity about whether or not people will take an interest in their self-interest, which the public often interprets as a kind of love, thinking, How could anyone withstand that much self-regard, it must spill out into the world just for me, a sharing of their private self (or selves), how brave!

And how brave, too, that what would be so embarrassing for the rest of us—singing, acting, dancing, telling jokes—would be the thing that would make the performer feel so present and available. Surely that is a gift. And it is. But there's something else that goes along with that (I know this because I can look at it now, not being a star, but being related to one): their self-interest isn't satisfied onstage. All the world's that for them, and every living room and every mother and all of a sister's love are swallowed up and eventually pissed on because you can't love them enough. Stars like my brother don't feel convinced of other people's concern and fidelity until God yells "Cut!"

Like Richard, Gary was fucked from the first because he was a star growing up in a neighborhood that hated him for it. Unlike Richard, he lacked the core of self-interest that would have made his charisma *pay*. What interested Gary about his allure was using it to make other people feel like star attractions, especially women. He encouraged them to overwhelm him with their charisma, but a lot of women—his mother, girls in high school, Fran—were confused by his desire, because they had been raised to be an audience for men. Gary was fucked because it's awful for women to be told they're stars when they've been raised not to believe it.

At first, Fran thought Gary's desire for her to be seen was just what she wanted. In their high school, Gary was one of the few boys who wanted to talk to Fran. Her confusion about his interest interested her for a while, so she pursued it.

When she was fifteen, she would go by the candy store where Gary worked after school, making sandwiches. An elderly Jewish couple owned the place. Some people thought the Jew people, as the colored people called them, were using Gary as a front to make the store feel more Negro friendly, but really everyone knew they only hired Gary so the colored people would feel friendlier toward *them*. Not rip them off so much. That's how bad the neighborhood was getting.

When Fran would go by the store, Gary would be wearing a starchy linen apron tied high above his waist. If it was summertime, as it was now, Fran would be wearing shorts, knee-high tube socks, and Candies, bergamot plastering her bangs to her forehead. For Fran, Gary's interest in her was like trying to learn a foreign language at a late age: frustrating and pointless but maybe there was something to it.

One summer day, near the end of the school year—they were sixteen now—she walked into the store and went up to him and said "Hey." Gary looked up from the hoagie bread he'd been slathering mayonnaise on. He said "Hey" back. Then he put his mind back on his work. Fran looked around at the cans of wieners and beans and saw nothing in them but dust on top of the lids. She was thinking about how to steal something she didn't want. "So how long you got to work here?" she asked, fingering the cellophane packaging wrapped around some pink and white Sno Balls. Gary was over near the store's cookie and candy section.

"Till eight. Then I stay to help them lock up."

"Oh," she said, less than mildly interested. She pulled one of her socks up; the elastic was loose. When she stood up again, she caught Gary looking at her tits or bra straps. That made her think about trying to act modest, because girls should, she'd heard that somewhere, but what did modesty mean when everything was so obvious, like dust on old cans of Chef Boyardee macaroni and such?

"So what you doing after work? I mean, after you lock up?" She scratched the back of her knee, still staring at him. He cut the sandwich in half.

"Homework; I mean, nothing."

"So, you want to hang out a little bit? It's nice out. You know Olivia?"

"That's the girl from your class? The one who beat her teacher up?"

"Yeah," Fran said, not bothering with the hurt in Gary's eyes. She was more interested in ignoring the Jew people who were staring at her, this girl who was taking up Gary's time. Gary wrapped the sandwich in wax paper, then put it in a brown paper bag and carried it to the front of the store, where the Jew people were waiting on a customer. Gary was back before Fran could shake the memory of the mayonnaise sticking to the wax paper. Upon returning, he offered her a little smile. Mayonnaise teeth. "I don't know if we should, Fran," he said. "That was an old lady she hit."

"So?"

"So if we went to her house, wouldn't that be bad? Like agreeing with a bad idea she had once?"

"Bad for who?" Fran asked. "That old white lady was getting on Olivia's nerves. I'm surprised it took her that long to get around to knocking her down. I would have fucked her up more, and before."

Gary bent his head low, started wiping breadcrumbs off the counter. He didn't like that kind of language. Fran was the best kind of actress: one who wouldn't take direction from some director who believed he had a right to her, no matter how nice he thought he was, or could be.

After he agreed to at least walk her over to Olivia's, she pulled on his heart a little more by stealing a package of Ring Dings. She didn't hide them in her shirt or socks. She just crushed them in her left hand, like a purse she kept forgetting to throw away. She didn't even want the cakes. What she wanted she got when she walked out the door with that mess in her hand: the look of incredulity on Gary's employers' faces as she sashayed past them, defying them to stop her for not paying. What Fran didn't see and never would was Gary motioning to his employers that he would take care of it, pay for the damage. And he did.

Opening the door to her house, Olivia—small, busty, doe-eyed—let her smile of greeting curdle noticeably when she saw Gary standing there. "What you bringing him up in here for?" she said. It wasn't a question, but a command. She eyed Gary, who was standing a little behind Fran. Fran didn't say anything at first. In that moment, she felt less like a woman than a wall he couldn't scale. Or write his name on.

"Gary," Fran said, after a while.

"I can see that. Why?"

"'Cause I want him to be here. I didn't want to walk over by myself."

"Why?"

"'Cause I didn't want to walk over here by myself."

"Does this look like a hotel? I can't be having all these people in my house, Fran."

"Shut up, girl. Nobody's trying to make you feel like anything." Fran didn't turn back to see if Gary was following her up the three white steps—an architectural detail germane to Baltimore, but who cared?—where Olivia stood sentry, but he did. Fran pushed past her. Gary followed. Olivia sighed, less annoyed than exasperated, and maybe something more. "I thought it was just going to be us," she said, closing the door after them.

"It *is* just us. Gary's just tagging along. What you got?"

"Enough for us. Nothing extra."

"That'll be fine. Gary, you don't do this shit, do you?"

They were in the living room now. Along one wall was a pink sofa made up in crushed pink velvet. It was covered in plastic. There were two pink chairs on the opposite wall. They were made up in the same fabric as the sofa, but the plastic the chairs were covered in was older, cracked, slightly yellowed.

Gary didn't know what Fran was referring to, but he shook his head no. They sat on the carpeted floor between the sofa and the chairs, in front of the living room table. The furniture looked as if it was reserved for grown-ups, or wakes. Olivia didn't have to tell them that. The table was littered with the signs of Negro respectability: doilies, a tall bowl filled with plastic fruit, a little hymnal. Gary sat across from the two girls. Fran fingered a doily on which a bowl of fruit rested, as if she was trying to recall where she had seen one before, a lace thing that felt as if it had been dipped in wax. For some reason it disturbed her, these artifacts of someone's idea of home.

"How can we spread our shit out with all this bullshit out?" Fran said, in a sudden fit of pique. She swept Olivia's mother—that is, her mother's bowl and hymnal—to one side of the table. The bowl partially obscured Gary's face. But he could see Olivia take a little brown envelope out of her pocket, tap it against the table's edge, and put a line of white powder down on the table. She handed Fran a little cut-in-half straw. All of this they did in silence. Gary watched it all in silence, too: Fran snorting up the mysterious substance in one nostril and then another; rubbing her nose; and just like an actress becoming the substance she imbibed.

She shivered; she laughed; she looked at Gary as if she had never seen him before. She stood up and stretched her arms out wide. For Gary, there was no other woman in the world, except at home. Fran hugged herself, asked Olivia for a little music. But before Olivia had a chance to get up off the floor, or put the straw down, Fran had turned the radio on herself. Optimism. That's what Fran looked like, dancing to the song that said: "Skip to my lou, my darling / I'd love to be the man who shares your nights / My name is Romeo if you'll be my Juliet / Let's pretend I'm the shoe that fits you perfectly."

Fran was dancing alone and not alone; the world, the man singing on the radio, the station's antenna, the airwaves, the sky bouncing with sound no one could see, were with her. It was the first time Gary had ever seen her attached to anything. He had never seen her clutch life before, unless she was stealing something from it that didn't matter to her much, like a cake or a boy.

Fran closed her eyes and extended her arms toward Gary in a way he'd dreamed of seeing one day. Now that day had come. But if he reached for her—reached for *it*, whatever "it" she represented—would every dream be fulfilled? And if they were, what would he be then? A boy without longing? How could he recognize himself otherwise?

There was the question of his body, too. If you prefer looking, and confer stardom on the thing you're looking at, you don't want to look at a different movie, one that features *us* instead of *you*.

"He won't dance 'cause he's a faggot," Olivia said. "Ha ha, didn't I tell you? A faggot or *white*. He *can't* dance." Olivia giggled, and Fran giggled, too, but drily. The weight of their sudden hatred weighed on Gary. He made a move to rise to Olivia's challenge, but the floor pulled him back. Maybe he *was* white. He could be anything. In any case, there was no room on the dance floor. It was filled with female meanness, the thickest substance known to man.

"Go white boy, go white boy, go!" Olivia started chanting in time to the bright beat, the singer's voice on the radio running at a clip underneath her. The singer was asking "Will you be my Juliet? / I want to be the shoe that fits you perfectly." They were dancing around him now. He could smell their girl bodies and drug scent. Fran pushed the table away from Gary; it was anchoring him and she wanted him to float free, too, near where the song was playing, near where she was, in the air. Pushing the table aside, she knocked some of Olivia's mother's fruit to the floor. It didn't bounce. Olivia, bending down to pick it up, said: "Girl, be careful. Banging shit up."

"Leave it."

"But she's going to kill me; it was a gift—"

"I said *leave it*."

Olivia drew her hand back, stood up again, and looked down at Fran, who was squatting in front of Gary, rocking on her heels, legs spread. Fran looked up at Olivia as if to say, "So?" Which was what Olivia looked to Fran for in the first place: a dare. And the threat of punishment—if you do or don't do this, this or that might happen—that gives the dare its spark.

Satisfied, Olivia turned to the radio and started flipping dials. Fran turned back to Gary. She asked him: "What you want to do?" He didn't take it as a dare, but it was. Fran laughed. "Come on, now, you gonna let all of this spoil and go to waste?" There was no music, just static, but she was rocking on her heels as if the static had a beat. That's what drugs made you hear: happiness and static. He thought: I wish I could hear it. Gary closed his eyes.

He was always waiting for love to be what he thought of it: an event informed by niceness, divorced from appeased egos, hatred, and pornography. Love would be his rescue one day, laying him down on a field of daisies, making him and his love lambs of Jesus.

He heard one of the chairs go *crunch*, followed by another of Olivia's giggles. She said, from across the room: "I told you he was a faggot." Opening his eyes, Gary found Fran standing above him. She was slapping her right thigh with her hand. She wasn't as interested in corroborating Olivia's statement as she was in going where the drugs were taking her: to the irritating realization that she didn't know what Gary was, since if there was to be no fucking, his perceived rejection of her preceded Fran's eventual rejection of him—and nearly everyone else. She couldn't face that. She wanted to do another line, but it had to be in front of someone it might make a difference to. Fran walked over to Olivia and said: "Get up." The radio was picking up reception from two stations simultaneously. Fran's voice was hard against some man crooning crossed with a woman's voice out of a commercial.

"What?"

"I said get up."

"Girl, get out of my face."

"I'm not in it. But it's about to get the back of my foot if you don't."

Olivia gave a helpless little cry, struggling for a laugh. "But why— you could sit on the sofa, over there." Fran stared her down. The radio played on; out of it came all the sounds that fall between love and advertising. Olivia got up, reluctantly; as she did so, the plastic made a depressed, *whoosh*-y kind of sound. Fran sat back in the seat, pulling Olivia toward her. Olivia opened her mouth and closed her eyes, like a baby baffled by its own hunger. Fran made her wait a while before she kissed her with her eyes open, looking to see whether or not envy would hurt Gary's heart. But she had miscalculated his optimism; to Gary, she was still the most beautiful woman he had ever seen. He was reveling in his senses being dwarfed by her movie moves, and its soundtrack: the radio playing between two stations, and the ladies slowly lapping tongues.

Fran pulled her mouth away first. She said to Gary: "Now you can leave. But you know I'll be rolling up in that store to take what I need again. Bitch." Gary understood what Fran meant: she was coming back to the Jew place, and for him; he was what she needed. *She was coming back*—one of the sweetest phrases ever. He tried not to smile, all in love, as Olivia shut the door behind him.

Another Kafka. In "Conversation with the Supplicant," the unnamed male narrator attends a church where a woman he loves goes to worship. One gets the sense that the narrator is not particularly religious; the young woman is his religion, inaccessible and therefore deifiable. In the church, the narrator notices, among the other supplicants, a young man who seems to take a particular interest in our narrator's comings and goings. They strike up a conversation. One could take the narrator's interlocutor as his double: the mystical voice to the narrator's all-too-human reason.

> The young man standing opposite me smiled. Then he dropped on his knees and with a dreamy look on his face told me: "There has never been a time in which I have been convinced from within myself that I am alive. You see, I have only such a fugitive awareness of things around me that I always feel they were once real and are now fleeting away. I have a constant longing, my dear sir, to catch a glimpse of things as they may have been before they

show themselves to me. I feel that must have been calm and beautiful…" Since I made no answer and only through involuntary twitchings in my face betrayed my uneasiness, he asked: "Don't you believe that people talk like that?"

I knew I ought to nod assent, but could not do it.

In other words, the narrator cannot agree or rather acknowledge the liminal, least of all in himself—the only "real" there is.

The scariest moment in *Psycho* is not when the people are getting hacked to death, but when Vera Miles, searching for the sister who is lost to her, walks into a bedroom and is taken aback by her own reflection in a floor-length mirror. I sometimes wonder if I am lost to Richard forever. Richard and I didn't see one another much after he became *Richard Pryor* in the seventies, because we couldn't *see* one another. That is, we see each other too clearly, and then past the actual seeing. I wonder what it would be like if I didn't have to wonder what he thought. It can make you lonesome, knowing that you're out there as another person with another name but still *yourself* and yet unavailable to yourself, traversing the trail of the lonesome pines littered with family memories. The way Richard and I are like now is like this, I reckon: being colored and walking into a restaurant full of white people and finding another colored person there. Genetics, politics, I don't know what, makes you seek that black person's eyes out as a way of acknowledging, yes, here we are, for good or ill, kind of together. Maybe I'm looking for a conversation among the supplicants. Invariably, the only other colored person in the restaurant doesn't want to acknowledge your presence, let alone your mind. So they turn away. Being Richard's sister was like that, sometimes. He'd look at me as if I were the only black person in the restaurant. And sometimes I was.

* * *

Gary felt that way all the time—like a supplicant—even without a sister. Skinny and strung out on his love for Fran, and the terrible responsibility he undertook when he decided to honor and obey her, he truly didn't have anyone to talk to. Certainly not his mother. From the beginning, Fran and Mrs. McCullough tolerated one another for Gary's sake, but there was no love lost between those two women he did it all for: the savings, the mortgages, pushing his sickening dick to the side so they wouldn't have to deal with it if they didn't want to. He understood that. They didn't want to hear about his love of other women, being women. And since he was interested in little else, he became conversant with himself—a supplicant who would have understood Kafka's tale of love, even if I don't. "He remarked that I was well dressed and he particularly liked my tie," Kafka writes at the end of his tale. He goes on: "And what fine skin I had. And admissions became most clear and unequivocal when one withdrew them." Maybe that's what Gary felt when he left Olivia's that night, the night of Fran's drug show: by leaving, he'd be able to feel those two girls clearly and unequivocally. Absence makes the heart think about what it's feeling. And since this is a DVD world, where the story-line is not equal to the star—I blame Richard and his kind for all that star-over-the-story stuff—maybe Gary would matter more to you now if Richard played him. I could coach him in the part: Gary, walking home from Olivia's, a supplicant talking to himself, wanting nothing more than to withdraw his feelings from himself so they existed in a world made perfect by his absence from everything.

Richard could play that. Part of his charm, if you want to call it that, was his ability to look defeated by the attention he craved. His persona, onstage, in movies, and elsewhere, was interesting, if you want to call it that, because you could never be quite certain if he wanted you to look at him or if he wanted you to look away. Like Kafka, like Gary, Richard couldn't play a pimp but he could play a pimple. Like Gary, once Richard understood that the women he craved loved to compete with him and one another for the rather dubious prize of head bitch of the Richard Pryor universe, he collapsed inside, became a stranger to himself, since he couldn't imagine he was much of a prize. Add colored to that kind of feeling and maybe you're totally fucked.

And like Richard, Gary thought his mother was above that kind of bitch shit, and so revered her. Neither Gary nor Richard could see it any different, because they couldn't feel any different than how they felt. This was their strength and their tragedy.

Gary found out that his mother was just another woman when he brought Fran home for the first time. He and Fran had been dating for about two years by the time that happened. They were about to graduate from high school, Gary still cutting sandwiches in half. He gave Fran money on the side. Immediately upon asking her home to Sunday dinner, he was apprehensive about it. But he could not say why.

Of course his mother knew Fran by sight and reputation. She knew Fran's entire family and blamed them for the dirt and drugs that were remaking their community. In the early nineteen-eighties, East Baltimore was swelling up in the middle and oozing slime on the sides; it was fat with the drug traffic that had been dumped there because God knows why. When Gary was a child, the white children only came to his neighborhood if their mothers told them to collect Mavis, her runny-nosed kid, and her bag of cleaning supplies. Now the white kids had red-rimmed eyes and runny noses themselves, looking to die a little, too. Rock n' roll, fashion, drugs—white people will follow your colored ass into everything. The McCulloughs tried to keep their white steps white, but fools like Fran's family were all too happy to get sick on those steps, thereby proving how ridiculous the effort to keep them clean was in the first place: what was the point of living in nigger heaven if you kept trying to scrub the clouds?

It was a Sunday in spring, fleecy-clouded. Even though Gary had been going out with Fran for two years and change, he hadn't fucked her yet. Fran didn't care as long as he kept giving her pocket change, and anyway, what was it to her, his old dick, the fact that it made him feel like a stupid interloper in her presence? He was too mother-soft for her anyway. There were plenty of hard motherfuckers around. She wasn't even boy crazy unless the boys were crazy. If she did have to fuck Gary one day, she reasoned, she could get high first. She knew he was dick-soft that first night at Olivia's, but she didn't care. Drugs made her hard enough for the both of them. Maybe all she meant for him to be was a brother.

So while Gary cut sandwiches, she dealt drugs. There was so much money to be made, you had to be stupid not to develop some angles. Fran'd take little schoolkids into someone's hallway and get them high on a variety of glues she'd mixed together and charge them fifty cents a pop. Or she'd buy bennies she got on Gary's straight dime and drop them in her older sister's hand for a dollar. She bought shoes with her money, too, but she didn't wear any of her new shit when Gary dragged her over to his mother's house for her first visit. Nor did she get high. She didn't want that woman—a mother—to know who she really was. In any case, getting high would have been redundant, she thought, once she got a look at his mother's Technicolor Jesus. It was such a trip.

"You like my Jesus?" Mrs. McCullough asked her, by way of an opening gambit. There was a pitcher of lemonade and three tall glasses on the kitchen table, with little rings of liquid sweat underneath them. Fran was standing in front of the stove, facing the kitchen windowsill. Jesus was standing on it. Gary sat across from his mother, not looking anywhere at first, and everywhere, as one does when one looks at a movie.

"He's all right."

Beat.

"I'm glad Gar brought you home for a Sunday, Fran. *After* church is the best time for visiting."

"Huh," Fran said.

"Don't you find it so, Gary?" Mrs. McCullough asked, turning to her son. Gary twisted in his chair, not looking at either woman. There they were, together, because of him; the realization prickled his skin with sweat and made him feel trapped and slightly sick.

"Gary?"

"Yes, Mama?"

"It's nice that you could bring Fran over on a Sunday."

"Yes, Mama."

"Fran, why don't you sit down, honey. You're making me nervous."

"Oh, I'm all right."

Beat.

Mrs. McCullough got up, brushing one of the wet glass rings off the table at the same time. It was something to do, and having done it she couldn't figure out what to do next, so she sat down. The kitchen was small enough without another woman standing up in it.

"Do you go to church, Fran?"

"No." Pause. "Ma'am."

"Oh, your mother—"

Fran cut her off.

"She just never—"

"I see."

"Pardon."

"Your mother."

"She just never mentioned him. Jesus and all. Too many kids, I guess."

"Well, it would be a shame if she knew what she was missing and still didn't do it. He is a comfort. And the church! People just enjoying being together in His name. People like us. Like me and Gary. We go together all the time. Of course, Gary's Daddy never gets to church, because he works so hard *every day*, doing something or another. Like today. He won't be here for supper." She turned to Gary. "He's working."

"Oh."

Gary thought he could say something, just on principle, but if he did, then the attention would be on him instead of the women, his two stars. So he shut up before he had a chance to speak. In this way, he was becoming a man.

"And you've lived here for how long?" Mrs. McCullough asked, knowing the answer. She was staring straight into the side of Fran's head. Fran couldn't stop looking at Jesus. If she wanted Him so much, Mrs. McCullough reasoned, then she might as well go on and take him, since she was in a taking mood.

"I don't know," Fran said. "A long time. Always over on Fayette."

"And how many of you are there?"

"You mean in my family?"

"Yes."

"Five."

"And I bet you're the baby!"

Mrs. McCullough knew as well as anyone that Fran's younger sister, Denise, had been the baby. But she had burned up in a fire. Fran didn't want to talk about that.

"I am now," Fran said. She fingered Jesus' long, shoulder-length plaster-of-paris hair.

"He's got good hair," Fran continued. "Does he always look like this?" she asked, turning to Mrs. McCullough, who said: "He looks like the person you imagine."

"I think he could be black."

"I mean, he should look like love," Mrs. McCullough said sharply.

There it was; there was no taking it back. She didn't equate blackness with love. Coloredness was so trying, why add love to it? And anyway, what did Fran know about praising anything? My son, my Jesus. Mrs. McCullough knew where Fran lived, all right; that's what accounted for her flat, trashy affect. It was due to her family tradition, too, and its legacy of smells. When she closed her eyes for a moment, as she did now, Mrs. McCullough could smell and then see Fran's parents smoking reefers while their children ate boogers, their nappy hair looking like hairy boogers on top of their idiot heads with their slack jaws underneath, dribbling snot from their flat, ashy noses, snot being what they fed on from generation to generation. And besides being nasty, Fran's family was tearing down the McCulloughs' neighborhood. Mrs. McCullough knew they were doing it out of nigger boredom and neglect. If that was the kind of love that Fran came from, what did she know about the Good, which was to say Mrs. McCullough's son Gary, who was, after all, herself?

Mrs. McCullough said: "Well, let me get my plates on the table. You children must be starved."

She got up. As she walked to the corner of the kitchen where the dishes were stacked, standing in neat rows, she rubbed Gary's head. It was a mother's gesture, an acknowledgment of this fact: if she had accomplished anything in this world by way of bettering the species, Gary was it.

Looking on, Fran felt something nasty-tasting well up in her throat. But it was too late to look away and not be sick. Mrs. McCullough called from the corner: "Honey, would you put a fire under those pots?" That first word, like Mrs. McCullough's gesture of ownership moments before, caught Fran off guard, and turned her saliva to tin. She did not know what that kind of female meant by anything. Words and gestures that are inexplicable to us annihilate the self, since we cannot prove we exist in a language we do not understand.

Fran was never one to be overwhelmed or discouraged, though. If being a girl in the presence of a boy-loving mother put her at a disadvantage, she wouldn't show it. Just to contradict everything, she took Mrs. McCullough's "Honey" as her own. She walked over to the stove. She turned the gas on when she was certain she was in Mrs. McCullough's and Gary's line of vision. She could tell, as they set the table, that they were surprised she was standing at the stove; they kind of flinched. But since Fran was a guest and they were colored, they didn't make any remarks about it. Then Fran did this: she pulled a leaf of collard greens out of Mrs. McCullough's big stew pot, ate it, and said, a star fully aware of her audience: "Needs more salt."

That's the worst thing one black bitch can do to another: say your shit needs any kind of seasoning. It's not we *don't* ever do it to one another, but being colored we never talk about it. That would be grandstanding. Mostly, competition and need stay in our hearts, until they kill us. That's just how our bodies work. Look at Richard, a perfect example of Negro genetics: all fucked on MS and living to crack jokes about it. What would Richard say about Fran looking into Mrs. McCullough's pot? He'd pretend he was Fran, and imagine getting all up in Mrs. McCullough's face with: "That your son over there? *Was*, I should say. He's mine now. Come on over here, baby, and say good-bye to Mama." Then, raising his voice, Richard would say: "I said *come over here and say good-bye to your Mama*—bitch. And bitch, say good-bye to your son, otherwise known as your *wuzband*." Richard could get away with stuff like that onstage because we don't say it in life. He was our id. Fran didn't know from a stage, but to her, everyone was an audience. And like any star, she was annoyed when other people didn't perform their parts in a way that complemented her own—or, worse yet, upstaged her. Mrs. McCullough as The Mother. Was that role greater than her own? She wouldn't know how to play that. And Gary letting Mrs. McCullough pat his head like a dog. What kind of performance was that? After leaving The Mother's home, she took Gary back to her own so-called home and made him fuck her.

* * *

They did it, after a fashion, in Fran's dirty room. Cranberry polyester sheets. The TV was on. I say they did it after a fashion, because it didn't feel real to Fran. When she'd been with a girl like Olivia, Fran did her in the boy way. She could even hate her in the boy way. But Gary was too gentle, using his fingers instead of his business when other guys would, you know, just hit it. He wouldn't even have known what she was talking about if she brought all of that up—other guys and such. If she did, maybe he'd go back to his mother. That would be worse than his hands.

Fran was quite the little performer, though, I can tell you. What she projected was a kind of Geraldine Page–like meanness. By the time she got to Gary, she'd been so evil for so long that she'd reduced her parents to sniveling roommates. She'd never quelled her desire to be a child, which is to say an actress, overtaken by a power greater than her own, told when to have the glass of milk and turn the light off: life as a stage direction. But now Gary was showing her what was inside her own body by pushing up against it—fear, which her meanness masked. He was using his mouth now. She could tell because fingers don't breathe. He was offering her what he presumed she wanted: love. Exhaling it all over her wet.

Most showgirls, I can tell you, are interested in the audience member they can't get at, the guy in the third row riffling through his program while you're pouring out your heart. Richard was that way. Even when he played stadiums, he could spot the guy in the fourth tier who wasn't amused, and work on him. Be an audience member that withholds and that tap-dancing bitch will beat the boards forever. Most showgirls, they'd get steamed if you told them they weren't particularly giving out of makeup. That wasn't Fran's fear—that someone like Gary would say she wasn't giving. She didn't mean to be. What she feared that afternoon was that he would make her play a part *he* thought was perfect for her: the supplicant's beloved. Before, boys had handled Fran like a passing moment descended from a larger moment starring them and the first woman they hated: Mother. Their hatred worked on Fran like the guy in the third row works on a performer: as the only lack of attention worth having. No matter how difficult or hard those boys thought she'd been when they were together, she was with them for their lack of attention. And now Gary was giving her nothing but.

He spent more time on her than any boy she'd ever known. That pushed her cowardice to the fore, plus her panic over not knowing how to act in relation to this slurping writer intent on making her play the role he'd written for her. His mother had been too much; now he wasn't even reading a script—*her* script—that she could follow. Her instinct was to drag him out of that dark mess—she could only imagine what he saw down there—but fear gripped her stomach before she could act. Gary pushed harder. So hard, in fact, that she believed she'd relieved herself. She wondered if her meanness, fear, and cowardice—shaped like bullet-shaped turds—were smashed against the cranberry sheets. She would not roll over and take a look. She didn't know how to act. She couldn't do anything, least of all see if she'd shat. In any case, Gary would have scooped her shit up, wrapped it up in Kleenex with a bow, and put it in her purse had he known that's what she was looking for, instead of the happy ending his imagination insisted upon.

I can tell you that despite what was in her mind, she would have won the Hot D'Or Award for her performance that afternoon anyway. Sometimes the camera is less interested in what's in your mind than in how you use your head. Eventually she got used to Gary's probing what she hated, because she could get high while he did it. Eventually the drugs she liked helped her not only bear the tedium and horror of their life together, but cultivate it. Billie Holiday once said that she knew she didn't want to be on junk anymore when she couldn't bear to watch TV. The flat sameness of it, you know. That's what Fran introduced into her marriage to Gary, almost from the first. An affectlessness—when she wasn't being evil—that was meant to squash Gary's Walt Disney approach to marriage. Are we happy? I don't care. Isn't our newborn baby a champ? I don't know. Isn't it amazing we got out of the old neighborhood and into this new house? Let's call it love. I don't care.

I have here the short article you wrote about Fran and the woman who eventually played her, in 2000. Now why can't I have that? I was up for the same part. So what if Miss Alexander is younger than me by some twenty years? I feel a certain resentment about the Diana Sands comparison you make, saying Miss Alexander reminds you of Cancer Bitch. I felt Fran when I read the book. So much so that I could make her backstory up. All I get is being a sister to celebrity. What am I supposed to do with that? Write children's books about Kwanzaa and hope my brother dictates a five-hundred-word introduction that would sell it? Write a memoir that betrays family secrets? Or produce a documentary with, let's say, Prince's sister, about star brothers who overwhelm their equally gifted, barely lauded siblings? That's what you want to hear. I am an actress. Maybe I could have done something different in this life, different than talking dirty to get you to be interested in me. I couldn't have worked harder on Fran. Everything I've told you about Fran—it wasn't even in the movie or the book. I know her so well, I could make her up and it would still be nonfiction.

An out-of-work actress is a terrible thing to see. They're always acting bright, ready, and available, because they're trying to seduce men—writers, directors, and so on—who can claim them and put their bodies and imaginations to work. Longing to be claimed, an out-of-work actress is always trying not to show her true desperation. They act more "girlish" than they would ordinarily, just to get some dick interested. That kind of girlishness always comes out as brittle tasting. You can smell their fear: about getting old, tits falling, work drying up. If you're not working, you can take classes, think about plastic surgery, do stuff that makes you think you're doing something. But what if you're an actress with no kind of access to show business? Auditions and the like? Take it from me.

An actress is a liar. An actress's soul is whatever you're paying her to shape it as at the time. Why do men fall for it? I can spot an actress a mile away—and then avoid her. I don't suppose it's because men like you find some general truth about women under the tits and feathers, is it? Look at all those men around Mary Tyrone—her two sons and husband—drinking themselves to death, waiting for her to be different, waiting for her to become less of a junkie and more of a mother. Why did they do that? Why did Gary? Can't Mary's sons and husband see that actress, junkie, mother—it's all the same? That all those roles are fueled by self-regard and self-pity? What kind of hope do men find underneath all that acting? Are you hoping that one day she'll stop acting and love you as herself forever? You might as well give that idea up. A mother doesn't give that part up until God yells "Cut!" Neither does a junkie. Neither does an actress. The hope you all have that women will act differently—somewhere, somehow—is just that: your hope. Actresses are themselves, if only they had one. Women are themselves, if only they could stop acting.

PHANTOMS

by STEVEN MILLHAUSER

THE PHENOMENON

THE PHANTOMS OF our town do not, as some think, appear only in the dark. Often we come upon them in full sunlight, when shadows lie sharp on the lawns and streets. The encounters take place for very short periods, ranging from two or three seconds to perhaps half a minute, though longer episodes are sometimes reported. So many of us have seen them that it's uncommon to meet someone who has not; of this minority, only a small number deny that phantoms exist. Sometimes an encounter occurs more than once in the course of a single day; sometimes six months pass, or a year. The phantoms, which some call Presences, are not easy to distinguish from ordinary citizens: they are not translucent, or smoke-like, or hazy, they do not ripple like heat waves, nor are they in any way unusual in figure or dress. Indeed they are so much like us that it sometimes happens we mistake them for someone we know. Such errors are rare, and never last for more than a moment. They themselves appear to be uneasy during an encounter and swiftly withdraw. They always look at us before turning away. They never speak. They are wary, elusive, secretive, haughty, unfriendly, remote.

EXPLANATION #1

One explanation has it that our phantoms are the auras, or visible traces, of earlier inhabitants of our town, which was settled in 1636. Our atmosphere, saturated with the energy of all those who have preceded us, preserves them and permits them, under certain conditions, to become visible to us. This explanation, often fitted out with a pseudo-scientific vocabulary, strikes most of us as unconvincing. The phantoms always appear in contemporary dress, they never behave in ways that suggest earlier eras, and there is no evidence whatever to support the claim that the dead leave visible traces in the air.

HISTORY

As children we are told about the phantoms by our fathers and mothers. They in turn have been told by their own fathers and mothers, who can remember being told by their parents—our great-grandparents—when they were children. Thus the phantoms of our town are not new; they don't represent a sudden eruption into our lives, a recent change in our sense of things. We have no formal records that confirm the presence of phantoms throughout the diverse periods of our history, no scientific reports or transcripts of legal proceedings, but some of us are familiar with the second-floor Archive Room of our library, where in nineteenth-century diaries we find occasional references to "the others" or "them," without further details. Church records of the seventeenth century include several mentions of "the devil's children," which some view as evidence for the lineage of our phantoms; others argue that the phrase is so general that it cannot be cited as proof of anything. The official town history, published in 1936 on the three-hundredth anniversary of our incorporation, revised in 1986, and updated in 2006, makes no mention of the phantoms. An editorial note states that "the authors have confined themselves to ascertainable fact."

HOW WE KNOW

We know by a ripple along the skin of our forearms, accompanied by a tension of the inner body. We know because they look at us and withdraw immediately. We know because when we try to follow them, we find that they have vanished. We know because we know.

CASE STUDY #1

Richard Moore rises from beside the bed, where he has just finished the forty-second installment of a never-ending story that he tells each night to his four-year-old daughter, bends over her for a goodnight kiss, and walks quietly from the room. He loves having a daughter; he loves having a wife, a family; though he married late, at thirty-nine, he knows he wasn't ready when he was younger, not in his doped-up twenties, not in his stupid, wasted thirties, when he was still acting like some angry teenager who hated the grown-ups; and now he's grateful for it all, like someone who can hardly believe that he's allowed to live in his own house. He walks along the hall to the den, where his wife is sitting at one end of the couch, reading a book in the light of the table lamp, while the TV is on mute during an ad for vinyl siding. He loves that she won't watch the ads, that she refuses to waste those minutes, that she reads books, that she's sitting there waiting for him, that the light from the TV is flickering on her hand and upper arm. Something has begun to bother him, though he isn't sure what it is, but as he steps into the den he's got it, he's got it: the table in the side yard, the two folding chairs, the sunglasses on the tabletop. He was sitting out there with her after dinner, and he left his sunglasses. "Back in a sec," he says, and turns away, enters the kitchen, opens the door to the small screened porch at the back of the house, and walks from the porch down the steps to the backyard, a narrow strip between the house and the cedar fence. It's nine-thirty on a summer night. The sky is dark blue, the fence lit by the light from the kitchen window, the grass black here and green over there. He turns the corner of the house and comes to the private place. It's the part of the yard bounded by the fence, the side-yard hedge, and the row of three Scotch pines, where he's set up two folding chairs and a white ironwork table with a glass top. On the table lie the sunglasses. The sight pleases him: the two chairs, turned a little toward each other, the forgotten glasses, the enclosed place set off from the rest of the world. He steps over to the table and picks up the glasses: a good pair, expensive lenses, nothing flashy, stylish in a quiet way. As he lifts them from the table he senses something in the skin of his arms and sees a figure standing beside the third Scotch pine. It's darker here than at the back of the house, and he can't see her all that well: a tall, erect woman, fortyish, long face, dark dress. Her expression, which he can barely make out, seems stern. She looks at him for a moment and turns away— not hastily, as if she were frightened, but decisively, like someone who wants to be alone. Behind the Scotch pine she's no longer visible. He hesitates, steps over to the tree, sees nothing. His first impulse is to scream at her, to tell her that he'll kill her if she comes near his daughter. Immediately he forces himself to calm down. Everything will be all right. There's no danger. He's seen them before. Even so, he returns quickly to the house, locks the porch door behind him, locks the kitchen door behind him, fastens the chain, and strides to the den, where on the TV a man in a dinner jacket is staring across the room at a woman with pulled-back hair who is seated at a piano. His wife is watching. As he steps toward her, he notices a pair of sunglasses in his hand.

THE LOOK

Most of us are familiar with the look they cast in our direction before they withdraw. The look has been variously described as proud, hostile, suspicious, mocking, disdainful, uncertain; never is it seen as welcoming. Some witnesses say that the phantoms show slight movements in our direction, before the decisive turning away. Others, disputing such claims, argue that we cannot bear to imagine their rejection of us and misread their movements in a way flattering to our self-esteem.

HIGHLY QUESTIONABLE

Now and then we hear reports of a more questionable kind. The phantoms, we are told, have grayish wings folded along their backs; the phantoms have swirling smoke for eyes; at the ends of their feet, claws curl against the grass. Such descriptions, though rare, are persistent, perhaps inevitable, and impossible to refute. They strike most of us as childish and irresponsible, the results of careless observation, hasty inference, and heightened imagination corrupted by conventional images drawn from movies and television. Whenever we hear such descriptions, we're quick to question them and to make the case for the accumulated evidence of trustworthy witnesses. A paradoxical effect of our vigilance is that the phantoms, rescued from the fantastic, for a moment seem to us normal, commonplace, as familiar as squirrels or dandelions.

CASE STUDY #2

Years ago, as a child of eight or nine, Karen Carsten experienced a single encounter. Her memory of the moment is both vivid and vague: she can't recall how many of them there were, or exactly what they looked like, but she recalls the precise moment in which she came upon them, one summer afternoon, as she stepped around to the back of the garage in search of a soccer ball and saw them sitting quietly in the grass. She still remembers her feeling of wonder as they turned to look at her, before they rose and went away. Now, at age fifty-six, Karen Carsten lives alone with her cat in a house filled with framed photographs of her parents, her nieces, and her late husband, who died in a car accident seventeen years ago. Karen is a high school librarian with many set routines: the TV programs, the weekend housecleaning, the twice-yearly visits in August and December to her sister's family in Youngstown, Ohio, the choir on Sunday, dinner every two weeks at the same restaurant with a friend who never calls to ask how she is. One Saturday afternoon she finishes organizing the linen closet on the second floor and starts up the attic stairs. She plans to sort through boxes of old clothes, some of which she'll give to Goodwill and some of which she'll save for her nieces, who will think of the collared blouses and floral-print dresses as hopelessly old-fashioned but who might come around to appreciating them someday, maybe. As she reaches the top of the stairs she stops so suddenly and completely that she has the sense of her own body as an object standing in her path. Ten feet away, two children are seated on the old couch near the dollhouse. A third child is sitting in the armchair with the loose leg. In the brownish light of the attic, with its one small window, she can see them clearly: two barefoot girls of about ten, in jeans and T-shirts, and a boy, slightly older, maybe twelve, blond-haired, in a dress shirt and khakis, who sits low in the chair with his neck bent up against the back. The three turn to look at her and at once rise and walk into the darker part of the attic, where they are no longer visible. Karen stands motionless at the top of the stairs, her hand clutching the rail. Her lips are dry, and she is filled with an excitement so intense that she thinks she might burst into tears. She does not follow the children into the shadows, partly because she doesn't want to upset them, and partly because she knows they are no longer there. She turns back down the stairs. In the living room she sits in the armchair until nightfall. Joy fills her heart. She can feel it shining from her face. That night she returns to the attic, straightens the pillows on the couch, smooths out the doilies on the chair arms, brings over a small wicker table, sets out three saucers and three teacups. She moves away some bulging boxes that sit beside the couch, carries off an old typewriter, sweeps the floor. Downstairs in the living room she turns on the TV, but she keeps the volume low; she's listening for sounds in the attic, even though she knows that her visitors don't make sounds. She imagines them up there, sitting silently together, enjoying the table, the teacups, the orderly surroundings. Now each day she climbs the stairs to the attic, where she sees the empty couch, the empty chair, the wicker table with the three teacups. Despite the pang of disappointment, she is happy. She is happy because she knows they come to visit her every day, she knows they like to be up there, sitting in the old furniture, around the wicker table; she knows; she knows.

EXPLANATION #2

One explanation is that the phantoms *are not there*, that those of us who see them are experiencing delusions or hallucinations brought about by beliefs instilled in us as young children. A small movement, an unexpected sound, is immediately converted into a visual presence that exists only in the mind of the perceiver. The flaws in this explanation are threefold. First, it assumes that the population of an entire town will interpret ambiguous signs in precisely the same way. Second, it ignores the fact that most of us, as we grow to adulthood, discard the stories and false beliefs of childhood but continue to see the phantoms. Third, it fails to account for innumerable instances in which multiple witnesses have seen the same phantom. Even if we were to agree that these objections are not decisive and that our phantoms are in fact not there, the explanation would tell us only that we are mad, without revealing the meaning of our madness.

OUR CHILDREN

What shall we say to our children? If, like most parents in our town, we decide to tell them at an early age about the phantoms, we worry that we have filled their nights with terror or perhaps have created in them a hope, a longing, for an encounter that might never take place. Those of us who conceal the existence of phantoms are no less worried, for we fear either that our children will be informed unreliably by other children or that they will be dangerously unprepared for an encounter should one occur. Even those of us who have prepared our children are worried about the first encounter, which sometimes disturbs a child in ways that some of us remember only too well. Although we assure our children that there's nothing to fear from the phantoms, who wish only to be left alone, we ourselves are fearful: we wonder whether the phantoms are as harmless as we say they are, we wonder whether they behave differently in the presence of an unaccompanied child, we wonder whether, under certain circumstances, they might become bolder than we know. Some say that a phantom, encountering an adult and a child, will look only at the child, will let its gaze linger in a way that never happens with an adult. When we put our children to sleep, leaning close to them and answering their questions about phantoms in gentle, soothing tones, until their eyes close in peace, we understand that we have been preparing in ourselves an anxiety that will grow stronger and more aggressive as the night advances.

CROSSING OVER

The question of "crossing over" refuses to disappear, despite a history of testimony that many of us feel ought to put it to rest. By "crossing over" is meant, in general, any form of intermingling between us and them; specifically, it refers to supposed instances in which one of them, or one of us, leaves the native community and joins the other. Now, not only is there no evidence of any such regrouping, of any such transference of loyalty, but the overwhelming testimony of witnesses shows that no phantom has ever remained for more than a few moments in the presence of an outsider or given any sign whatever of greeting or encouragement. Claims to the contrary have always been suspect: the insistence of an alcoholic husband that he saw his wife in bed with *one of them*, the assertion of a teenager suspended from high school that a group of phantoms had threatened to harm him if he failed to obey their commands. Apart from statements that purport to be factual, fantasies of crossing over persist in the form of phantom-tales that flourish among our children and are half-believed by naïve adults. It is not difficult to make the case that stories of this kind reveal a secret desire for contact, though no reliable record of contact exists. Those of us who try to maintain a strict objectivity in such matters are forced to admit that a crossing of the line is not impossible, however unlikely, so that even as we challenge dubious claims and smile at fairy tales we find ourselves imagining the sudden encounter at night, the heads turning toward us, the moment of hesitation, the arms rising gravely in welcome.

CASE STUDY #3

James Levin, twenty-six years old, has reached an impasse in his life. After college he took a year off, holding odd jobs and traveling all over the country before returning home to apply to grad school. He completed his coursework in two years, during which he taught one introductory section of American History, and then surprised everyone by taking a leave of absence in order to read for his dissertation (*The Influence of Popular Culture on High Culture in Post–Civil War America, 1865–1900*) and think more carefully about the direction of his life. He lives with his parents in his old room, dense with memories of grade school and high school. He worries that he's losing interest in his dissertation; he feels he should rethink his life, maybe go the med-school route and do something useful in the world instead of wasting his time wallowing in abstract speculations of no value to anyone; he speaks less and less to his girlfriend, a law student at the University of Michigan, nearly a thousand miles away. Where, he wonders, has he taken a wrong turn? What should he do with his life? What is the meaning of it all? These, he believes, are questions eminently suitable for an intelligent adolescent of sixteen, questions that he himself discussed passionately ten years ago with friends who are now married and paying mortgages. Because he's stalled in his life, because he is eaten up with guilt, and because he is unhappy, he has taken to getting up late and going for long walks all over town, first in the afternoon and again at night. One of his daytime walks leads to the picnic grounds of his childhood. Pine trees and scattered tables stand by the stream where he used to sail a little wooden tugboat—he's always bumping into his past like that—and across the stream is where he sees her, one afternoon in late September. She's standing alone, between two oak trees, looking down at the water. The sun shines on the lower part of her body, but her face and neck are in shadow. She becomes aware of him almost immediately, raises her eyes, and withdraws into the shade, where he can no longer see her. He has shattered her solitude. Each instant of the encounter enters him so sharply that his memory of her breaks into three parts, like a medieval triptych in a museum: the moment of awareness, the look, the turning away. In the first panel of the triptych, her shoulders are tense, her whole body unnaturally still, like someone who has heard a sound in the dark. Second panel: her eyes are raised and staring directly at him. It can't have lasted for more than a second. What stays with him is something severe in that look, as if he's disturbed her in a way that requires forgiveness. Third panel: the body is half turned away, not timidly but with a kind of dignity of withdrawal, which seems to rebuke him for an intrusion. James feels a sharp desire to cross the stream and find her, but two thoughts hold him back: his fear that the crossing will be unwelcome to her, and his knowledge that she has disappeared. He returns home but continues to see her standing by the stream. He has the sense that she's becoming more vivid in her absence, as if she's gaining life within him. The unnatural stillness, the dark look, the turning away—he feels he owes her an immense apology. He understands that the desire to apologize is only a mask for his desire to see her again. After two days of futile brooding he returns to the stream, to the exact place where he stood when he saw her the first time; four hours later he returns home, discouraged, restless, and irritable. He understands that something has happened to him, something that is probably harmful. He doesn't care. He returns to the stream day after day, without hope, without pleasure. What's he doing there, in that desolate place? He's twenty-six, but already he's an old man. The leaves have begun to turn; the air is growing cold. One day, on his way back from the stream, James takes a different way home. He passes his old high school, with its double row of tall windows, and comes to the hill where he used to go sledding. He needs to get away from this town, where his childhood and adolescence spring up to meet him at every turn; he ought to go somewhere, do something; his long, purposeless walks seem to him the outward expression of an inner confusion. He climbs the hill, passing through the bare oaks and beeches and the dark firs, and at the top looks down at the stand of pine at the back of Cullen's Auto Body. He walks down the slope, feeling the steering bar in his hands, the red runners biting into the snow, and when he comes to the pines he sees her sitting on the trunk of a fallen tree. She turns her head to look at him, rises, and walks out of sight. This time he doesn't hesitate. He runs into the thicket, beyond which he can see the whitewashed back of the body shop, a brilliant blue front fender lying up against a tire, and, farther away, a pickup truck driving along the street; pale sunlight slants through the pine branches. He searches for her but finds only a tangle of

ferns, a beer can, the top of a pint of ice cream. At home he throws himself down on his boyhood bed, where he used to spend long afternoons
reading stories about boys who grew up to become famous scientists
and explorers. He summons her stare. The sternness devastates him,
but draws him, too, since he feels it as a strength he himself lacks. He
understands that he's in a bad way; that he's got to stop thinking about
her; that he'll never stop thinking about her; that nothing can ever
come of it; that his life will be harmed; that harm is attractive to him;
that he'll never return to school; that he will disappoint his parents and
lose his girlfriend; that none of this matters to him; that what matters is
the hope of seeing once more the phantom lady who will look harshly at
him and turn away; that he is weak, foolish, frivolous; that such words
have no meaning for him; that he has entered a world of dark love, from
which there is no way out.

MISSING CHILDREN

Once in a long while, a child goes missing. It happens in other towns,
it happens in yours: the missing child who is discovered six hours later
lost in the woods, the missing child who never returns, who disappears
forever, perhaps in the company of a stranger in a baseball cap who
was last seen parked in a van across from the elementary school. In our
town there are always those who blame the phantoms. They steal our
children, it is said, in order to bring them into the fold; they're always
waiting for the right moment, when we have been careless, when our
attention has relaxed. Those of us who defend the phantoms point out
patiently that they always withdraw from us, that there is no evidence
they can make physical contact with the things of our world, that no
human child has ever been seen in their company. Such arguments
never persuade an accuser. Even when the missing child is discovered
in the woods, where he has wandered after a squirrel, even when the

missing child is found buried in the yard of a troubled loner in a town two hundred miles away, the suspicion remains that the phantoms have had something to do with it. We who defend our phantoms against false accusations and wild inventions are forced to admit that we do not know what they may be thinking, alone among themselves, or in the moment when they turn to look at us, before moving away.

DISRUPTION

Sometimes a disruption comes: the phantom in the supermarket, the phantom in the bedroom. Then our sense of the behavior of phantoms suffers a shock: we cannot understand why creatures who withdraw from us should appear in places where encounters are unavoidable. Have we misunderstood something about our phantoms? It's true enough that when we encounter them in the aisle of a supermarket or clothing store, when we find them sitting on the edge of our beds or lying against a bed-pillow, they behave as they always do: they look at us and quickly withdraw. Even so, we feel that they have come too close, that they want something from us that we cannot understand, and only when we encounter them in a less-frequented place, at the back of the shut-down railroad station or on the far side of a field, do we relax a little.

EXPLANATION #3

One explanation asserts that we and the phantoms were once a single race, which at some point in the remote history of our town divided into two societies. According to a psychological offshoot of this explanation, the phantoms are the unwanted or unacknowledged portions of ourselves, which we try to evade but continually encounter; they make us uneasy because we know them; they are ourselves.

FEAR

Many of us, at one time or another, have felt the fear. For say you are coming home with your wife from an evening with friends. The porch light is on, the living room windows are dimly glowing before the closed blinds. As you walk across the front lawn from the driveway to the porch steps, you become aware of something, over there by the wild cherry tree. Then you half-see one of them, for an instant, withdrawing behind the dark branches, which catch only a little of the light from the porch. That is when the fear comes. You can feel it deep within you, like an infection that's about to spread. You can feel it in your wife's hand tightening on your arm. It's at that moment you turn to her and say, with a shrug of one shoulder and a little laugh that fools no one: "Oh, it's just one of them!"

PHOTOGRAPHIC EVIDENCE

Evidence from digital cameras, camcorders, iPhones, and old-fashioned film cameras divides into two categories: the fraudulent and the dubious. Fraudulent evidence always reveals signs of tampering. Methods of digital-imaging manipulation permit a wide range of effects, from computer-generated figures to digital clones; sometimes a slight blur is sought, to suggest the uncanny. Often the artist goes too far, and creates a hackneyed monster-phantom inspired by third-rate movies; more clever manipulators stay closer to the ordinary, but tend to give themselves away by an exaggeration of some feature, usually the ears or nose. In such matters, the temptation of the grotesque appears to be irresistible. Celluloid fraud assumes well-known forms that reach back to the era of fairy photographs: double exposures, chemical tampering with negatives, the insertion of gauze between the printing paper and the enlarger lens. The category of the dubious is harder to disprove. Here we find vague, shadowy shapes, wavering lines resembling ripples of heated air above a radiator, half-hidden forms concealed by branches or by windows filled with reflections. Most of these images can be explained as natural effects of light that have deceived the credulous person recording them. For those who crave visual proof of phantoms, evidence that a photograph is fraudulent or dubious is never entirely convincing.

CASE STUDY #4

One afternoon in late spring, Evelyn Wells, nine years old, is playing alone in her backyard. It's a sunny day; school is out, dinner's a long way off, and the warm afternoon has the feel of summer. Her best friend is sick with a sore throat and fever, but that's all right: Evvy likes to play alone in her yard, especially on a sunny day like this one, with time stretching out on all sides of her. What she's been practicing lately is roof-ball, a game she learned from a boy down the block. Her yard is bounded by the neighbor's garage and by thick spruces running along the back and side; the lowest spruce branches bend down to the grass and form a kind of wall. The idea is to throw the tennis ball, which is the color of lime Kool-Aid, onto the slanted garage roof and catch it when it comes down. If Evvy throws too hard, the ball will go over the roof and land in the yard next door, possibly in the vegetable garden surrounded by chicken wire. If she doesn't throw hard enough, it will come right back to her, with no speed. The thing to do is make the ball go almost to the top, so that it comes down faster and faster; then she's got to catch it before it hits the ground, though a one-bouncer isn't terrible. Evvy is pretty good at roof-ball—she can make the ball go way up the slope, and she can figure out where she needs to stand as it comes rushing or bouncing down. Her record is eight catches in a row, but now she's caught nine and is hoping for ten. The ball stops near the peak of the roof and begins coming down at a wide angle; she moves more and more to the right as it bounces lightly along and leaps into the air. This time she's made a mistake—the ball goes over her head. It rolls across the lawn toward the back and disappears under the low-hanging spruce branches not far from the garage. Evvy sometimes likes to play under there, where it's cool and dim. She pushes aside a branch and looks for the ball, which she sees beside a root. At the same time she sees two figures, a man and a woman, standing under the tree. They stare down at her, then turn their faces away and step out of sight. Evvy feels a ripple in her arms. Their eyes were like shadows on a lawn. She backs out into the sun. The yard does not comfort her. The blades of grass seem to be holding their breath. The white wooden shingles on the side of the garage are staring at her. Evvy walks across the strange lawn and up the back steps into the kitchen. Inside, it is very still. A faucet handle blazes with light. She hears her mother in the living room. Evvy does not want to speak to her mother. She does not want to speak to anyone. Upstairs, in her room, she draws the blinds and gets into bed. The windows are above the backyard and look down on the rows of spruce trees. At dinner she is silent. "Cat got your tongue?" her father says. His teeth are laughing. Her mother gives her a wrinkled look. At night she lies with her eyes open. She sees the man and woman standing under the tree, staring down at her. They turn their faces away. The next day, Saturday, Evvy refuses to go outside. Her mother brings orange juice, feels her forehead, takes her temperature. Outside, her father is mowing the lawn. That night she doesn't sleep. They are standing under the tree, looking at her with their shadow-eyes. She can't see their faces. She doesn't remember their clothes. On Sunday she stays in her room. Sounds startle her: a clank in the yard, a shout. At night she watches with closed eyes: the ball rolling under the branches, the two figures standing there, looking down at her. On Monday her mother takes her to the doctor. He presses the silver circle against her chest. The next day she returns to school, but after the last bell she comes straight home and goes to her room. Through the slats of the blinds she can see the garage, the roof, the dark green spruce branches bending to the grass. One afternoon Evvy is sitting at the piano in the living room. She's practicing her scales. The bell rings and her mother goes to the door. When Evvy turns to look, she sees a woman and a man. She leaves the piano and goes upstairs to her room. She sits on the throw rug next to her bed and stares at the door. After a while she hears her mother's footsteps on the stairs. Evvy stands up and goes into the closet. She crawls next to a box filled with old dolls and bears and elephants. She can hear her mother's footsteps in the room. Her mother is knocking on the closet door. "Please come out of there, Evvy. I know you're in there." She does not come out.

CAPTORS

Despite widespread disapproval, now and then an attempt is made to capture a phantom. The desire arises most often among groups of idle teenagers, especially during the warm nights of summer, but is also known among adults, usually but not invariably male, who feel menaced by the phantoms or who cannot tolerate the unknown. Traps are set, pits dug, cages built, all to no avail. The nonphysical nature of phantoms does not seem to discourage such efforts, which sometimes display great ingenuity. Walter Hendricks, a mechanical engineer, lived for many years in a neighborhood of split-level ranch houses with backyard swing sets and barbecues; one day he began to transform his yard into a dense thicket of pine trees, in order to invite the visits of phantoms. Each tree was equipped with a mechanism that was able to release from the branches a series of closely woven steel-mesh nets, which dropped swiftly when anything passed below. In another part of town, Charles Reese rented an excavator and dug a basement-size cavity in his yard. He covered the pit, which became known as the Dungeon, with a sliding steel ceiling concealed by a layer of sod. One night, when a phantom appeared on his lawn, Reese pressed a switch that caused the false lawn to slide away; when he climbed down into the Dungeon with a high-beam flashlight, he discovered a frightened chipmunk. Others have used chemical sprays that cause temporary paralysis, empty sheds with sliding doors that automatically shut when a motion sensor is triggered, even a machine that produces flashes of lightning. People who dream of becoming captors fail to understand that the phantoms cannot be caught; to capture them would be to banish them from their own nature, to turn them into us.

EXPLANATION #4

One explanation is that the phantoms have always been here, long before the arrival of the Indians. We ourselves are the intruders. We seized their land, drove them into hiding, and have been careful ever since to maintain our advantage and force them into postures of submission. This explanation accounts for the hostility that many of us detect in the phantoms, as well as the fear they sometimes inspire in us. Its weakness, which some dismiss as negligible, is the absence of any evidence in support of it.

THE PHANTOM LORRAINE

As children we all hear the tale of the Phantom Lorraine, told to us by an aunt, or a babysitter, or someone on the playground, or perhaps by a careless parent desperate for a bedtime story. Lorraine is a phantom child. One day she comes to a tall hedge at the back of a yard where a boy and girl are playing. The children are running through a sprinkler, or throwing a ball, or practicing with a hula hoop. Nearby, their mother is kneeling on a cushion before a row of hollyhock bushes, digging up weeds. The Phantom Lorraine is moved by this picture, in a way she doesn't understand. Day after day she returns to the hedge, to watch the children playing. One day, when the children are alone, she steps shyly out of her hiding place. The children invite her to join them. Even though she is different, even though she can't pick things up or hold them, the children invent running games that all three can play. Now every day the Phantom Lorraine joins them in the backyard, where she is happy. One afternoon the children invite her into their house. She looks with wonder at the sunny kitchen, at the carpeted stairway leading to the second floor, at the children's room with the two windows looking out over the backyard. The mother and father are kind to the Phantom Lorraine. One day they invite her to a sleepover. The little phantom girl spends more and more time with the human family, who love her as their own. At last the parents adopt her. They all live happily ever after.

ANALYSIS

As adults we look more skeptically at this tale, which once gave us so much pleasure. We understand that its purpose is to overcome a child's fear of the phantoms, by showing that what the phantoms really desire is to become one of us. This of course is wildly inaccurate, since the actual phantoms betray no signs of curiosity and rigorously withdraw from contact of any kind. But the tale seems to many of us to hold a deeper meaning. The story, we believe, reveals our own desire: to know the phantoms, to strip them of mystery. Fearful of their difference, unable to bear their otherness, we imagine, in the person of the Phantom Lorraine, their secret sameness. Some go further. The tale of the Phantom Lorraine, they say, is a thinly disguised story about our hatred of the phantoms, our wish to bring about their destruction. By joining a family, the Phantom Lorraine in effect ceases to be a phantom; she casts off her nature and is reborn as a human child. In this way, the story expresses our longing to annihilate the phantoms, to devour them, to turn them into us. Beneath its sentimental exterior, the tale of the Phantom Lorraine is a dream-tale of invasion and murder.

OTHER TOWNS

When we visit other towns, which have no phantoms, often we feel that a burden has lifted. Some of us make plans to move to such a town, a place that reminds us of tall picture books from childhood. There, you can walk at peace along the streets and in the public parks, without having to wonder whether a ripple will course through the skin of your forearms. We think of our children playing happily in green backyards, where sunflowers and honeysuckle bloom against white fences. But soon a restlessness comes. A town without phantoms seems to us a town without history, a town without shadows. The yards are empty, the streets stretch bleakly away. Back in our town, we wait impatiently for the ripple in our arms; we fear that our phantoms may no longer be there. When, sometimes after many weeks, we encounter one of them at last, in a corner of the yard or at the side of the car wash, where a look is flung at us before the phantom turns away, we think: Now things are as they should be, now we can rest awhile. It's a feeling almost like gratitude.

EXPLANATION #5

Some argue that all towns have phantoms, but that only we are able to see them. This way of thinking is especially attractive to those who cannot understand why our town should have phantoms and other towns none; why our town, in short, should be an exception. An objection to this explanation is that it accomplishes nothing but a shift of attention from the town itself to the people of our town: it's our ability to perceive phantoms that is now the riddle, instead of the phantoms themselves. A second objection, which some find decisive, is that the explanation relies entirely on an assumed world of invisible beings, whose existence can be neither proved nor disproved.

CASE STUDY #5

Every afternoon after lunch, before I return to work in the upstairs study, I like to take a stroll along the familiar sidewalks of my neighborhood. Thoughts rise up in me, take odd turns, vanish like bits of smoke. At the same time I'm wide open to striking impressions—that ladder leaning against the side of a house, with its shadow hard and clean against the white shingles, which project a little, so that the shingle-bottoms break the straight shadow-lines into slight zigzags; that brilliant red umbrella lying at an angle in the recycling container on a front porch next to the door; that jogger with shaved head, black nylon shorts, and an orange sweatshirt that reads, in three lines of black capital letters: EAT WELL / KEEP FIT / DIE ANYWAY. A single blade of grass sticks up from a crack in a driveway. I come to a sprawling old house at the corner, not far from the sidewalk. Its dark red paint could use a little touching up. Under the high front porch, on both sides of the steps, are those crisscross lattice panels, painted white. Through the diamond-shaped openings come pricker branches and the tips of ferns. From the sidewalk I can see the handle of an old hand mower, back there among the dark weeds. I can see something else: a slight movement. I step up to the porch, bend to peer through the lattice: I see three of them, seated on the ground. They turn their heads toward me and look away, begin to rise. In an instant they're gone. My arms are rippling as I return to the sidewalk and continue on my way. They interest me, these creatures who are always vanishing. This time I was able to glimpse a man of about fifty and two younger women. One woman wore her hair up; the other had a sprig of small blue wildflowers in her hair. The man had a long straight nose and a long mouth. They rose slowly but without hesitation and stepped back into the dark. Even as a child I accepted phantoms as part of things, like spiders and rainbows. I saw them in the vacant lot on the other side of the backyard hedge, or behind garages and toolsheds. Once I saw one in the kitchen. I observe them carefully whenever I can; I try to see their faces. I want nothing from them. It's a sunny day in early September. As I continue my walk, I look about me with interest. At the side of a driveway, next to a stucco house, the yellow nozzle of a hose rests on top of a dark green garbage can. Farther back, I can see part of a swing set. A cushion is sitting on the grass beside a three-pronged weeder with a red handle.

THE DISBELIEVERS

The disbelievers insist that every encounter is false. When I bend over and peer through the openings in the lattice, I see a slight movement, caused by a chipmunk or mouse in the dark weeds, and instantly my imagination is set in motion: I seem to see a man and two women, a long nose, the rising, the disappearance. The few details are suspiciously precise. How is it that the faces are difficult to remember, while the sprig of wildflowers stands out clearly? Such criticisms, even when delivered with a touch of disdain, never offend me. The reasoning is sound, the intention commendable: to establish the truth, to distinguish the real from the unreal. I try to experience it their way: the movement of a chipmunk behind the sunlit lattice, the dim figures conjured from the dark leaves. It isn't impossible. I exercise my full powers of imagination: I take their side against me. There is nothing there, behind the lattice. It's all an illusion. Excellent! I defeat myself. I abolish myself. I rejoice in such exercise.

YOU

You who have no phantoms in your town, you who mock or scorn our reports: are you not deluding yourselves? For say you are driving out to the mall, some pleasant afternoon. All of a sudden—it's always sudden—you remember your dead father, sitting in the living room in the house of your childhood. He's reading a newspaper in the armchair next to the lamp table. You can see his frown of concentration, the fold of the paper, the moccasin slipper half-hanging from his foot. The steering wheel is warm in the sun. Tomorrow you're going to dinner at a friend's house—you should bring a bottle of wine. You see your friend laughing at the table, his wife lifting something from the stove. The shadows of telephone wires lie in long curves on the street. Your mother lies in the nursing home, her eyes always closed. Her photograph on your bookcase: a young woman smiling under a tree. You are lying in bed with a cold, and she's reading to you from a book you know by heart. Now she herself is a child and you read to her while she lies there. Your sister will be coming up for a visit in two weeks. Your daughter playing in the backyard, your wife at the window. Phantoms of memory, phantoms of desire. You pass through a world so thick with phantoms that there is barely enough room for anything else. The sun shines on a hydrant, casting a long shadow.

EXPLANATION #6

One explanation says that we ourselves are phantoms. Arguments drawn from cognitive science claim that our bodies are nothing but artificial constructs of our brains: we are the dream-creations of electrically charged neurons. The world itself is a great seeming. One virtue of this explanation is that it accounts for the behavior of our phantoms: they turn from us because they cannot bear to witness our self-delusion.

FORGETFULNESS

There are times when we forget our phantoms. On summer afternoons, the telephone wires glow in the sun like fire. Shadows of tree branches lie against our white shingles. Children shout in the street. The air is warm, the grass is green, we will never die. Then an uneasiness comes, in the blue air. Between shouts, we hear a silence. It's as though something is about to happen, which we ought to know, if only we could remember.

HOW THINGS ARE

For most of us, the phantoms are simply there. We don't think about them continually, at times we forget them entirely, but when we encounter them we feel that something momentous has taken place, before we drift back into forgetfulness. Someone once said that our phantoms are like thoughts of death: they are always there, but appear only now and then. It's difficult to know exactly what we feel about our phantoms, but I think it is fair to say that in the moment we see them, before we're seized by a familiar emotion like fear, or anger, or curiosity, we are struck by a sense of strangeness, as if we've suddenly entered a room we have never seen before, a room that nevertheless feels familiar. Then the world shifts back into place and we continue on our way. For though we have our phantoms, our town is like your town: sun shines on the house fronts, we wake in the night with troubled hearts, cars back out of driveways and turn up the street. It's true that a question runs through our town, because of the phantoms, but we don't believe we are the only ones who live with unanswered questions. Most of us would say we're no different from anyone else. When you come to think about us, from time to time, you'll see we really are just like you.

THE GLORY OF KEYS

by PATRICK CRERAND

O N MONDAY BRIAN SULLIVAN did not sleep well, so he sent his Pontiac Sunfire to take his plane-geometry exam for him and never returned to Brookhaven High School. After lunch, Brian's math teacher, Ms. Florida, had to find a new desk for the Sunfire and sharpen its pencil. She opened a window to air out the exhaust, but the kids warmed to the smell of gasoline and oil and overall enjoyed the steady hum of its 2.2-liter Ecotec I4 engine. When Principal Dillard stopped by the classroom at two-fifteen for his daily check—he and Ms. Florida had been caught canoodling during the Sadie Hawkins dance earlier in the semester—the car was in the back row, with one headlight shining on the purple ink of the dittoed exam.

"Could I have a word, Ms. Florida?" he said.

Ms. Florida stepped out to the hall. The students started to shout the way they would if they were riding a roller coaster. Brian Sullivan's Sunfire honked and flashed its lights so as not to be left out of the hullabaloo.

"How long has there been a car parked in your classroom?" Mr. Dillard asked.

"Just this period," Ms. Florida replied. "But I heard from Mademoiselle Jeanne that it sat in during French class as well."

"Her Intro to French?" he asked.

"No," Ms. Florida replied. "Advanced French."

"Funny," Mr. Dillard said. "That car doesn't seem older than a '98."

"No," Mrs. Florida said. "It's a '95. My brother had one just like it, in pearl blue."

Mr. Dillard walked back to his office and rechecked the attendance sheets for the day. Sure enough, in each of Brian Sullivan's classes, the teacher had crossed out his name and written in '95 *Pontiac Sunfire, white with red trim*.

Mr. Dillard thought about calling the Sullivan home, but there had been a surprise locker check that afternoon, and three students had been arrested for felony narcotics. A fourth had been caught with a firearm on school grounds. One of the drug-sniffing dogs had left a trail of runny shit down the halls. The Pontiac Sunfire, Mr. Dillard thought, was a stable vehicle. He recalled a commercial featuring a cherry-red two-door convertible with a buxom brunette behind the wheel, a woman not unlike Ms. Florida. The commercial's slogan had been *We build excitement*. Ms. Florida's face glowed in his mind. Some things, he thought, were better left as they were.

That first semester, Brian Sullivan's Pontiac Sunfire struggled in the academic arena. Its French accent was a bit throaty, and without the ability to grip a pen properly it had a hard time finishing most of its composition assignments. On the sports field, though, Brian Sullivan's Pontiac Sunfire dominated. In November the football team fitted it with a blue and gold bra, the colors of the Brookhaven Bearcats, and spray-painted a number on each door. Coach Tibbets found himself singling out the car during two-a-day practices for its effort in tackling drills. The greatest insult he could lob at his players became "You run like a goddamned Corolla."

Against their rival, East High, Coach Tibbets strapped chains onto the Sunfire's tires and gave the team a ferocious pep talk that had to be cut short due to the fumes from the car's exhaust. That night, under the klieg lights of Welcome Stadium and the Steadicam of the local NBC affiliate, Brian Sullivan's Pontiac Sunfire set a new record for touchdowns in a half (seventeen). It seemed to know exactly where to be to make a play. The senior girls painted its number on their lithe bellies in black shoe polish. A few college scouts were there as well, watching as the Pontiac literally drove circles around East High's elite Tiger defense.

"Do you think it can learn the option?" a scout from Bowling Green State asked.

"Forget it," the man from Ohio State said. He pointed to a smoldering puddle of darkness in the end zone. "We want three yards and a cloud of dust, not ten miles and an oil leak."

But their critical gaze did not inhibit Brian Sullivan's Pontiac Sunfire's good time. At the homecoming dance in the gym later that night, it deejayed a blistering set of trance music, opening its doors and blasting its radio until its battery wore down. Coach Tibbets popped the Sunfire's hood to jump it alive again with his Ford Bronco, and all the girls gathered around to watch. Even Ms. Florida stopped making eyes at Mr. Dillard to sneak a glimpse at its greasy block. After two jolts, Brian Sullivan's Pontiac Sunfire sent an arc of light sparking from its battery and set a wall of crepe-paper flowers aflame. The girls swooned.

At the after-party, Marty Greyerson, the captain of the team and leading receiver, shotgunned beers with the Sunfire in the garage while the rest of the team cheered. They had set the head of the Bearcat mascot on the Sunfire's hood like a grotesque ornament. A few girls rested on the bumper as it revved its engine. The good times rolled.

As the night wore on, though, the crowd thinned. The other kids roamed the upstairs bedrooms of Marty's house, raiding the liquor cabinet and stealing CDs. They pawed and sucked face. Brian Sullivan's Pontiac Sunfire tried to drive inside the house, too, but Marty's mother had white carpet, and the Sunfire was still dripping green and black blots from the game. Plus someone had jammed a Doors cassette into its deck, and Marty could hear Jim Morrison's mad voice grow louder when the Sunfire rolled closer.

By three, the garage had grown colder. The somber timbre of Jim Morrison echoed off the walls. The Sunfire was deciding whether it felt safe to drive when Betty Heller walked in.

Brian Sullivan's Pontiac Sunfire waited as she walked a slow circle around the edge of the garage. Betty Heller was a nice girl, but with the guys on the team she had a reputation. When she came to the headlights she laid a hand across its hood.

"I feel like…" she said, and paused. "If I could just drive you a bit, maybe. Your paint is so soft." She pressed her left breast against the windshield.

Eventually Betty stroked the wiper until Brian Sullivan's Pontiac Sunfire turned on its emergency flashers and squirted a bit of blue washer fluid on Betty's hand.

"It's okay," Betty said, caressing a dent on its hood. "Leave it there."

There were few corners of Brookhaven High where Brian Sullivan's Pontiac Sunfire did not leave an impression. In Mr. Janney's Physics class, the Sunfire often volunteered for demonstrations, and once let Mr. Janney shoot a potato out of its tailpipe. It tutored Freshman Math in the courtyard before football practice, though most of its pupils struggled to decipher the elaborate system of honks and dings Mr. Ritzenfelter, the enrichment teacher, had laboriously cataloged into a kind of car alphabet. After gym, weaklings without pubic hair took refuge in the Sunfire's trunk when it came time to shower. During Mr. Cappello's Civics course, Brian Sullivan's Pontiac Sunfire led a moment of silence for the victims of an earthquake in Malaysia.

But the sporting arena was its true stage. In the spring, it ran track and threw the shot put. At the district meet, over the protests of the other teams, it took first prize in the hundred-yard dash and ran the mile in just over three minutes. The hurdles proved a bigger challenge, but it placed a respectable fifth, and the *Columbus Dispatch* named it to the All-District team.

So it was no surprise that when votes were counted for the class valedictory speech, Brian Sullivan's Pontiac Sunfire was the overwhelming favorite. Even Betty Heller, who had held a grudge when the Sunfire had stopped returning her calls, could see the logic.

"He's touched so many lives," she told her best friend Carol.

Still, it faced its fair share of detractors. One day, driving to Woodshop, the Pontiac overheard Brookhaven High's guidance counselor, Jerry Whalen, speaking in his office with Principal Dillard. They had just received the results from the Pontiac's employment-aptitude test.

"It says here it should look for a job in the engineering sector," Principal Dillard said. "What's so wrong with that?"

"It leaked a few dots on a Scantron," Mr. Whalen said. "Now we're supposed to believe it's college material? Maybe a Grand Am—but a Sunfire? Its Kelley Blue Book isn't even $2,400, and that's not going anywhere but south. I mean, look, Harry—I'm not in the dream-dashing business, but come on. We'd be better off selling it to East High and buying that new couch for the guidance room."

"It did show promise in Mr. Schneider's art class," Mr. Dillard offered, pointing to the mural of tire tracks on the wall outside. But Mr. Whalen rolled his eyes.

"You'll be the fool of the Principals' Ball, letting it speak at graduation," Mr. Whalen said. "And then who will you come crying to, stinking drunk? You're the one who let this car into everyone's life. Face it, Harry: some cars have it and some don't. Don't build up its hopes that it could be something other than a Pontiac Sunfire."

In the end Mr. Dillard brushed this talk off. During commencement, Brian Sullivan's Pontiac Sunfire walked with the other kids, its tassel secured tightly to its rearview, next to its pine-cone-shaped air freshener. It gave a rousing valedictory, according to Mr. Ritzenfelter, who translated it afterward and emailed it to the entire district under the subject heading THE GLORY OF KEYS. Principal Dillard taped a Certificate of Attendance onto the Pontiac's back window, and all the teachers signed their names in soap.

Two weeks later, at the Principals' Ball, Mr. Dillard danced with his wife while Ms. Florida blinked in his mind like an electric sequin swirling on the disco ball. The other principals called him "VTec" and made childish *vrooms* behind him when he walked to get punch. That night he sat hunched over the telephone in his dark kitchen, speaking in hushed tones to Ms. Florida about how it was her soft shoulders he'd wanted to rest his cheek against. But she had other worries on her mind. She had gotten a flat coming out of the teachers' lot that afternoon and had sat there crying for hours. Instead of changing the tire she had written a note to Principal Dillard's wife. Whenever she felt guilty she did this, he knew; she used it as a way to level them both. The notes were never mailed. With the confession written, she always said, there was no reason to lie anymore.

"I just sat there with grease on me and felt like I would never come clean, Harold," she said.

"About the affair?"

"No," she said. "That car. What kind of world have we sent him out into?"

"The car?" Principal Dillard said. "I don't know. You're just upset. You always get depressed after graduation. But come August it'll be just the same. The excitement will build again. We'll build the excitement together, Jan."

"Stop with the fucking commercials," Ms. Florida said.

In the fall, Brian Sullivan's Pontiac Sunfire enrolled at Ohio State and tried to walk onto the football team, but the campus was enormous and not at all impressed with the fantastic abilities of cars. It wasn't strange to see a microwave cart doing shuttle runs on the lacrosse fields by Lincoln Tower, or to catch the tail end of a juggling performance by the Manda, a double-jointed half-man, half-panda who entertained all comers on the corner of High and 15th. Before the Saturday-morning tailgate at Triangle House, Brian Sullivan's Pontiac Sunfire watched its roommate Charlie and his pledge brothers construct a metallic Holstein that shit stadium mustard and suckled actives with Coors Light from its teats. The Sunfire did a few doughnuts on the front lawn, but the brothers tired of those antics quickly. When it came time to go to the game, Brian Sullivan's Pontiac Sunfire couldn't fit through the turnstiles at the Horseshoe and ended up giving its ticket away to a scalper.

The Sunfire never really felt comfortable among the Buckeyes. It was hard to move around most of the hallways on campus, which had been remodeled in the late sixties based on a narrow, labyrinthine floor plan designed purposely to discourage sit-ins. After a month of frustration, the Pontiac stopped getting its oil changed. One morning it awoke in a pool of its own transmission fluid and Charlie reported it to the RA.

"That leak ruined my DVD player," Charlie testified at the dorm hearing. "And I think it's wearing my best polo shirt without asking." He held a tartan plaid shirt up for the jury to see. "That's oil on the collar. I can smell it."

Brian Sullivan's Pontiac Sunfire didn't wait to hear the verdict. After the fall break, it parked in front of the Sullivans' house back in suburban Columbus and didn't return to campus. But Brian Sullivan, who had spent the past year studying to be a peripatetic, had long ago stopped thinking of it as his car. He left its keys on a hook in the kitchen cupboard near the oatmeal and went east to study under a Sufi mystic in Vermont.

Sometimes the Sunfire took rides past the high school. Once, when it tried to enter the front door, two security guards it didn't recognize demanded to see a visitor's pass. The Sunfire honked for Principal Dillard, but Principal Dillard was no longer there to greet it. It was only Mr. Ritzenfelter, who was passing by on his way to lunch, who averted a greater misunderstanding by explaining that Mr. Dillard had shamed himself and the school by cheating on his wife, and had resigned. Since then there had been several bomb threats, and now no one could enter the building without a guest pass. The Sunfire backed down the stairs and sat humming in neutral until the security men finally threatened to tow it off school property.

In the spring, a reckless cousin of Brian's borrowed the Sunfire one night and drove it to HempFest '02, somewhere near the Buckeye Lake amphitheater, where a huckster convinced him to trade the battery for a bag of low-grade marijuana. The huckster spent the rest of the day selling electrical shocks from the battery to stoners, who jerked and moaned against a background of seamless guitar arpeggios echoing off the smoky hillside. Powerless and distraught, Brian Sullivan's Pontiac

Sunfire managed to roll down into the woods near a meth shack. A drifter or two used it as a bathroom, or a place to get high for while. One night a mutt with pups burrowed under the driver's seat and shook through the cold dark hours. Sparrow shit painted the Sunfire's windshield white. The junkies sold the springs from its seats and used the foam to start fires in the rain.

A year passed, and the police raided the meth shack. The city towed the Pontiac back to Columbus and left it in the impound lot under the 315 overpass. The car sat parked next to an old Dodge Dart for two months, until it was auctioned to a retired nun who drove it a hundred miles a year, all in the same circuit: from her home to the Kroger to Saint Agatha's and back home again. After one trip she left a carton of milk in the trunk for several weeks and the kids in the neighborhood started calling Brian Sullivan's Pontiac Sunfire the "Vomit Comet" because of the musty smell. When they notice it now, it's only to toss rocks at its side or grind their skateboards on its bumper, unaware of that year at Brookhaven when it was king. Such is the fate of cars.

1,000 LUNCH BAGS

I've always felt an instinctive, impossible responsibility to protect my children from the types of sadness and misfortune I've encountered in my own life. For me, grammar school in the early 1940s was a bleak experience. The personalized lunch bags on these pages represent one father's attempts to brighten his daughters' school days.

The bags were born the morning after my daughter Corby's unmarked lunch was stolen in third grade. (This must have been 1982 or '83.) The day after the theft, I wrote CORBY on a new lunch bag. The CORBY got a little more elaborate each day until, eventually, a sort of narrative form developed.

By the time my youngest daughter, Victoria, began carrying a lunch herself, the bags had become a daily chronicle of adventures at home and at school, encompassing subjects as varied as world history, dance recitals, schoolmates, grades, holidays, and assorted griefs and joys.

Of course, the advent of middle school pretty much ended each girl's individual saga—the bags no longer being sufficiently cool or sophisticated for anyone by seventh grade or so. But until they outgrew them, the girls almost always saved the bags and brought them home. I reckon my wife and I still have over a thousand in the attic. Digging through the crinkled mass, we can relive those days—sometimes puzzling over a bag's meaning, but feeling revived all the same, in spite of our receding memories.

I suspect that the bags may be reborn someday for a new generation of young school trudgers.

—*Robert Barnes*

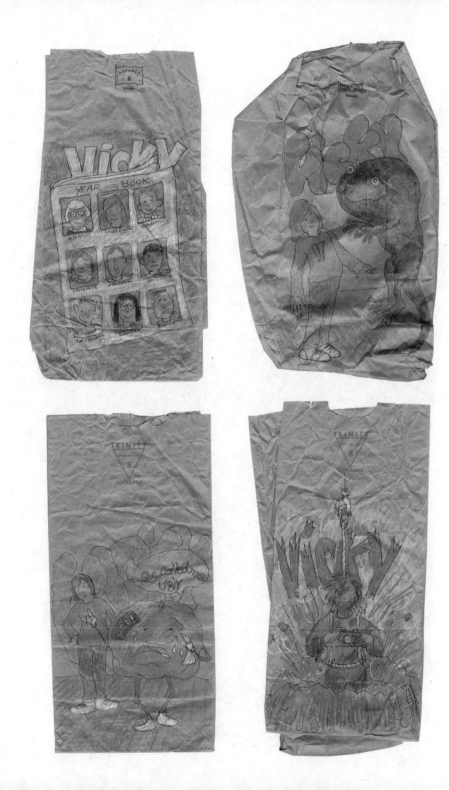

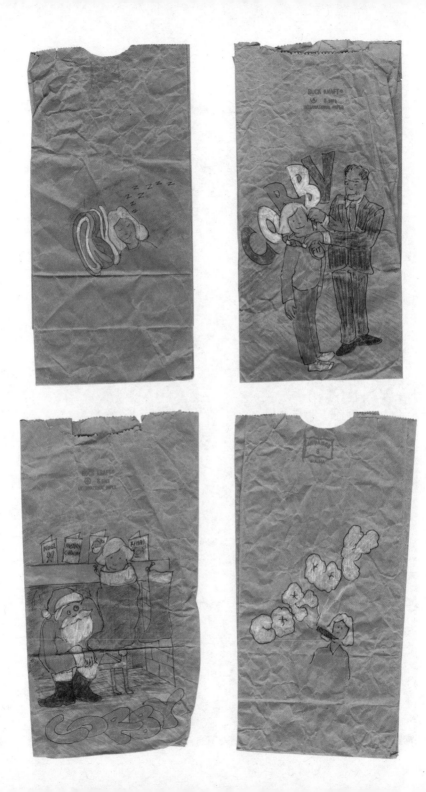

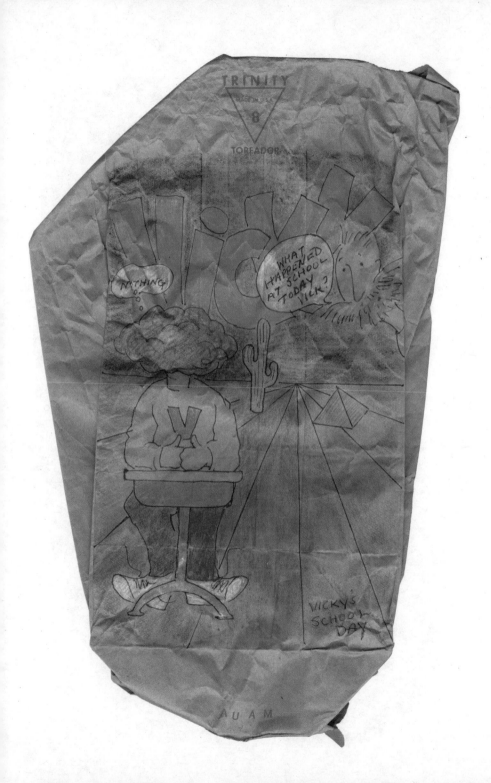

ENTRY-LEVEL NORWAY
A SMATTERING OF NEWISH
NORWEGIAN FICTION

by JOHN ERIK RILEY *and* MIKKEL BUGGE

K RISTIAN RILEY—the brother of one of this essay's authors— has a saying that he enjoys offering to foreigners interested in our nation. To anyone considering a visit to this particular northern European rocky outcropping, he'll say: Winter in Norway is not entry-level Norway.

As we edit these texts at the end of March, winter very much still with us, his words seem undeniably true. The roads in Oslo are clear, but there is still ice in the driveway and a foot of snow in the yard. Experience informs us that it will not be diminishing anytime soon.

Of course, even in warmer months, Norwegians like to think of their nation as unlike anywhere else. With great pride they refer to Norway as *annerledeslandet*, which can be loosely translated as "the different place." If you ask Norwegians what they mean by this, you will get a different answer every time. Some will point out that Norwegians don't like to adapt; that they are skeptical and like things the way they are. Others will make reference to the extreme nature of our immediate surroundings, and our ability to deal with said extremes. The land, they will tell you, has made Norwegians deter-mined and shy.

There is certainly something to be said for this perspective. Norwegians are, indeed, very good at dealing with the worst of climates. In Norway, winter can stretch into spring, and summer can seem more like fall. Most Norwegians know how to cross-country ski. They also know how to dig a snow cave when the weather turns from bad to terrible. All of this means that there is a certain tinge of irony that goes with the term *annerledeslandet*. It is an expression of that most common of Norwegian pastimes: complaining and gloating about one's suffering at the same time.

On the surface, though, Norway resembles a block of unhewn black granite encrusted with gold and diamonds. The urban centers seem to be brimming over with modern architecture and shops offering designer furniture. The state has constructed deftly engineered tunnels and bridges leading to even the tiniest islands and hamlets. Most cars on the highways are new or newish and well maintained.

Two factors are important in understanding the high standard of living: (1) Norway is an oil-producing nation, and (2) Norway is not a member of the EU. We have certainly had our share of economic nosedives over the last ten years, and some people have had to face serious misfortune. For the most part, however, Norway has sailed along smoothly, seemingly untouched, like a party boat floating on a sea of oil.

What, then, does any of this have to do with literature? Well, for one, Norway has made good use of its oil money. The state spends much of its acquired wealth on health care, development, aid to other nations, and plenty else that is good and wise—including funding for the arts, with literature amongst them. All but one of Norway's eight major political parties support public funding of the arts to a degree that would surprise even the most left-leaning American. (The lone holdout here is the rightist Progress Party.)

As part of this program, the Norwegian state buys one thousand copies of every domestically published work of fiction. There are certain requirements for being considered, of course, but the bar is relatively low. The standard royalty for a novel or story collection, as a result, is very high indeed.

The state also spends hundreds of millions of kroner every year (that's tens of millions of dollars) providing authors with stipends, travel scholarships, and grants. Millions more are spent on literary festivals, book tours, and similar events. Today, thanks in no small part to this government funding, Norwegian literature is being spread to much of the world. And writers have the opportunity to experiment in ways that would otherwise be quite difficult in such a small market. (The population of Norway is smaller than that of Wisconsin.)

To outsiders, then, Norway may seem like something of an author's paradise, at least if you ignore the high cost of living. Our writers, by and large, have the freedom to retreat to their cabins. There are certainly writers who do exactly that, devoting themselves to the production of carefully wrought stories about skiers and fishermen. And they do this extremely well.

As one may imagine, though, any Norwegian writing today is faced with a glaring paradox. On the one hand, we live in an extreme climate on the very edge of Europe, a country of recovering survivalists. On the other, we are well-off members of a smoothly functioning society, with little economic worry. We are members of a floating minority. Claiming that the present state of affairs has led to an identity crisis may be pushing it, but there is little doubt that the cultural moment has brought with it some interesting tensions.

There is an undercurrent of concern, even aggression, flowing through Norwegian art. (The most extreme expression of this being Norwegian black metal, which has its own infamous history.) Perhaps Norwegians know that they are the exception to the rule, and that the present state of affairs cannot last. Perhaps they fear that something terrible is brooding just below the surface.

Still, the Norwegian willingness to experiment comes not just from the aforementioned government funding and the accompanying existential unease. It's also a direct consequence of what Norwegian authors read. They relate to their own national literature, of course, from the first Viking sagas to still-important figures like Knut Hamsun and Henrik Ibsen to more recent genre-bending concept fiction, but they are also heavily influenced by literature from other countries.

Most Norwegians can read Swedish, Danish, and English without much effort. Many speak either French or German, as well. Ask a set of writers what they like and you'll get a different answer from every one. Some are fans of Swedish poetry. Others focus more on magical realism from South America. Among younger writers, American authors such as Don DeLillo and David Foster Wallace have been influential. All of this and more gets tossed into the literary melting pot.

Today, various movements and aesthetics seem to exist side by side. The novel, relatively speaking, is rather traditional in form and scope; as is the case in most countries, coming-of-age stories, historical tableaux, and memoirs make up much of what is published. One peculiar theme that seems to pop up, again and again, is the question of what it means to be Norwegian. What is our national identity? What has history done to us? How have we changed? What has remained the same? Whom do we want to be?

When it comes to the short story—our primary focus here—one

can observe two major tendencies. Historically, there has been a certain leaning toward modernist minimalism, especially in the 1980s and 1990s, due to the influence of Kjell Askildsen, whom many consider a master of the short form. (Think Samuel Beckett meets Raymond Carver.) On the other hand, a growing number of writers have been moving in another direction: Hans Herbjørnsrud, included here, has a maximalist approach to fiction that has inspired some writers to cross boundaries and revamp the genre.

Still shorter forms—such as poetry, the prose poem, the short-short story, etc.—are even more varied in scope. In fact, one could make the claim that poetry is the most diverse genre in Norwegian literature. Virtually every imaginable style is being explored, from realistic beat-generation ramblings to the sonnet corona. We've invited the small press Flamme Forlag to curate a selection of very short contemporary prose and poetry, and they've chosen to include some of the youngest writers we have. They are not representative of Norwegian literature in its entirety (who is?), but they are writing in a way that seems genuinely fresh and new. Their sense of form and meter is free and casual. But there is also, in their work, a feeling of longing, of apprehension—maybe even a need for control.

As such, they are, perhaps, more indicative of what Norway has become in the past few decades. From Hans Herbjørnsrud's story of the seventeenth century's Blind Margjit to Rannveig Revhaug's *Sims*-influenced texts, we move from the ghosts of the past to a glimpse of the near future.

...Which brings us to why we chose these particular stories for this particular issue of *McSweeney's*. Strangeness—cultural, literary, or otherwise—seemed more important to us than familiarity. Originality trumped cohesion. Complex maximalism outweighed austere minimalism. There is a grab-bag aspect to any collection of fiction, and we were indeed tempted to just grab whatever we happened to like the most. But we have attempted to restrict ourselves to work that conveys something about contemporary Norway, and that has an off-chance of seeming good even after being forced through the brutal gears of the translation machine.

The earliest texts are from the mid-1980s; the newest ones are from the so-called naughts. We have focused solely on short stories (or, in some, cases, *short*-short stories), and for this reason, some truly great novelists have not been included. All of the authors, excepting one, are alive and working today; all have been lauded with critical acclaim, and most have received prestigious awards.

We have collected these texts out of love, both for strange Norway and for its even stranger literature. Our anthology is far from comprehensive, little more than an entry-level introduction. If we have succeeded, though, it should seem more rewarding than a midwinter visit. We sincerely hope that you, its English-speaking readers, will find something of value here.

Translations of Ingvar Ambjørnsen, Laila Stien, Roy Jacobsen, and Per Petterson have been published with the financial support of NORLA. "On an Old Farmstead in Europe" © Gyldendal Norsk Forlag AS 1992. Translation © Liv Irene Myhre 1994. "Loophole" © Gyldendal Norsk Forlag AS 2008. "Out in the Open" © Tiden Norsk Forlag 1994. "Alarm" © Cappelen Damm. "Interlude XXIV" © Gyldendal Norsk Forlag AS 2001. "Another Star" © Cappelen Damm 2005. "Two by Two" © Cappelen Damm 2005. "Small World" © Flamme Forlag 2009.

ON AN OLD
FARMSTEAD IN EUROPE

by HANS HERBJØRNSRUD

THE VERY FIRST PERSON known to have lived on our farm was Blind Margjit, who died in 1616.

In the 1620s a cottar named Jon made his home here. The sources give only one piece of information about him: Jon was in reduced circumstances. Poor, in other words.

The tax ledger of 1645 indicates that Wise Ragnhild lived on the farm that year, and paid six shillings in taxes.

The land registry of 1665 lists the farm as being leased from an estate. It owed half a barrel of grain and produced two and a half barrels, kept two cows, broke no new land, and was charged with growing hops for beer brewing. In the census of 1665 the farm is not mentioned.

At the time of Blind Margjit, Jon, and Wise Ragnhild, the farmhouses were located in an area we now call Gamletun. The old site and the surrounding fields are low-lying, on the basement floor of the valley, and in the 1600s they were surrounded by bogs and wetlands. The farmstead lay down there, exposed to floods and water damage, for more than two hundred years.

Not until 1864 did the residents give up the hopeless battle against the water. At that time the main house, summer kitchen, storage houses, cowshed, and barn were all dismantled, log by log, and carted higher up and rebuilt, house by house, on the ridge where our farm sits today. But even up here, on the main floor of the valley, the houses sit so low that the great flood of 1927 would have dug out the ground beneath the foundations had it not been for the rock barriers the residents were able to hurriedly erect.

After the houses were moved, the original foundations were leveled. The old farmstead was converted into fields and meadows. That parcel now has a deeper layer of topsoil and yields more crops than other fields on the farm. In our time the surrounding wetlands have been drained, cultivated, and planted. Hydroelectric dams have tamed the river, and the little creek that used to scurry about in the bogs has been channeled and now stretches like a taut plumb line through its old meandering course. These days we grow barley or wheat at Gamletun. And every time I till the fields there in spring, the harrow clanks against foundation stones forced into the light.

In earlier years these stones would always remind me of something absurd and alien. Either they would be the color of blue clay and flat like flagstone, resembling the plates and armor of an armadillo, or they would be pale yellow, and curved, and look more like the weathered bones of dinosaurs. Three years ago I found two rocks that looked like ostrich eggs.

But early this morning, a windy April morning in 1991, when I heard two angry clanks from below me and jumped down from my seat on the tractor, I pulled two head-size stones from the harrow's teeth and immediately felt there was something strangely familiar and appealing about them.

With my nails I scraped moist black soil from their sides. It had taken the ground frost 127 years to bring them to light. Both were bone-colored and head-shaped and resembled the skulls sometimes unearthed by a gravedigger's shovel.

With the diesel motor idling, I stood there in the field with one stone in each hand. How strange: they had eye sockets and cheekbones and jawbones. When I looked a little closer, I could make out nasal bones and ear cavities as well. I imagined I could even see a few amber-yellow teeth. The stones were evenly and smoothly curved from the forehead, over the crown and down the back. They resembled heads created by a sculptor more than they did skulls.

But still, how different they were, these two stone heads.

One had a high forehead with eye sockets close together in a narrow facial oval. It had to be Blind Margjit, I decided. This is how that singular woman might have looked beneath the skin. Her barren sockets stared at me with an empty, introspective look.

The other head was broad-jawed and coarse, with high cheekbones and a bumpy forehead. It seemed to glare at me with a querulous and menacing expression. This was how I had always imagined Wise Ragnhild, without her gooseberry-green eyes and large, full-lipped frog mouth.

The stone heads were still caked with soil. I knocked their foreheads together, hard, so that lumps of dirt and sand flew off. The collision produced an eerie stone note; it made me listen with excitement and curiosity. What was I hearing?

I banged the skulls together again. And again. And again.

And as I loudly knocked the heads together—*clack! clack! clack!*—I heard a heavy, dark, ancient sound, stone music that traveled up the bones of my arms—*clack! clack! clack!*—a bone music that sent electric sparks through my collarbone and spine and reverberated throughout my limbs—*clack! clack! clack!*—a skeletal score for vertebrae and shoulder blades, for hip sockets and shins, for hammers, anvils, and stapes—*clack! clack! clack!*

I stood at Gamletun clacking and making skeletal music until my teeth began to chatter along. The heads seemed to knock out the beat of a moldy old folk song that centuries ago had come into being here from thundering floods and trickling brooks and tinkling rain. And soon they began to produce word after word of a refrain:

And the Man with the Eyes
Keeps searching for his sight.

I stood at Gamletun knocking out a folk song that the ground frost had forced out of the field and into the sunlight early on this morning. When the harrow found it, the song was still dormant. I lifted it up and shook it awake. Music and words that had lain hidden and forgotten under the dirt for centuries flew like sparks from the stone heads as they crashed together:

And the Man with the Eyes
Keeps searching for his sight.

At that point I had to stop. I didn't have the strength for more. Knocking the heavy stone heads together was becoming too strenuous. I was able to uncover only the refrain of the song. Breathing hard, I set the heads down on the furrow. There they began to resemble two women struggling in floodwater up to their necks.

I bent all the way down to Blind Margjit's head and gently stroked her brow. Then I began to puff like a bellows—*whoosh, whoosh*—into her eye sockets. I was coaxing her. I was urging her on:

"Whoosh, Margjit, whoosh, whoosh! I'm bringing you back to life. Whoosh, Margjit, whoosh, whoosh. Tell me what your song was about. Whoosh, Margjit, whoosh, whoosh."

At that moment a whirlwind as tall as a tree came reeling through Gamletun. It swayed around the tractor, careening across the field, and headed straight for me. The whirlwind had kicked up a veil of swirling dirt, and now it came toward me like a tall, ungainly ghost with a swarm of dry leaves for a head. I was sucked into a mad reel and sandblasted by a hurricane of dirt.

And then, abruptly, the wind let go. Everything was still, deadly still and silent. For an endless moment I was in the quiet eye of the storm. The tornado had sucked the air right out of me, as if I were about to be vacuum-packed. Now I was wrapped inside a cocoon of perfect peace and calm. All around me the currents raged.

In another moment I was yanked back into the dance and took a few more turns with the wind.

When the whirlwind lurched on at last, I once again found myself in the field, exhausted and blinded by the dust. I sat on the furrow, clutching the stone heads, unable to see a thing. And while I sat like that—disoriented, stunned, and in total darkness, like blind Blind Margjit—I saw for the first time Gamletun as it must have looked centuries ago.

On the farm, people staggered back and forth across the twenty-two wading stones that spanned the wetlands.

In late summer evenings a mist scented with white bog cotton drifted up from the dykes and hollows and puddles, wrapping the farmstead in a woolly blanket until only the top of the ash tree in the yard peeked up out of the haze.

Sometimes the spring or autumn floods would snatch the broom from the front steps, extinguish the fire in the open hearth, and toss away wooden vessels and the churn, leaving wiggling carp behind on the dirt floor. One flood left the houses completely submerged for days, those that were not set adrift and carried off along with a few outhouses and summer barns and logs and driftwood from huts and farms farther up the valley.

My grandfather learned from his grandfather that during a spring flood in the 1560s the young Margjit sat perched for one day and two nights in the farmyard ash tree that stood there with trembling branches and parted the onrushing torrents. Only the crown of the ash tree was visible above the floodwaters, making it look like a bush. The rowan tree by the cowshed resembled an upturned broom. Above the main house the water simmered and bubbled like a boiling pot.

Margjit sat in the ash tree feeling as if the whole valley had come rushing at her like a landslide. The water surface had no waves. It heaved, trembled, and quivered like fine linen in the bleaching yard on a breezy day. Through the driving rain she could hear its sound: it was low, rustling, and almost inaudible, but as frightening and piercing as a hissing snake. The rain battered her like a wet birch switch.

Seventeen-year-old Margjit was the only one left on the farm by then. Her father and two younger sisters had succumbed to disease in midwinter. Shortly before the flood, her mother had fallen dead while gathering herbs by the bog. She had been buried on the day the drenching rain began to fall.

Legend has it that Margjit's mother was a medicine woman to the whole district. She was the one people turned to when evil crept in through someone's eyes and mouth and settled in the body as illness and pain. Her mother treated the sick with healing lotions made from bat blood, baby fat, beaver glands, corpse sweat, ear wax from virgins, semen from swains, werewolf spittle, and many other things that she knew to have healing powers. She concocted potions for them made from henbane, celery, aspen leaves, juniper berries, and other powerful herbs and plants that only experts like her were familiar with.

Ever since she was a little girl, Margjit had sat by her mother's side as she urged and beseeched the evil to let go of tormented bodies. All the pain and misery that little Margjit saw fell like heavy burdens upon her. She would sit there observing, wide-eyed and attentive, taking it all in. All the pain and suffering, the bitterness and rancor of others, sank to the bottom of her soul. It made her sullen and sad. Gradually she became snake-eyed and ill-natured.

Her thoughts and gaze could injure others. Her mother was unable to exorcise the evil, no matter how many of her balms, brews, and incantations she tried. Nor did anyone else know of any remedies. Margjit had seen too much evil and horror as a young child, they said.

As a result Margjit was feared and disliked by everyone. If she stared at a pregnant woman, the fetus died in the womb. If she stared at cattle, they began to milk blood. If she watched when anyone churned, the cream turned to water instead of butter. Her gaze could scorch a neighbor's green pastures. It could ignite houses and trees. It could stop birds in flight. That's how much she had seen. So heavy was her heart. So piercing were her eyes.

Margjit lived under a blackened sun; she could no longer shed tears. Thus she could not cry while she sat shivering and shaking in the top branches of the ash during the flood. Her life was as dark and empty and desolate as the rushing water she sat watching.

In the farmyard ash tree, she watched the roof of the house slowly disappear. Finally the current sputtered white over the roof's peak, lapping and licking at it like tongues of fire. Then it died down, and the house vanished. Water bulged over it like a big black hump.

With each log of the house wall that had disappeared into the water, Margjit had climbed one branch higher into the tree. Her frock and blouse were dripping wet. Her numb, stiff hands gripped the tree's branches like claws. When the flood swallowed the main house, she stopped screaming for help. Her cries had fluttered over the rapidly moving water like the squawks of injured birds. None had reached shore. No one had arrived to help.

Eventually she rested her tired head against the trunk of the ash tree and stared upstream. Her jaw was clenched, her mouth a gash, and her protruding brow strangely white and shiny on her dirty face. She was so exhausted and weak that she could no longer scream. Only her eyes still glowed with life. They were the color of dewberries, hateful, burning. Poisonous. Her gaze hissed like red-hot iron in water when it fell upon the bulging current over the vanished roof.

At dusk on the first evening she saw a drowned sheep drifting downstream. The body was swollen, heavy in the water, and in the soft silvery light it resembled a floe of foam. Not until the sheep was close to her tree did she see the two crows pecking away at the cadaver, their claws buried deep in the wool.

When the mist had wrapped itself around the sheep, she climbed another branch and settled down like a bird seeking shelter for the night. Darkness was falling. All around her she could hear the flood. It muttered and mumbled like tattles and tales; it sighed and sobbed like all the world's torment and torture, and its whine was as cold as a whetstone grinding against the edge of a scythe.

But whenever she stared down into the raging current below, she flew like a great loon, neck outstretched, over an endless field of water, alone and screaming.

In the middle of the night a big cowshed came bobbing toward her. The shed seemed even blacker than the pitch-black darkness from which it had emerged, and the doorway gaped blacker than the blackest misery she had ever seen. It seemed like a nightmare: the cowshed came out from the night like a mountain of solid darkness. When the branches of the ash tree began to scrape along the side of the shed she wanted to scream with terror, but she was so hoarse and cold that she couldn't make a single sound, not even a cough.

The branches pushed at the shed. It dipped and curtsied in the water, slowly spinning around. Then it disappeared into the darkness.

*   *   *

In the morning, when she was so hungry that she began to nibble on buds and bark, she spotted a man astride a log hurtling right at her. In the swirls of current over the house roof the log reared like a spooked horse, spun around, veered off to the side, and rushed past the ash tree.

In a flash Margjit looked into a wild-eyed face. She exchanged a hasty look with the man, but no words. Then he disappeared into the rainy haze.

She did not know him, and she never saw him again. The man on the log had only had time to cast his eyes at her as he rushed past, down the watery slope.

And she had accepted them.

From then on, everywhere she went she would ask about this unknown man who had ridden a runaway log in the flood. No one knew who he was, or where he had come from, or if he'd survived.

He had given her the only thing he had to offer at that moment— his gaze—and she had caught it in flight and kept it with her for the rest of her life as if it were a part of herself.

Legend has it that Margjit lost her sight in old age. She is said to have stated that it was not until she became Blind Margjit that she understood what she had seen at seventeen. It was that long before she truly grasped the insight given to her by the nameless man from the spring flood in her youth.

She called him the Man with the Eyes.

In the summertime, when the old Blind Margjit sat on a stool under the farmyard ash tree, she told anyone willing to listen about the great flood. Margjit's words must have been strong and durable, for some of what she said underneath the tree survived for generations—

remembered for 375 years—and was not written down until now, by me, on a windy and rainy April night in 1991. And her words still have sap and substance, for when I close my eyes and try to think back, there is no face I see as painfully clear and prominent as that of the seventeen-year-old Margjit sitting in the farmyard ash, staring out over the shiny black water.

What did she say? Blind Margjit recalled that the log that the Man with the Eyes rode was a log from a house, and that it made a leap into the air before it spun around in the swirling current over the roof and tore past the tree where she sat. And she remembered seeing his back as it disappeared into the mist.

But how the Man with the Eyes looked, and how he was dressed, she had altogether forgotten. Or maybe in the rush of it all she'd never noticed. She didn't know if he had been young or old, if he had light or dark hair, if he was heavy or slender. She didn't even know if his eyes were brown or black or blue. The Man with the Eyes was simply a look cast from a runaway log in a furious current.

And a back swallowed by the mist.

Probably just an ordinary man, fighting for his life in the flood.

Yet their meeting became the one single moment that she was able to wrest from the flood. It was a wide-open eye that lay buried deep in her soul, staring at her all her life.

But what really happened?

Everything happened, as already indicated. Margjit and the Man with the Eyes exchanged glances, and faster than one dream can turn into another she was transformed.

She had been snake-eyed and mean-spirited. Her eyes were evil; they could kill and torment. Her thoughts were evil; they could bite and sting. She had been a victim of the belief in the evil mind and the evil eye that was the basis for understanding fellow human beings in the old farming community.

But all at once she turned kind-eyed and mild-mannered. She had been hexed and shunned; now she was released and became accepted and liked by all. She had been sullen and sad; instantly she became cheerful and spirited. Her hair had been coal black and her eyes dark as dewberries. Suddenly her hair turned the color of corn silk and her eyes blue as cornflowers in a ripe wheat field. From that day and that moment she was changed. No one recognized her, nor did she recognize herself.

In fact, she did not recognize her community or her neighbors at all. She saw everything and everybody with entirely new eyes. It was as if she had been held captive until that moment, and was brought into the light for the first time.

But how did this happen?

I simply do not know. Nor does anyone else. These things sometimes happen to young girls, or so I hope.

The legend may both see and describe what happened to Margjit in the top of the ash tree, but it doesn't explain or expound on her transformation. It says or reveals nothing further about itself or her. It may be that the legend knows itself to be a legend. Still, it survived throughout the centuries because it was able to keep the wonderment of its listeners alive; it has served as a misted mirror in which generation after generation has dimly glimpsed its own reflection. It is precisely what the legend conceals and our own surprise and puzzlement that give the young Margjit the freedom she needs to become transformed.

According to the legend, the light in Margjit's eyes burned slowly down until finally it died out. But when everything became pitch-dark inside her and around her, Blind Margjit called upon the sight she had kept hidden since her youth. And in the middle of her darkest night, the eyes of the Man with the Eyes were kindled again; they flickered and shone and lighted her path. She was blind, but the Man with the

Eyes gave her sight. He became her eyes and gaze. Blind Margjit saw better than when she had had her sight. She saw everything around her, and she saw herself from the outside. She both saw and was seen.

This is according to the legend, which also says that in the last year of Blind Margjit's life she became either mad or psychic. She withered and then rejuvenated herself. She broke into a thousand pieces, which she scattered like stardust across the sky. She broke into pieces and made herself whole again. Perhaps she was both psychic *and* mad.

She began to see things that no one could or would see. She swallowed the sun and crowed. She was everyone and she was no one. Her gaze danced deliriously through the centuries.

It was then, in the year of her death, 1616, that she completed the ballad "Margjit and the Man with the Eyes," which she had been composing since the great flood in the 1560s. She could neither read nor write, but where she lived the oral folk-song tradition was still alive. Her neighbors listened to her and memorized the words and the tune.

The ballad describes a moment that grows and grows and becomes longer and longer and lasts and lasts until finally it spans her whole life, from birth until death. She is born and dies at the same moment. Her cradle is her grave, I think it says in one of the last verses.

Blind Margjit was consumed and possessed with the idea of time and mortality. She was not the only one among her contemporaries to feel this way. It was the early 1600s. Elsewhere in Europe the gods of war were about to be unleashed and run berserk for thirty years. Cervantes and Shakespeare died. The medieval geocentric world image collapsed, and soon Pascal would stare with horror into a desolate and ice-cold cosmos and exclaim, "The eternal silence of these infinite spaces terrifies me."

The 1600s was the obscure period between the Renaissance's confident and self-assured concept of time and the new notions of the 1700s and the Age of Enlightenment. It was a century when the Europeans became aware of a chilling isolation, as the French philosopher Georges

Poulet writes in his work about the perception of time from the baroque period to Proust and Henri-Louis Bergson. A world so far divinely ordered began to list and capsize. Time came unhinged. The individual was trapped in the moment or in his memories and became the victim of time and mortality.

Someone once said that the baroque poets of the 1600s were nostalgic about the past and walked backward into a threatening future. In their poems the word *history* is synonymous with decline and dissolution; life is compared to a shimmering soap bubble about to burst. The past becomes a lovely dream, the future something ominous, and the present an open grave.

The Europeans of the 1600s were robbed of their sense of permanence and continuity. The strand was broken and the pearls scattered in every direction. Time no longer followed a straight line divinely determined. It overflowed its banks and flooded a large bog and carried everything away.

Poulet uses another image: the European of the 1600s felt at the mercy of a flood of disjointed moments. Time became a huge quagmire that must be traversed by stepping from one precarious foothold to the next, from one moment to the next, never knowing whether you would land on safe ground or be pulled under.

In the outskirts of this Europe, on a swampy and impoverished little farm in Norway, the illiterate Blind Margjit circles the farmyard ash tree in the year of her death, 1616, leaning on her cane while humming and crooning a ballad that was to live on after her for another 180 years. When she was finished putting the ballad together it was twenty-nine verses long, just as many as there were letters in the alphabet she did not know.

The first part of the ballad describes, interprets, and explains what happened during the spring flood between the snake-eyed girl in the ash tree and the courageous, stalwart Man with the Eyes who rides on the wild current. Then the ballad goes on to describe how the blind

Man with the Eyes doddered from farm to farm and from valley to valley in search of his sight.

Finally, when he is old and white-haired, the Man with the Eyes knocks one moonlit autumn night on the door at Margjit's farm. When Margjit opens the door and steps outside, she sees an old, blind man underneath the ash tree. She recognizes him immediately and walks over to him. At the moment Margjit takes his hand and looks into his moonlit face, she loses her sight and becomes blind. But in the same moment the Man with the Eyes is able to see the stooping Blind Margjit standing before him.

The ballad ends with Blind Margjit saying she has lived her entire life within one incredible moment. In the end she sits folding baby nappies along with a shroud for an old man.

As the years and decades passed and the 1600s turned into the 1700s, people added new words to her ballad and left some existing ones out. New verses were added and old ones were dropped. The ballad became a folk song.

But after 1790 the song began to disintegrate. It dissolved into stanzas, which then dissolved into verses and words, which in turn dissolved into letters.

When Norwegian folk songs, fairy tales, and legends were collected in the middle of the last century, only bits and pieces remained of the song about Margjit and the Man with the Eyes. Not one stanza had been written down.

The song had returned to the Latin alphabet from whence it came. When I see the twenty-nine letters of the alphabet all in a row, they remind me of a cemetery where the song about Margjit and the Man with the Eyes lies buried. Each of the twenty-nine verses has one letter on top as a memorial.

Perhaps the song also lies buried in the foundations at Gamletun. I was able to knock out the refrain with the help of the stone heads:

And the Man with the Eyes
Keeps searching for his sight.

Perhaps the song was not meant for life. It died, but the legend survived.

Everyone who lived on the farm after Blind Margjit heard about and may even have imagined the Man with the Eyes, who was no more than a glance cast at a young girl in the great flood.

But there may also be those who have been touched, accidentally, by this glance from an obscure place in history.

We excavate foundations, and we study church registers and court records, and we try to uncover the past.

And sometimes we are caught by surprise when a glance from the past suddenly meets our own.

Perhaps we are seen.

Perhaps history sees us.

Then the glance glides by and disappears in the rainy mist.

Whoever searches long enough in history will finally be found.

I am writing this late one April night in 1991. On the table in front of me are the two stone heads that my harrow found in the field this morning. From time to time I put the pen aside and lean over the papers to gently stroke Blind Margjit's brow. Her eye sockets gaze at me with a distant and vacant stare.

Before I began to write, I sat caressing her lovely head for a long time. And that is when the glance from the unknown man on the log quite unexpectedly met mine, sharp, piercing, and painful.

The next moment his glance had vanished into the mist and the rain.

History had seen me, and I could begin to write.

Translated by Liv Irene Myhre

LOOPHOLE

by JOHAN HARSTAD

WORK'S ROUGH, WHICH is why I brought the family to a vacation spot by the ocean, where I don't stand a chance of being sent to monotonous meetings or asked about unpaid invoices. We get up early and spend most of the day on the beach, where we are offered overpriced refreshments by underpaid salesmen. In the evenings, when the kids are in bed, my wife and I walk down to the local tavern and talk about all the reasons we love one another. But then, one very hot morning, while the children are building sandcastles by the water and my wife is reading a book about laser treatment for wrinkles, I decide to swim past the floating balloons along the border of the official swimming area. Seconds after I pass the first balloon, I sense a deep and unavoidable urge to dive underwater for reasons I don't quite understand. I dive anyway, and to my surprise, as I swim, I notice a blank, rectangular hole at the bottom of the sea. Without thinking twice, I swim toward the hole, then into it. I kick my legs and float, then glide, through the water, curious about how deep the hole is, amazed by how deep it appears to be. Perhaps a minute later, maybe less, at the very moment I consider turning around because I'll soon be out of breath, I notice a blurry light ahead. I kick harder and harder, paddling as fast as I can toward the light, excited to see how far away from the beach I am. I make my way through the hole and out of the water, breaking the surface with an enormous gasp. Everyone looks at me. An entire family, husband, wife, children, stands there with water up to their necks, staring at me with such a perfect mixture of love and loathing that for a moment I am unsure what to do. But then the man of the family throws his arms around me and pats me on the back. They all talk at once, I have trouble following, I seem to understand only the woman's hand gestures, which indicate that I should join them on land, and so I follow. I walk behind them to the place they have chosen, they put up a parasol, and the children lay out a towel on the sand, motioning that I should lie down. I'm worried that I might do something wrong, perhaps offend them, so I accept their suggestion and lie down, carefully, while glancing around to see if I can spot my own family. Familiar faces I have seen here and there gaze at me, and wave their hands. I wave back, self-consciously, as I continue to look for my wife, but she is nowhere to be seen. The whole situation is embarrassing, I want to get up and leave, but whenever I try to sit up or move about I am met with harsh stares and a screed of meaningless words that can be interpreted only as stern admonitions. I remain in my place. During the course of the afternoon, I am offered sandwiches and Coca-Cola, and in the evening, I follow my new family to their bungalow. I shower with the other children. The husband and wife wrap us up in cotton pajamas and put us to bed before they go for a walk on their own, presumably to the local tavern. The days after that are more or less identical: the other children wake me up, painfully early, and we proceed to the beach, where I lie on my towel in the sun and wait for someone to give me something to drink. I have tried, several times, to tell them that I don't belong here, but every time I open my mouth the man waves me away as though my words only irritate him. And since I am deeply afraid that I'll cause trouble, not to mention make a scene, I choose to remain calm and take things as they come. Over time I grow aware of how my new family observes me with a certain amount of skepticism. They make me sit at the far end of the table when we eat dinner, the lady of the house won't lend me her sunscreen, the children keep their comic books to themselves even though they have enough for every person on the beach. I gradually realize that something awful must have happened when I swam through the hole at the bottom of the ocean, and that I am trapped, at least for the time being. I force myself through several more days of boredom and intense sunburn before it occurs to me that stasis is no longer an option. Rather, I need to use all my wit, all my smarts, to plan an escape. The perfect moment arrives a few days later, while the family is busy preparing lunch, handing out sandwiches and so forth: when I see my chance I bolt toward the water and dive in. Desperately, I swim back and forth between the arms and legs of the other vacationers, searching for the hole that I came out of; finally, relieved, I find it. It has shrunk a bit, it seems, but it's still large enough for me to squeeze through, and so I push forward along the claylike walls. Once again I notice a light at the end of the passage and swim toward it, out and up, ready to embrace my family and tell them what happened. But as soon as my head breaks the surface of the water, I realize that I am not at home at all. Next to me two retirees, a man and a woman of indeterminate age, are standing, smiling. As before, I am welcomed into the fold, they lead me toward the sand and place me on a soft sun chair in the shade of a parasol. They cover me in sunscreen and hand me a deck of cards, which I am asked to shuffle. The man then takes the cards from me and deals a game of gin rummy. I look around, the same people I have seen before wave to me, but my family is nowhere to be seen. The old woman mumbles some incomprehensible words and pours me a glass of lemonade. When the sun is about to go down, the old man and woman collapse their parasol and their chairs and pack their things and together we walk to their car, climb in, and set off, as far as I can gather, for Miami. And that's when I make my decision: I will no longer fight, no longer try to return to my family. Instead, I lean back and let my eyes rest on the blur of the road whizzing past, and think about how I might use the inheritance when my new guardians finally leave this world.

Translated by John Erik Riley

OUT IN THE OPEN

by LAILA STIEN

SVEIN AND I HAVE always loved nature. There's nothing like a fishing lake and a glass of sweet vermouth, is what I always say. Nothing like a proper mountain hike, Svein always says. We say it whenever someone starts preaching about the Mediterranean. Everyone preaches about their trips to the Mediterranean these days. It's Fuerteventura this and Ibiza that, not to mention Palma Nova and how fabulous it is there with all the newly renovated hotels, the air-conditioning, and the nightclubs that are open till early morning. And then there are all those celebrities! Else Britt saw Tina Turner and Prince in Palma Nova. They were performing in a hotel only three blocks from where she and Per Sture were staying—an experience for life. Those hips! she says, whenever Prince is mentioned. And people mention Prince often. Whenever they sit down to eat. She has learned one of his songs by heart: "We wanna play in the sunshine, we wanna be free," she sings, and rolls those green eyes of hers.

* * *

Svein and I have also been to the Mediterranean. We went to Gran Canaria during our Christmas vacation two years ago and were almost rained away. "Never again," Svein says, "never in my whole life."

I agree completely. I much prefer the porch. It's free of charge. Or we can go for a drive, pack frankfurters and a camp stove. We enjoy our trips enormously, Svein and I. There's something special about nature; you feel so balanced, in a way. I've said it to Else Britt: "Why don't you go for a drive?" I've said. She and Per Sture are always fighting— *discussing*, she calls it. "All right, then," I say, when she tells me that, but think to myself that those two will never get married, the way they keep fighting and bickering. Svein and I, we can lie on a blanket out in the open for hours and just enjoy the stillness and peace.

"You'll find peace in the graveyard, when the time comes," Else Britt is in the habit of saying. "You have to kick up your heels while you're here. Experience something." She gives us long lectures about the stimulating life she shares with Per Sture—they're always seeking out new places, expanding their horizons. Next year, when they've saved enough money, they're going to Crete. They're staying at home until then, they lack the funds to travel, but of course they have to go out. "You've got to go *out*," she says, and looks at me.

Svein and I don't sit inside and mope all the time, the way she seems to think. We have lots of experiences. You don't have to go to a disco and damage your hearing and become an asthmatic to experience something big. For instance, we drive up to Sogns Lake quite often. And it was while we sat and cooked frankfurters on the camp stove at Sogns Lake one Sunday in May that we decided to go north for our holiday. Neither of us had been farther than Trondheim before.

It would be the vacation of the century. The Land of the Midnight Sun, endless mountain plateaus, reindeer, glassy mountain lakes brimming with fish. Nothing like the overcrowded Mediterranean hotels with hollering Swedes outside your bedroom window, cockroaches in the bathroom, E. coli in the swimming pool, and poisonous jellyfish in the sea.

I could barely wait to tell Else Britt about our plans.

We set out on the first of July. It rained all the way to Dovre. But then the weather cleared, and it got better and better the farther north we came. In Trondheim the sun was shining. It had taken us seven and a half hours, but we felt as fit as foals. We had to keep up our pace, though, as Svein said; we didn't have a single hour of vacation time to waste. Every minute felt valuable. If you spend a couple of weeks outside, you can save up enough energy for at least two winters.

The roads in Northern Trøndelag were narrow, with sixty-kilometer speed limits pretty much everywhere. We had planned an overnight stop in Mosjøen, but had to turn in upon arriving in Grong. It was late, and we thought we could rent a small cottage for one night, take a last glance at civilization.

But there were no vacant cottages in Grong. The attendant at the camping site called around and told us that we could get a room in a motel if we drove twenty-five kilometers back down the road. We said no thank you and asked for a campsite to put up our tent.

"Help yourselves," he said, and gestured with his arm.

There were RVs with huge awnings everywhere. People sat in the openings, barbecuing their dinners and drinking beer. We drove around a bit more.

"Might as well get it over with," Svein said.

"I agree," I said.

I felt mortified when we began to put up our little two-man tent between all those huge RVs. We hauled in a few things, pulled up the zipper. Svein went to the bathroom right away, but I waited until everything was silent and I was sure that our neighbors had gone to bed.

* * *

"Oh, I know of a place, far up north in the land, with a glittering fjord, between mountains and sands, where I… hum hum hum hum where my hum hum hum hum with the finest the finest hum hum," Svein sang as we crossed the county border into Nordland.

"Leave that to the local pop star, will you," I said, and put on Madonna.

We ran into a few problems on our way farther north. In Mo i Rana we had to fix an oil leak. Problems make themselves known on long journeys. Everything is revealed. Clearly the car wasn't as flawless as the ad had claimed. Once we reached the Arctic Circle, we stopped taking pictures of one another.

Svein was adamant about getting that certificate they give you up there. It costs fifty kroner and he had to wait for fifteen minutes to get it signed. It saved our lives, I'm sure of that—I've hung it up above the fireplace and there it shall remain—because when we came back to the car after the photo session and the signing, we saw that the left rear tire was flat. If it had blown on the way down the mountain, on the steep hills, on the winding roads, it would've been our last mountain crossing.

We reached our destination two days late. There was quite a bit of traffic along the way, and the usual roadwork and so forth. On Hamar Island, which isn't an island at all, a trailer with flowers from Amsterdam had overturned on a tight curve. It took more than an hour to get it upright, and when we came to Bognes (or whatever it's called) we'd missed the last ferry. We had to put up the tent again, but didn't feel so embarrassed this time around. A lot of people were much worse off than we. They slept in their cars with their parents-in-law, their dogs and kids, mess and mayhem.

* * *

We arrived in the early evening, on the fourth day of our journey. When we parked in a pocket along the highway, it felt as though we had reached the top of the world. Nothing but heath and moss, low hills and small, scattered birches. The landscape stretched endlessly in all directions, bathed in sunshine beneath a cloudless sky. It was beautiful.

The lake we had chosen was only a couple of hours away by foot. Svein had plotted it on the map in May, selecting it from among the 15,999 other fishing lakes on the Finnmark plateau. We had brought new red anoraks and professional hiking boots, and now we put them on and hefted our bags and off we trudged. Svein walked in front, with the map and the compass in his hands.

We had walked for hardly an hour when I started to get a blister on my heel.

"Svein," I called.

He turned. His upper lip was sweaty and he was out of breath.

"I've got a blister on my heel," I said.

"You're joking," he said. "Those boots are made for walking any kind of distance. Seven hundred and fifty kroner worth of specialty boots."

"They still hurt," I said.

"Then have a cigarette," he said.

Despite his complaining, he stopped and got the Band-Aids out of the side pocket of his backpack. It was after I took my boot off and he had begun to bandage it that the first mosquitoes showed up.

"Where did they come from?" I asked.

"They were just waiting for the right moment to welcome us," Svein answered.

"Give me the spray," I said.

"We've got to save it," he answered.

"I said give me the spray!"

Everything felt much better once the Band-Aids were on. The backpack was pretty heavy, and the small of my back and my thighs were aching, but I didn't say a word. A bit of hard work never hurt anybody. The soft wind brushed our faces as we walked. The reindeer moss was as soft as a sponge to step on and shone white as far as our eyes could see.

"Isn't it beautiful?" I called to Svein.

He turned and nodded. He looked strange. His face was sort of crooked. He looked the way he did when I gave him that bolo tie for his twenty-fifth, the one with a knot made of silver and onyx.

When we had walked for a little over three hours he waved with the map and pointed. I hurried to catch up; Svein was striding ahead on his long, thin legs. "There it is," he grinned. At the shore, when we stripped off our backpacks, it felt like we were floating up into the air. Our arms shot up on their own, like wings or propellers. We put up the tent in no time, despite the strong wind. We'd had enough practice by now.

The lake! To sit like that, on rubber mattresses, leaning against the sleeping bags, pulling the cork on a bottle of vermouth! All we could hear was the rustling of the leaves. All else was silence.

"I wish Else Britt could see us now," I said cheerfully.

"Stop going on about Else Britt. You're completely obsessed with her."

"Obsessed! I'm just annoyed, is all. She's always bragging about everything. I didn't know being annoyed was illegal."

"Cheers," he said, and lifted his mug.

"Cheers," I replied.

There was a small, sandy beach nearby, and we took a bath there. I swept the mosquitoes away with my washcloth. Then we fetched water in the saucepan for soup. Our plan was to base most of our meals on fish in the coming days, fish and berries and instant mashed potatoes, but packets of soup are easy to carry in the summer heat.

We had a wonderful night, to put it meekly. There's something about nature that... yes, it brings something out in you...

Tap tap tap tappety tap. I awoke to drumming on the tent roof, barely able to breathe. Svein was panting right in my ear. His hair was sopping wet.

"Open it," I moaned. My throat was grating, totally dry. Svein turned over, reached up, and unzipped the tent canvas. The air cooled. We groaned.

What happened next was indescribable. Truly indescribable. In less than a minute the tent was full. They swarmed, buzzed, and sizzled, seethed and stung, big gray clouds billowing in front of our eyes, almost blinding us. One mosquito flew up my nostril. I blew my nose on my T-shirt and got it out at the very moment another stung me under the eye. I smacked at it, waving my arms around, then coughed another one up and killed two on the back of my hand.

"*Svein,*" I wailed.

"Would you calm down," he answered through clenched teeth.

He had zipped the tent canvas back up and was wiping at it with both hands. I saw that he got the better of quite a few that way and began to do the same.

In time, we killed all of them. We could still hear buzzing, but the sound was outside the canvas now. We sank down onto the mattresses, tried to catch our breath. It was difficult. It had to be at least thirty degrees Celsius in the tent, maybe more. The sun was sizzling out there.

"What time is it?" I whispered.

"Three o'clock."

"Three o'clock?"

"Hmm."

"Have we slept for that…"

"Three in the morning," he interrupted.

"What?"

He didn't answer.

"Christ."

For a while we didn't talk, just lay there instead, quite still. Now and then I knelt and breathed through the valve in the tent.

"I have to pee," I said around quarter past five.

"Okay," he answered, his voice short and dry.

I gave him a hopeful look, poured my entire soul into it. Svein is so practical. There's nothing he can't fix. I can't stand men who can't hit a nail on the head before they've tried twenty times, or who bend the nail on the first strike. Svein would have a clever answer.

"Get at it," he said, and stayed where he was, calmly staring up at the ceiling, where the tapping was getting worse and worse: *tap tap tap tappety tap tap tap.*

"Where?"

I could barely manage to get a sound out.

He nodded toward the tent opening.

"*Out there?*"

"Where else?"

True enough, where else.

"Just give yourself a good spray," he added.

He didn't say we had to save it, not this time. Svein is such a nice, good guy. I took the can, opened the tent door, and slipped out.

"Close it!" he roared from inside.

"Close it yerself!" I hissed back, clamping my teeth together so the little bastards wouldn't fly down my throat.

"Did it go all right?" he inquired when I returned.

"Oh yes," I said.

He grabbed the can and crawled outside.

Svein said the bugs were there due to a lack of wind. It's not often there's no wind on the Finnmark plateau, apparently. We just had to wait. The fine breeze that had been in the air when we arrived would surely return.

By the third day the breeze still hadn't come back. The air was quiet. Time stood still. We were lying quite still, too, waiting. The mosquitoes were the only thing moving. They tapped and drummed on the roof, streamed inside in huge swarms at the sight of the slightest crack. But the buzzing sound was worse. It pierced you to the bone.

Svein stopped eating. I had stopped already, the day after we arrived. There were digestive issues.

"Does he write anything about that, this prophet of yours?" I wondered.

"About what?"

"The toilet situation." I giggled. A few moments later, I was laughing hysterically. I laughed so hard my stomach muscles felt like they were being torn off. Svein wedged the vermouth bottle between his backpack and his rolled-up sleeping bag. His face was expressionless, as disapproving as a freshly minted sergeant's. He had been reading a book called *Life in the Wilderness* all spring. It had been written by a man who had been fishing in all the sixteen thousand lakes on the Finnmark plateau and knew every tuft, every mouse hole, in the entire wilderness. I had the impression that Svein knew the book by heart. He quoted from it often: "There is always something special about the first sunset around the bonfire at the campsite." That's the sentence he used to serve me after the evening news, just before we went to bed. At the dinner table—when we were eating fish cakes, spaghetti, frankfurters, or whatever we had available—he would sometimes say: "I've been fishing in many a place for many a year, but have never seen a nicer trout!"

"Does your author write anything about going to the bathroom or doesn't he?" I wanted to know when I had caught my breath.

"Shut up," he snarled into his mattress, his back toward me.

We emptied half the vermouth bottle and read *Woman's Day* from cover to cover twice, horoscopes and recipes and everything. I'd been crying my fair share over the terrible sun, which wouldn't leave us alone, and Svein had been annoyed and yelled at me quite a bit when we suddenly, in the evening on the third day, heard the drone of an engine in the distance. At first we weren't sure if it was moving toward us or away from us; the sound rose and fell, rose and fell. Svein sat up, almost upending the camp stove, which stood near the tent opening, hardly used. After a couple of minutes there was no doubt—the vehicle *was* coming toward us. The droning grew stronger and louder. I sat up, too, my heart beating so hard that it almost drowned out the engine. The sound wasn't falling any longer, only rising. Soon it was right up close. And then, suddenly, it was silent. A branch groaned. The dry heath cracked.

"Hello? Hello, is there anyone in there?"

A man's voice. Rather high-pitched.

"Yes," we answered simultaneously.

The steps came closer.

Svein pulled down the zipper, peeped his head just outside.

"Hi," he said in a friendly voice.

The guy came up close, bent down, and peered in, grinning. "So you're inside in the fine weather," he said when he saw me, too.

Svein smirked. Both of them were smirking broadly. Svein a little artificially, but I was the only one to notice.

"You've got some coffee?"

"Yes, oh yes, won't take long, just come in," Svein answered, hospitality incarnate.

"No-o-o, why don't you have a bonfire?"

"We, well, we've just arrived," Svein stammered.

"Oh. I see. But you'll need a bonfire."

"Of course. Sure, of course we will."

Svein flung his anorak on, grabbed the spray box, and crawled outside. I dressed myself, lacing up the anorak hood so tightly that only my nose was sticking out. Then I crawled out, too.

There was a breeze blowing, so the mosquitoes had died down a bit. Our visitor was well dressed, in a military jacket and trousers. He had a knife as long as a sword hanging in his belt. He pulled it out and started to cut branches off of the bushes.

"You'll find birch bark over there."

He turned to me and pointed to a group of slightly larger bushes some distance away. I snatched the spray box and hurried off. I was careful when I inhaled and exhaled, trying to keep the bugs away from my face and mouth as much as possible.

"Don't you have a knife?" he asked when I came back with a handful of bark. He walked over to the bushes himself, then came back with a whole forest.

Later we sat in the smoke and sliced bread and slurped hot coffee and chewed the dried meat he had brought. The guy cut thin slices of it with his huge knife and gave them to us. I brushed the mosquitoes away with my left hand and ate with my right. The meat was salty and hard. I don't believe I've ever eaten anything as delicious. The dry, flat bread was delicious. The coffee was delicious. I squeezed my eyes shut to protect them from the smoke and didn't give two hoots about my digestion. "You gotta have a bonfire," our visitor said again.

The man's name was Nils, and he was seventeen years old. Svein asked if he was out looking for his reindeer flock, perhaps. No, he laughed, he didn't have any reindeer, and besides, they didn't actually stay around here, inland, in the summer.

"No, of course not," Svein said.

The lack of reindeer meant that we would miss out on some fine photographs, but I was relieved that at least we would not be trampled. At night, say, while we lay sleeping.

"You on a fishing trip, perhaps?" Svein asked.

"No."

"All right."

"Antlers."

"Antlers?"

"Yeah, I'm collecting reindeer antlers."

"I see. You sell them?"

"Yep."

There were many buyers, he said, in Sweden. They cut them up and sold them for a good price.

"I see."

"They grind 'em and send them to Japan."

"I see."

"Yes, they have... they've got a problem with that, the Japanese, you know, they have trouble with their..."

Svein grinned as though he knew more than he was letting on. Nils rolled a cigarette, held out the packet of tobacco. We could have some if we wanted to.

* * *

I almost burst into tears when he left. It was totally crazy, but I couldn't help it. I felt so alone. I don't think I have ever felt so abandoned before in my life.

"What's going on with you? Have you fallen in love, or what?"

"Don't be silly," I said. "He's seventeen years old. You heard what he said, didn't you?"

"Fresh meat," Svein grinned. "Lamb chops."

That's when I slapped him.

I didn't quite realize what I'd done until a moment later. I had never in my life done anything like that, not even when I went out with Geir Jøran, as awful as he was. I had slapped Svein. The sound reverberated.

Afterward he wouldn't even talk to me. We were lying next to each other in the tent, staring at the ceiling. Patterns were forming up there, changing with the movements of the swarm. The tapping and the drumming didn't bother me anymore; it just meant that they weren't inside. But the buzzing, the buzzing almost made me crazy. Dentists' drills and chainsaws and kids screaming in the apartment next door at five o'clock on a Sunday morning are nothing in comparison. I put cotton wool in my ears, as much as I could cram in, but it didn't help. The wool only made it more uncomfortable to lie on my side. I began to cry again.

"For fuck's sake shut up!"

My heart almost popped out and rolled down from the rubber mattress, that's how startled I was.

He got a little friendlier toward evening. Asked if I wanted some vermouth. I nodded. He poured some into the mug and handed it to me.

"Thank you," I said.

I'd better be a bit nice, too, I thought, and lay down on my side and stroked his arm and chest. I stroked for a long time. He didn't react, didn't move, didn't even budge an eyelid.

Maybe we, too, had a problem now.

* * *

We must have been asleep. At least, my throat was terribly dry when I looked at my watch around two o'clock. It was suffocatingly hot. The tent cloth was sweaty on the inside, slippery. There was no movement, not a puff of wind. Only the bloodthirsty swarms and that sun, the terrible sun and *zum zum zum*.

I sat up, pressed my hands against my ears. It didn't help. It was as if whole swarms had forced themselves into my head, drilled their way through the eardrums, and filled my whole skull with *zum zum*.

I fumbled and rummaged in my backpack, my hands shaking. I found the vermouth. Didn't have time to look for a mug.

"What the hell are you doing?"

Svein bored his bloodshot eyes into mine and snarled. He was ugly there, where he was lying, his hair disheveled, his face bearded and sweaty. Not a chance in hell I'm going to marry that man, I thought, and took another sip.

"Stop, for fuck's sake!"

He flung out his arm, twisted the bottle out of my hands, put the cork back, and stuck the bottle under his mattress.

I lay down again. I was itching everywhere. My forehead, my scalp, even beneath one of my feet where a damned beast had stung me. I scratched and scraped, clawed holes in my skin. It helped because it made the pain sharp, and that was a thousand times better.

I woke up again feeling nauseous. Sweat was breaking out on my forehead, something was grumbling in my body, churning, pushing its way—upward.

"I have to throw up."

"What?"

Svein was delirious.

"I have to throw up," I repeated.

"That's all we need," he mumbled, and turned over on his other side.

I crawled toward the opening, pulled the zipper down, and stumbled out. I didn't have time to grab the spray. I made it a few meters before I collapsed and up it came. Bits of meat and red liquid. And even more red liquid. I bent forward on the heath while the swarm attacked from all sides, under my neckband, around my ankles, into my ears, through my knickers, my T-shirt, everywhere. I screamed and started running.

"Have you gone totally mad?"

Svein. He was there somewhere. I heard him. Not too far away. I was lying on the ground, one of my palms bleeding. Got up. Retched again. Kept going. I stumbled on a root, but didn't fall. Kept going. The swarm was there, buzzing, stinging, sucking. The black swarm—

The lake! I stumbled over to the edge.

Then he was there. Pulling me away, holding on to my hands, hauling me up.

He was quite nice to me when we came back to the tent. Hung my underwear out to dry. Held me so I could get my warmth back, mumbled something about cramps and the ice that had just melted. He fetched water so I could rinse my mouth, and afterward he folded my damp T-shirt and pushed it against the mosquito bites.

"We're pulling ourselves together, okay? Let's take it easy now."

His voice was gentle. When he'd hauled me up, he'd barked a bit, said it was because of my lousy vermouth, that it was totally uncalled for to drag along crap like that and I should've listened to him and brought the cognac.

It was still early in the morning when we heard the engine droning.

"It's Nils," I said. It slipped out of me. "With the tractor!"

"Bike," Svein corrected me. "It's called a quad bike, a four-wheeler."

My skin had stopped itching. We were utterly still, almost not breathing. Svein sat with his mouth open and squinted, looking perfectly stiff, as if he had turned around and looked at a city and turned to salt or stone. Yes, it was coming closer. Coming this way. It buzzed and droned and purred. It was Prince and Tina Turner simultaneously, the Moonlight Sonata and Sissel Kyrkjebø, the most beautiful music, I thought, but remained careful not to say anything that could be misunderstood. I threw some clothes on. We put our heads outside.

It was him. It was Nils. He sat in the middle of a huge heap of jagged horns.

"Good morning!"

"Morning," we said.

"What've you done with the coffee bonfire?" he grinned.

Soon the fire was crackling, but I stayed inside the tent. I could hear them, though, heard Svein telling him I was sick.

"Sick? But then she can't stay here."

"No-o-o."

Nils asked if I couldn't even have a cup of coffee.

"Don't know... The mosquitoes are quite bad."

"The skeeters? Ye-es, oh ye-es. Want me to roll another cigarette?"

I heard him stand up and walk away a little. He came back again.

The fire hissed out there, crackled and rustled.

"You can come out now," he called after a while.

I peered out of the opening. Thick smoke was rolling up. I tied my shoelaces, found my anorak and trousers, sprayed myself from top to toe. Then I took a deep breath and walked out.

"No, she's not well," he said when he saw me. "Perhaps you should pack up."

I shook my head.

"Too many mosquitoes," I said, and tried to smile.

"We'll fix that," he said.

From then on, everything transpired quickly. Nils unzipped his jacket, put his hand in an inner pocket, fished up a walkie-talkie, got connected, and chatted for ages in Sami. He finished with "Okay." That was the only word we understood.

An hour later a seaplane landed on the lake, right outside the tent. Or, rather, next to the luggage, because we had already dismantled the tent and rolled it up. A fit young man with a Poco Loco sweater leapt ashore. He was wearing black leather trousers and had a knife in his belt identical to the one Nils had.

"Hello," he said.

"Hello," Svein said. He seemed embarrassed. "My girl here, she… she's… she's not all that well," he began.

That was all he had to say. Nils took over. They began to lift the horns and the luggage on board. Svein helped. I went and stood close to the bonfire, facing the smoke. Twenty minutes later we were flying over the marshes.

We drove home via Sweden. The roads are better there. We stopped in Luleå. Spent two nights in a camping cabin and sunbathed in a studio we found in the city center. Svein bought cognac in the bottle shop and stayed in the cabin and drank. Drank and slept. Slept and drank. He was miserable, and I told him so.

"Not a chance in hell I'm going to marry you," I said.

"Did I ask you?"

I tried half my wardrobe and decided to settle for a sporty image for my first day back at work. Long trousers and a shirt. My newly washed hair was shining, and I'd used foundation on the mosquito bites.

"Nice vacation?" Else Britt asked. I saw at once that she was more tan than I.

"Fabulous!" I said. I did it pretty convincingly. Then I turned toward the copy machine and began to sing that song—"We wanna play in the sunshine, we wanna be free." I sang the whole first verse, I knew it by heart by now, swaying my upper body, the machine spewing out paper. I started the second verse, I didn't know the words, but I hummed and grinned until she was grumpy. She took her green cat eyes and her gaudy paper folder and her cigarettes and her lighter and strode into her own office and closed the door.

"One day every day will be a yellow day let's play," I sang as loudly as I could.

It was very silent in there. I was sure that she could still hear me.

Translated by May-Brit Akerholt

ALARM

by ROY JACOBSEN

JAKOB TOTTERED DOWN the stairs. The steps hadn't multiplied, but Jakob was getting frailer. He was already in his eightieth year, an arduous age.

But the steps were far from his greatest concern—he was more worried about the era he was living in. His neighbor Kristian had been robbed as he sat there in his dumb gullibility over a tray of waffles at the co-op. A girl had been run over by a sports car on her way to school. And then there was something else as well: the fact that Jakob couldn't give a damn about any of it. It was a feeling that was new to him.

He had six letters from the head of the health center in his kitchen drawer and a brochure he'd already read eleven times. He took out the papers again, put on the coffee kettle, and pulled his glasses out of their case. They were keen to sell him a medical alarm, and had pointed out that if he wanted to live without both home care and supervision and not install an alarm on top of that, then the local authorities could not guarantee his safety any longer. They had made some vague threat about throwing him into a nursing home, of course, together with all the other idiots, but Jakob had managed on his own for thirty years and wasn't afraid of breaking his thigh bone or gangsters or the ocean storms that now and then tore at his house. He would remain upright as long as the place was still standing.

But these days his legs wouldn't carry him much farther than the mailbox. He read the brochure again, studying the picture of the little alarm button with the orange stripes, an object he could hold in his hand as he lay there like a slaughtered animal, frightened by a heart attack or alcohol poisoning, and he wondered why he always grew so stubborn whenever somebody tried to help him. All those educated people throwing away their lives down there at the health center, and he didn't even use the telephone anymore. That's how he was thinking this particular morning.

The weather wasn't all that bad; the roads were wet and icy, nothing unusual this time of year, and a corner of blue was peeping out from behind billowing clouds. The sound of silence in his deaf ear was like a rumble from the ocean. Jakob got dressed, deciding that he might as well get going. He could collect his thoughts on the way there. You don't make such a grave decision over a cup of coffee. You think it through, then you go home again if you change your mind.

The bus was leaving, and he had to stand in the road and wave his arms around until a young man stopped, someone from the neighborhood, or so he claimed, although Jakob had never seen him before. The young man drove him all the way to the health center, and fortunately the footpath had been sanded, the stairs were flat and broad, the railing solid.

Jakob's thoughts were still a mess. He sat in the waiting room, holding a number and studying the other weaklings and cowards; he saw a young mother and her kids, who were howling and stacking blocks on a small table in a corner, and an old carcass like himself, who made an effort to say hello. Jakob waved him off. He had more important things to think about. It was terribly hot inside. It was the old man's turn, now, and Jakob shifted away—what was he supposed to say, anyway? People came and went, and then they called his name, too; it was Gudrun, smiling as usual. She probably understood that he'd finally given in to her nagging, but her attitude no longer irritated him, not in the least.

"Well, I'm here about the alarm."

"How sensible of you, Jakob. In here, please…"

He strode into something resembling a doctor's office, a room with a desk and a few glass cupboards. He didn't get a real look at them before the nurse arrived. She was new, and he had to describe the fine points of his case several times while she made notes, seemingly unaffected by the fact that he'd finally reached a decision. Jakob could feel his reluctance growing again, but he was whisked away before he could say anything: returned to wait once again in the stifling waiting room with the mothers and kids and old fogies. Eventually Gudrun called him again.

"Okay, Jakob, you're on the waiting list—"

"What do you mean, waiting list?" He didn't quite understand.

"Yes, well… We don't have any alarms at the moment—you'll have to wait for one to become available. It may take two or three months…"

Jakob felt the urge to sit down so he could think things through. He knew that some old person would die soon enough, and then he or she wouldn't need their alarm any longer. The thought embarrassed him so much that he could barely get a word out. He coughed, and stole a cautious glance at Gudrun, hoping that she would do something to dampen the burning shame he felt, and sure enough, she nodded and smiled, but didn't say anything, just repeated that he'd made a wise decision. It didn't seem to help. He left the room and the shame behind, feeling like a beggar.

Outside he found himself on the stairs, fumbling with his

crampons, no need for them now that the ice had melted. He tore them off and tossed them into the ditch. The feeling of shame remained, all the way home, and over time, he felt a seething rage growing, as well.

He put on the coffee kettle and fell into a chair by the kitchen table. He didn't undress and he didn't light a fire. He wouldn't stand for this anymore—where did the shame come from? He never called anyone, there was the telephone, it had all happened so fast that he hadn't managed to make up his mind—what a mess, a fraud from start to finish, no one called him either, not even his son. He lifted up the receiver and dialed Gudrun's number. His worn-out voice whispered that he, Jakob, was in trouble, he puffed and rattled like a dead man, then he banged the receiver a couple of times on the tabletop before he snorted and tore out the extension cord.

He noticed that he had stood up while all this was happening, and he smiled, tore off his coat, and tottered up the stairs, took out the shotgun and shells just in the nick of time, as it happened, because he could already hear the sound of a car engine, he had just managed to lock the door when he heard a knock, the voice was unmistakable, it was the head of the health center.

"Jakob? Are you in there? Are you hurt, Jakob, has something happened...?"

"No," he groaned, opening the door and inspecting his visitor, a bald man in his late forties, a man of letters, wearing an anorak, rubber boots, and a cap, as if he were going hunting.

"Gudrun called me on my cell phone," he panted. "She said you'd—"

Jakob wasn't listening. He pointed the shotgun at the left front tire of the car and pulled the trigger.

"Come in."

The head of the health center stared speechlessly at the car, then at the smoking barrel. Jakob thumped him quickly on the head, and dragged him into the kitchen.

"What on earth are you doing?! You'll be arrested for this, you have to realize—"

"I want an alarm," Jakob said calmly, and pointed the barrel at the man's chest. "Sit down!"

"An alarm?"

The head of the health center fell down in a chair, seemed to collapse for moment, but then suddenly rose back to life.

"Of course you'll get an alarm. We just don't have any available at the moment. We—"

"I want an alarm now!" Jakob insisted. "You've been pestering me about getting this alarm for years, then I come and say that I want one, and it turns out that I have to wait for some other poor geezer to die!"

"Listen, Jakob, I'm not a magician. We've got the alarms we've got, that's all we've got—"

Jakob cocked the gun, put a new shell into the barrel, and sat down. He could see that the head of the health center was sweating.

"Do you actually understand what I'm saying to you?" the man said. Jakob nodded.

"I've paid taxes all my life," he said. "It's not like money's an issue. I've never been sick, you yourself have kept pestering me about this damn alarm, but now I can't have one?!"

"I've... I've told you you'll get it—what's really bothering you, Jakob?"

Jakob shook his head. Where was all this coming from, he wondered? He wanted to say that he'd been thinking about this alarm for months and years, damn it, back and forth forever, weighed the pros and cons, for and against, and hadn't been able to make up his mind, he'd filled his head with all this rubbish until he felt exhausted by it, ruined, old, they'd done away with him, that was what he wanted to say, but now the head of the health center was beginning to exaggerate the situation, he was lying across the table like a wreck, moaning:

"But Jakob... You've never acted like this before, what happened?"

Jakob stood up and pointed the barrel at the man's face, saw his guest lifting his arms like a puppet, only to let them fall again and start babbling about how he'd only have to wait for a few months.

"Yes, I've heard that, but I want an alarm now. Don't you understand? Now! Immediately!"

"But it's past four o'clock, Jakob—"

"You'll just have to work overtime! That's what *I've* done all my life!"

He shook the shotgun. The head of the health center fumbled with his cell phone.

"They're coming," he said after a short exchange. "They'll be here immediately. Can I take off my coat?"

"Go ahead."

Jakob opened a tin of fish balls and wolfed down three, then pushed the tin across the table. His guest shook his head and started to speak, but Jakob wasn't listening, the tone of the man's voice was friendly and something was definitely being expressed, but outside evening was approaching, it was getting windy. He asked his guest to make some coffee while he himself fetched a bottle of liquor. He poured himself a glass and drank.

"If they don't come, I'll shoot you," he said, and nodded to the bottle. "But I don't suppose you drink, either, you fat fuck. What do they pay you, by the way? And do you understand what you've done? Of course you don't, you're surrounded by fogies who can't make a single decision. Do you know what that does to you? Of course you don't."

He heard the sound of a car, stood up, and went into the hallway. A young man in a coverall entered, water streaming from his long hair, a toolbox in his hand. He was talking, probably about the weather. Heavy sleet blew into the hallway.

"I want it installed on the top floor," Jakob said, and closed the door behind him. "Next to the bed."

The man tried to glance into the kitchen, they could hear a chair fall in there. Jakob pointed his shotgun at the stairs and the electrician cautiously started up them, then disappeared into the bedroom.

He found the head of the health center lying on the kitchen floor, trembling, holding his throat as though he were choking. Jakob kicked him in the back until he went quiet, and helped him into the chair.

"Can't you take hard liquor?"

"Jakob, Jakob..."

"I've never been scared of anything, but when I got up this morning I tried to appreciate that this alarm was a sensible thing. I really tried, and I started to walk, I got all the way to—"

The coffee kettle simmered. "I'm sure it wasn't God, I don't believe in things like that, but there was something, a warm something—"

"You're sick, Jakob. Don't you understand—"

He let his fingers slide along the barrel of the shotgun. They could hear rummaging noises from the floor above.

"I was born in this house. We built the road ourselves, a children's parade came past here once on Constitution Day, what good did it do, and no one has ever, ever—"

A clear voice announced that the installation was complete, the alarm was ready, he lifted the kettle and steaming coffee flowed nicely into the cup, steps on the stairs, Jakob nodded obediently, stood up, and went into the hall, the sleet blew into the house again, two men ran for their lives toward the car. I'll forget to lock the door, he thought, and turned toward the never-ending stairs, but I'll show them, I'll get into bed.

He could feel the little plastic thing in his hand, with a knob at the top, all you had to do was push. He did. A few howls hit his ears, a harsh light was reflected in the black windows, all this nonsense they invent, he thought, and pushed again, of course nothing happened, you can't even take your last breaths in peace, he wanted to throw the stupid thing away, but all he had to do was push. Another violent tremor went through the house, a new red flare.

He got to his feet again and went over to the window. Across the way he could see the health center ablaze, flames reaching all the way to the sky. He smiled and pushed again and the town hall exploded. Then the administration building. The fires gained ground until the whole village was a mass of live embers. He heard voices just below his window, there they were, standing in the slush, the head of the health center and Gudrun and the idiot who'd installed the alarm, the mayor and that awful nurse who didn't understand what it means to make a decision, all of them staring up at him, panic-stricken.

The spit in his mouth had dried, he couldn't find the words, a last wish, he thought, no wonder they didn't want to give me this thing, he squeezed the button again and kept on holding it.

Translated by May-Brit Akerholt

INTERLUDE XXIV

by TOR ULVEN

WHEN I FELL ASLEEP, it was August. When I woke up, it was March. I couldn't understand what had happened, and since I despise winter, it was with great concern that I walked through the snow-filled city streets, past the theater and the subway station, toward who knows where. A dreadful premonition prompted me to seek out a hospital. Deep inside the building, I met a representative of the medical profession. He was sitting behind a desk. I asked him politely if he might answer a question or two, purely on a general basis. He nodded kindly. I asked if it was possible for memory loss to stretch across several months, and was told that it was. I then asked if it was this or that year. With a kind, only mildly ironic smile, he replied that the number indeed had a four in it, but that the correct date was 3064. I realized that my memory loss had not only wiped out everything between August and March, but had extended for more than a thousand years. I felt dangerously ill. I was terrified. And then

Translated by John Erik Riley

ANOTHER STAR

by INGVAR AMBJØRNSEN

L ESTER CALLED AROUND ten o'clock. It was the night before Christmas Eve, and the city streets were about to disappear under all that snow. I had been sitting in my chair by the window, drinking red wine. A strong wind was blowing in from the fjord, whipping crystals into the smallest cracks, forming a fairy-tale landscape out in the backyard, and something of a boy's joy over the heavy snowfall was blossoming in me. It was lovely to see the neighbor's gateway being slowly choked, covered with all this whiteness. The woodstove whistled and hissed as the moisture in the birch logs was squeezed out through the flue. I didn't want to answer the phone, but then I remembered that I had a frail mother in another part of the country.

As I mentioned, it was Lester calling. He felt it was high time we shared a Christmas star or two. And to my surprise, I said yes. I got dressed at once and walked outside.

The town was almost deserted. Only from the bars could I hear noise and laughter. Lester lived in one of the old shacks down by the river; the streets were not plowed, and I was walking in snow halfway up to my knees. When I arrived, I brushed the worst off before I went into the stairwell. He had left the door open a crack on the first floor, and I could hear him rummaging around in the kitchen.

"You were sitting in your chair again, weren't you?" he said. He was making himself a huge packed lunch. Slices of bread covered the whole table, and he was cutting long yellow strips off a block of cheese.

"Yes," I said.

"That chair will eat you someday. I'm not the only one who's worried."

I sat down on the log crate.

"This weather's quite a gift," he continued. "And the forest stands exactly where it stands, indeed." I tried to get him to see that he had, indeed, gone mad.

"Just make the tea," he continued. "Water's boiling." He piled the slices of bread on top of each other and made two huge parcels. Later we filled two two-liter thermoses with tea.

"I'm not dressed for a North Pole expedition," I said.

"No," he said. "I know that."

I really shouldn't have been surprised; I had known him for so long. Lester was a man of objects. In the bedroom he had a wardrobe the size of my own living room, and the whole house was filled to the brim: furniture, lamps, brass candleholders, paintings, carpets, ornaments. But when he showed me the two Italian pilot uniforms from World War II, I was a little dumbfounded. I'd never seen an Italian pilot uniform before. It was sewn as one piece, and from the crotch a zipper ran all the way up to the neck. The hood could be pulled down to just above the eyes and tied up. The uniforms were fully lined, both the legs and the sleeves; they had a waxy coating that made them stiff. When I'd managed to get into mine, I looked like the Michelin Man. The boots were original, too. They were also lined, and made of thick leather, which Lester had greased with pork fat. They reached up to my knees, and when I folded the trouser legs over the tops and tied the laces, I felt armed for the Pole expedition I had always dreamed of. I helped Lester put on his outfit, and then we took our backpacks and waddled back to the kitchen. It was hard to move. Our arms were pushed out from our bodies, and we had to walk with wide steps.

Lester found the two red stars. They were tiny, and lay sparkling in his sweaty hand. I recognized them from last time, and felt they were safe. It was strong stuff, but with a somewhat speedy engine, which made it quite easy to keep control. We ate one each. Then we packed our backpacks and left.

Outside the weather had gone totally crazy. We had to lean into the wind. Now and then the gusts hit us with such force that we almost toppled over, but I was still feeling warm and cozy behind my impregnated shield. When we were halfway to the town center, Lester stopped and pulled off his backpack. He rummaged through it and pulled out two pairs of goggles that matched our uniforms. We now looked completely and utterly like two Italian pilots from World War II; the only thing missing was the plane. I even had a pair of stripes on my sleeves, and a distinction of some sort above my left breast pocket.

We caught the very last bus from the bus terminal. Every time it stopped to pick up new passengers, there were people who thought they were seeing things. And slowly the bus rose up above the town, which lay flickering beneath us in the sea of snow. In between the heavy trees we caught glimpses of lit-up windows in villas we couldn't see. We were the only ones who got off at the last stop. When we did, the bus turned and drove back.

There weren't any houses up here, nothing but dark forest and white snow. When we took our first steps into that eerie witch's wood, I felt the LSD seep through me with a warm, electric quiver. Here there were no paths. We cut in through the spruce trunks, and the snow came up to our thighs. The contrast between the black forest and the white snow was overwhelming. We were moving inside a black and white film. The colors had died, and that gave us a sense of great peace. We didn't talk—it wasn't necessary, and besides it was impossible to say anything. The wind would have swept our words out into the nothingness before they reached the other person's ears. I thought it was good this way. Good to walk in this wordless landscape of friendly spruce trees and piercing wind. It was colder up here in the hills, but the snow was dry, and it was easy to wade through it. The thought that only a couple of hours ago I had been sitting in an armchair drinking wine seemed absurd. This is where I belonged.

As we got deeper into the forest, the snow reached up to our chests. We let ourselves fall forward, and sank down into the whiteness. I became a pupa, a fluid solution encapsulated in a shell; soon I would step forth as something new, something different. How utterly fed up I was with all those years I had behind me, years in the pupa phase, all the time that had been lost to meaningless word-wrangling.

After more than two hours we arrived at a cleared forest path. We brushed the snow off our pilot uniforms and continued on into the nothingness. We had no idea where we were, just that we had found ourselves at quite a distance from the social-democratic thought system.

Toward five o'clock in the morning we stopped somewhere to eat our sandwiches. They hit the spot—I can't describe it, but I understood that it was the first real *bread* I had ever had in my mouth. I could feel the nourishment forcing its way into my body as I swallowed.

We kept going, and the twists of fate led us once more in the direction of civilization. The forest path turned into an avenue of villas, and we found ourselves among the most expensive properties at the top of the ridge. One villa after the other became visible through the snowfall; they looked like huge UFOs, mansions from another planet.

The yellow outdoor lights in entrances and entryways danced in front of our eyes, pulsated, grew, contracted. The tops of the snow banks were above our heads; it was like walking in a glittering tunnel.

Here! Lester thought. He didn't say it, I'm absolutely sure of that. At the same moment I noticed how tired I was. We'd undergone a massive amount of physical exertion, and now our legs were giving in. The acid was thumping around in my consciousness; I saw myself from outside, my own batteries almost flat, the aura contracting around my body. I couldn't go on. I just wanted to sleep until next year.

Lester took off his backpack and retrieved a collapsible spade of light metal. It seemed so natural, I remember. Like all Norwegians, the idea was planted in us with our mothers' milk: trouble in heavy snow? Dig yourself down.

We attacked the snow bank, Lester using the shovel and I using my hands to help. He cut out neat blocks first, and put them aside; they would form the outer wall. Then we dug ourselves straight in, before continuing at a right angle.

It was another world. Another star. We lay next to each other on Lester's ground pad. The round cave-roof above us made me think of the uterus I came from. It wasn't cold. We lit a candle, and lay and watched the flame, the shadows playing across the smooth walls. A thin layer of ice, a fine glazing, was forming over the walls and the ceiling. It was utterly impossible to grasp that we were lying in a cave on one of the town's most exclusive residential streets. Outside it was still dark, but now and then the odd car drove past. As they passed our cave entrance their lights threw a warm glow into our room. There was something almost physical about that light; we could put our hands into it, fetch warmth from it.

Lester took out two more tabs. We had one each. Then we fell asleep.

*　*　*

I had never experienced anything like it, waking up from an LSD high. It's a state beyond anything else, because the memory of what you have ingested is completely gone. When you wake up in a snow cave under such conditions, you're instinctively one with the cave—it's a part of you. It has always been there. For an infinite time, I, along with this strange figure next to me, the one who is another aspect of myself, have been here. The muffled sounds from outside, the lights sweeping across the arched ceiling every time something passes out there in the strangeness, are a part of another world. Unknowable. I felt like a caveman. An embryo. But I had no desire to be born again; I remembered in detail the sound and light shocks from the last time, the intense discomfort of physical existence in time and space.

Lester woke up, too. He said something, I don't know what, but it was green and pink. He lit the candle again, and I happened to throw a glance at my watch. It was an amusing watch. When I moved my left arm back and forth, the green light from the luminescent hands trailed behind like thin threads. For some reason the watch showed four-thirty, which didn't tell me much. I had no idea that I'd slept for almost twelve hours. In a residential area. In a snow cave in a snow bank.

Time passed. Or time stood still. I don't know: we were in a vacuum. The candle burning. The sound of our own breaths. Our heartbeats. I was utterly and fully present in the here and now, relieved of morals, ideas, doubts, beliefs. I was here. In what was my own. The wall was smooth when I moved my hand over it. There was something sensual about this cold, this wetness. Now and then we could hear voices from people out on the road. They approached. Then they went away again. I didn't understand a word, but I enjoyed lying like this in half-darkness, listening to the melody of the language.

Eventually we heard a new sound. Heavy turns of a shovel. Someone was digging us out.

"Hello? Is anyone there?"

Language and understanding returned. I was almost in tears. There was something painful about the fact that the picture of myself as a caveman, an embryo swaddled in white, had disappeared.

"Hello?"

We didn't answer. We sat utterly motionless in the glow of the candle.

It was the voice of an adult man. He swore and continued to dig.

The breakthrough came a moment later. We saw a glimpse of the shiny spade; then the wall fell into space, and the winter evening revealed itself to us. In the garden, three people were standing in snow up to their knees. A man and a woman and a girl aged five or six. The man rested his arms on the spade and looked at us, shaking his head.

"I don't believe it," he said. "I refuse to believe what I'm seeing."

"My god!" said the woman.

The child began to cry.

I could understand their reaction. I won't claim otherwise. I can see why the child cried, why the woman called on the Lord, why the man would not believe his own eyes. It's not every day you happen upon two Italian pilots from World War II in your own garden, sitting in a snow cave.

"Take it easy," Lester said. "We're leaving."

The man wanted to know who we were, and we explained it to him as best we could, even if I, personally, was not totally sure.

"Did you sleep there last night?" the woman asked.

Yes, we did.

The child cried and cried.

"There, there," the father said, and rumpled his daughter's hair. And to us:

"It was Helene who found you. She saw a glint of light in the snow."

"Thanks a lot," Lester said. "You remember the story about the three wise men, who followed the light from the star?"

She nodded, sobbing.

"It's Christmas Eve," the woman said. Then she checked herself, and dove into deep religious waters. "You shall not walk away from here on an empty stomach. The turkey's in the oven."

The man looked embarrassed, but did not protest.

"Nothing much happens up here," she said when we were all inside. "Everything stands still. It..." She had been drinking quite a bit, and quickly, and the hand cutting the turkey was not quite steady. The table was swimming in colors; I was clinging to a wineglass. Over in a corner of the living room the lit-up Christmas tree pulsated with electric lights and glass beads. The little lady had long ago waved good-bye to her fears; now she was drinking soda and studying us with curiosity. We had taken off our Italian pilot uniforms, but we were still from another planet.

"Nothing much's happening anywhere," Lester said. "It's snowing and blowing. Now and then Christmas comes."

"Well, cheers!" the man said.

We clinked glasses. It was good wine from their own cellar.

"I must say!" said the man. "When I'll tell them this at work. That you..." He laughed happily.

The turkey swelled in my mouth. For some reason the burning candles on the table made me think about Christ.

"Imagine!" the woman said. "That you slept there all night."

"Yes," I said. "And you slept in here. It's a strange world."

"Afterward we must dance around the Christmas tree," the child said. "And sing all the songs."

"You can bet on it," Lester said.

And so we danced around the tree. We sang all the songs. The woman got drunker and drunker, but she had good manners, and always pulled herself together.

Then there were the presents. The sound of crackling paper. The colors crackling in my brain. The man of the house had, inexplicably, managed to smuggle two bottles of vintage wine under the tree. This touched me, and I burst into tears. Lester was already building a medieval castle with the little girl's LEGO set. I walked into the hallway and cut the distinction out of my pilot uniform. I gave it to the man, and explained that he now had a new hobby. I gave my knife to the little girl, who was now Lester's best friend and master builder. I wanted to give my silver ring to the woman, but she had withdrawn. I saw her in my mind's eye, lying across a double bed somewhere far inside the enormous villa.

The man and I sat and talked past each other for a few hours while we laboriously worked our way through his wine cellar. I became more and more sober with each glass; it was the LSD draining out of me. Lester was still high, far into his own world of buildings. He was working on the eastern tower now, constantly reeling off intricate fairy tales about the castle. The little girl sat there with big round eyes and an open mouth.

Finally I'd had enough. The man had a good heart, but a social intelligence that only encompassed French vineyards and imported luxury cars. Besides, as he got more and more drunk, he entered into a self-reproaching phase, during which he tried to make me understand that he regretted having organized his life the way he had. From now on, to hell with material comforts. To hell with status, stress, and false friendships. As a young man he'd been very good at drawing; now he wanted to start drawing again. He wanted to shove the whole job where it belonged, and become like Lester and me. He probably took it for granted that we dabbled in the arts, as our hair was so messy, and we were walking around in Italian pilot uniforms from the Second World War. I had to say good-bye.

I decided to give up on Lester; he'd become a little boy again, and would probably stay like that for the rest of the night.

Outside there was utter silence. Starry sky, crackling cold. I looked forward to the long walk down to the town center. But when I passed the snow cave, I saw that the candle was lit again.

The woman was crouching, dressed in Lester's pilot uniform, a bottle of sherry in her hand. Her lips were moving constantly. It was impossible to hear what she said, but at times since then I've imagined that she was trying to invent a new name for herself.

Translated by May-Brit Akerholt

TWO BY TWO

by GUNNHILD ØYEHAUG

A T TEN MINUTES to one one night in November, Edel loses it. She has been standing by the window with her arms crossed since ten past twelve, alternately looking down the drive and at the watch on her wrist. A few hours earlier, she had been lying on the bed clutching a book to her chest with her eyes shut tight, feeling good, strong, and completely open. Then she got up to clear the snow, so that Alvin could drive straight into the garage without having to stop and clear the snow himself. She had wanted to *reach out* to him— that was the expression she'd used when she thought about what it was she'd wanted to do. It was a cliché, but that was okay, it was what she wanted. She imagined her own small hand reaching out and being taken by Alvin's hand, Alvin's big, strong hand. Her eyes filled with tears when she thought of their two joined hands and everything they symbolized. And clearing the snow—it dawned on her that clearing the snow symbolized that she was making room for him again. She was making room for him again after he had asked for forgiveness and said that from now on, she was the only one, there would be no others; she had let him stay in her life as Thomas's father, as someone she shared her home with, someone she refused to look in the eye at the breakfast table and whose shoes she occasionally kicked as she passed them in the hallway. So she cleared the snow, and as she shoveled she looked up at the double garage and thought that it symbolized her goal. She was clearing the way for him—she was the garage that he could come home to. Her small car was already parked on one side, and when his car was on the other side things would be as they should be. Her small car parked alongside his big car. She ran up the driveway through the uncleared snow and turned on the light and looked at her little car standing there all alone, waiting, and then cried as she cleared the rest of the driveway to the garage.

That was forty minutes ago. It is snowing hard again now, snowing so much that it looks like the snowflakes are falling together, two by two, three by three, four by four, falling through the air until they land suddenly and mutely in the snow. In only forty minutes, the driveway has been covered again. And the man that she cleared the way and made room for is not here. He should have been here forty minutes ago. The last ferry docked at twenty past eleven and it takes three quarters of an hour to drive here from the ferry—and that's being generous. In other words, he should have been here at ten past twelve, when she finished clearing the snow and stood waiting, red-cheeked, by the window, with a magnanimous, nearly loved-up look on her face.

Every minute that passed after ten past twelve pulled this look of love from her face, like a net being dragged from the water. By the thirtieth minute past twelve, when she called his mobile and heard it ringing in the bread box in the kitchen, her face was no longer remotely magnanimous. She screamed with rage, she who had felt no rage one hour earlier as she'd lain on the bed feeling good, strong, and open, before she'd decided to get up and clear the snow. At twelve-thirty there was nothing left in her that was in any way still touched by the good, light magnanimity she had felt blossom in her heart just over an hour ago, as she'd lain on the bed and read *Birthday Letters* by Ted Hughes. Ted Hughes wrote the book for his deceased wife, Sylvia Plath. In the book he expresses his love for Sylvia, who took her own life largely because she felt that this love was lacking—she believed that he did not love her, that he was unfaithful, which he was, and on 11 February 1963 she put her head in a gas oven and took her own life. In the years that followed, the English press and many others held Ted Hughes responsible and criticized him for not talking about it, for not expressing any regret, not even asking for forgiveness, nothing. He received prizes for his poetry, but people looked at him with eyes that no doubt clearly expressed what they really thought of his behavior. Edel is one of those who have held it against him. She loved Sylvia Plath and she has borne a grudge against Ted Hughes, though she has found some solace in the fact that even among famous poets there are those who share her experience. She, a small bookseller in a rural community, can see herself in a famous poet, Plath—there *are* bonds between people, she has thought; even successful poets in big cities wander around in their homes in desperation, even they rage and throw things against the wall. The fact that they have cried and felt small, small and betrayed, that they have wanted to be stones that sink to the bottom and stay there, has been a huge relief to her. And yet it was awful that Sylvia had suspected Ted and was right. Because that meant it was possible: to suspect and to be right.

But then she read *Birthday Letters*. With great resentment, she picked the book with the red poppies on the cover from the cardboard box of books that she had ordered, and with great reluctance she opened the book and read the first poem. She did not know how it happened, but as she read the book, it struck her: even though he betrayed her, he must have loved her. He *saw* her, saw all the big and small things that she went around doing and feeling—and if only she had known *that*, as she went around doing all those things that she did not think were noticed! When Edel got to the last poem, she discovered that the red poppies on the cover referred to this poem about the red poppies that Sylvia had loved and seen as a symbol of life; and this evening, as she, Edel, lay on the bed reading this last poem, she felt she was the one who saw all this for her belovèd Sylvia, in a stream of warmth and the dark timbre of the voice that *saw* and *said*, that twisted and twisted down and down until finally she could barely breathe, suffocated by a pressing joy, or sadness: This Is Life, You Are Loved and You Are Betrayed, I Must Accept It, I Accept It: Life Is Good, Painful, and Awful! She thought to herself: This is *Acceptance*! The notion of *acceptance* radiated inside her like the sun suddenly staring through the clouds, forcing them open and covering the fjord like an iridescent bridal veil. This is *God*, thought Edel, and she felt like she was about to explode; she clutched the book to her breast and closed her eyes and felt completely open. She felt over-whelmed by something else, too, and had to scribble down some words on a piece of paper: *The power of literature.*

The reason that Edel let go of this good, magnanimous feeling, of the notion of "acceptance," and has now lost the plot instead, is that she suspected, but could not see, the scene that was unfolding in a house by the ferry, forty-five minutes' drive from the double garage, around the same time that she was clearing the snow from the driveway. The scene that Edel suspected but could not see looked like this: her husband, Alvin, was standing behind Susanne, who lives in the house that stands alone by the ferry, forty-five minutes' drive from the double garage. They were both naked. Susanne was bending forward and holding on to a window ledge. Alvin was standing behind her and holding her hips. Alvin thought to himself that this was not what was supposed to hap-pen, this was not what he had intended, he should have driven straight home, he should never have stopped at Susanne's, just to say hallo, to find out if she was very sad because he had stopped coming, if she had been all right in the last six months, and to say that it was difficult, nearly impossible, just to drive by her house when he finished work, to say that he stood up on the bridge of the ferry and tried to see if he could see her every evening when she had the lights on and it was dark all around, and her house twinkled at him like a small star in the night sky, but that it could not carry on, he had a family to consider, Edel had threatened to leave him and take Thomas with her and he could not bear that, he had to sacrifice their love for Thomas, that was just the way it was, that was what he'd wanted to say, he'd wanted to take responsibility for his family, that was what he had chosen, having spent a long and painful period thinking and doubting, he could not come in and stand here like he was now, holding her by the hips and pressing his cock between her legs.

Thomas—for whom Alvin was going to sacrifice his love and not stand as he was standing now, for his sake—is asleep. He was out all afternoon selling raffle tickets in the snow and spent the whole time thinking about Noah's ark, which he'd learned about at school. He thought about giraffes and leopards. He thought about rhinoceroses and dreamed of stroking them and sitting on their backs, touching their horns. He thought about how enormous the boat must have been, as the teacher had said yes when he'd asked if it was bigger than the hotel. He wondered whether there were also two ants on board. And two lice! And now he is lying curled up like a small fetus, dreaming about crocodiles. Because there were crocodiles on board, he had asked about that. He is dreaming about a big crocodile that has laid a crocodile egg in a nest, while Edel storms through the sitting room and pounds up the stairs to the bedroom. She throws on a pair of trousers and a sweater, puts on a pair of shoes, and hurls *Birthday Letters* at the wall as hard as she can. Alvin comes all over Susanne's buttocks. In the crocodile nest, the first baby crocodile breaks through the hard shell of its egg. A rhinoceros stands for a long time looking at another rhinoceros, then suddenly walks away, out of the ark's big front door, and the rhinoceros that is left behind does not know why. Thomas shouts to Noah: Wait! Wait for the other rhinoceros! He tugs at Noah's tunic. Then he runs toward the door to bring back the rhino that has walked away. The one that was left behind falls to the ground with a great thud.

Thomas stands in the doorway with tousled hair.

"Something went bump, Mummy," he says.

"It was a book that I threw against the wall," replies Edel.

"Why did you throw it against the wall?" asks Thomas.

"I was angry," says Edel. "It was a bad book. A terrible, terrible book. Put your clothes on, Thomas, we have to go and get Daddy."

"Why?" asks Thomas.

"His car has broken down and he can't get home. Hurry up," she says, and Thomas says that he does not want to, he has to sleep! If he does not go to sleep now, the rhinoceros might leave forever!

"You can dream in the car," says Edel.

"But I might not have the same dream!" says Thomas.

"Of course you will. Come on, I'll help you get dressed," she says, and takes him firmly by the arm, her whole body shaking.

"I want to have the same dream!" whines Thomas.

Susanne is shaking. She stammers. "Alvin," she says, and turns toward him, wanting him to put his arms around her. "I love you," she whispers into his neck. "I knew that you'd come back." He holds her tight, but says nothing. "I can't say it," he says finally. "You know I have said that I can't. It would be wrong. It would build up your hopes, you know I would love to... but Thomas..." She nods and looks at him, he can see that she is not entirely happy. But she tells herself that she can cope with anything and that he must be able to see that, on her face, how big and generous she is. Maybe that will make him understand that deep down, he loves her, and that it would be impossible, impossible to leave her. She looks at him with understanding on her face.

"Bloody hell, I have to clear the snow again," shouts Edel. "Bloody, fuck, shit, *shit!*"

She drives through the village through the snowstorm, her windshield wipers racing furiously back and forth. A triangle of snow builds up under one of them; in a while she will undoubtedly have to get out and brush it off. A triangle! Naturally, a symbolic triangle had to appear right in front of her eyes! She snorts, that she could be so stupid. Oh, *Life*—right. Oh, Terrible, Oh Good, Oh Pain, it is none of that, it is pure and simple lunacy and shit. And the outside is just bodies, skeletons packaged in flesh, doing this and that and nothing makes sense. That, thinks Edel, and laughs a sad laugh aloud for herself, is what I will say at the seminar on Monday. "Muuummmmyyy," complains Thomas. She has woken him, he is lying across the backseat with his duvet over him. She let him lie down without putting the safety belt on. "Go to sleep," she says. She has been taking courses in English literature at the college in the next village and up until now has enjoyed her current one, "Symbolism in Literature." She felt that it was true that you should not scorn symbolism and simply look at it as antiquated, romantic thought, things should make sense, the expression and the content, she believed that something could stand for something else, a rose for love, an ocean for life, a cross for death, but now it just irritates her, because now she realizes that of the two lanes on the road along the fjord toward the ferry, only her side has been cleared. She immediately thinks: *Is that how it is*, is that what this means, is his path closed, will he not come back, is it only she who can reach out to him, and he cannot reach her, is his lane full of snow, is that how it is? She feels helpless, is that what this means? No, she refuses to read it that way! It is just a road, she thinks, a stupid road, without any symbolic meaning. Crap and idiocy, and on top of that: asphalt. She wished she had fuzzy dice hanging from the mirror, or an air freshener, a Little Tree, the most pointless thing she can think of, when she gets back to the village she will stop at the gas station and buy a Little Tree to remind her of this, to mark this evening when she said good-bye to symbolic thinking and to—what, what else is she going to say good-bye to? Her marriage? But she is on her way to collect him, why, why is she doing this, shouldn't she drive back home instead and lock the door, let him sleep in the garage, should she stop driving, should she just stop, why did she react in this way, it has to be the least reflective thing she has ever done, she just did it, and what should she do now, should she carry on driving? She slows down as she swings into a wide bend, she sees an orange light pulsing in the trees on the other side of the road, it must be a snowplow, she is frightened of snowplows, she comes to a near standstill and lets the snowplow sail past on the other side of the road, the snow blasting over the barrier beyond the plow and hitting the trees, and tears come to her eyes, spontaneously, *because now his lane is also being cleared.*

Alvin looks at Susanne's face. The pleading in her eyes makes him feel ashamed. He kisses her on the cheek and goes to look for his pants. "What have you been up to recently, then?" he asks, and Susanne tries to hold in her stomach as she picks up her bra from the floor. "Not much, same as always, really... no, hang on..." She has thought of something. "Give me a second," she says, and with a sparkle in her eyes she pulls on her knickers and practically runs to the CD player. Alvin thinks suddenly that there is something helpless about her body dressed only in underwear, as she bends down to put on some music, he feels like he can't breathe, he tightens the belt on his trousers and pulls on his jacket. "Susanne, I'm going to have to leave. Edel will flip if I'm not home soon, I'm sorry, Susanne," he says. But Susanne does not listen, she has put on a CD of salsa music and starts dancing in front of him. He must not go. She must get him to stay. She must get him to say something nice to her before he goes. "I've been going to salsa classes!" she says, and dances closer and closer to him, with a provocative, slightly coy look on her face. She takes him by the hands, he says "Nooooo…" then she lets go and turns her back to him, rolling her hips. She's a bit nervous, so her dancing feels contrived. Alvin is so embarrassed on her behalf that he goes over to the dancing back and puts his arms round her and says that he really *must* go now, but that she's good at dancing, and she should carry on with it. "I'm a fool, Susanne," he says. "No, you're not," she says. "You are the best person I know." He kisses her on the forehead. "I might go to Cuba soon," she says, even though it's a lie. "Well, I hope you have a good time, then," he says.

Edel shakes her head, she doesn't want to think about it anymore, she doesn't want to interpret things symbolically anymore. We have rejected nature, that is what we have done, thinks Edel, as she drives slowly forward on the newly cleared road and the snowstorm gradually dies down, yes, nature has been abandoned and we are to blame, we have focused on language and become complicated. We have to get back to nature, we have to stop reading books, we have to stop interpreting everything, we have to stop thinking figuratively, we have to live like animals, we have to eat food and sleep. We must renounce symbolism. We must stop thinking altogether. We must live in one simple dimension. Ah! She is happy. She feels crazy. Or perhaps she has actually been crazy up to this moment and has now regained her sanity. She has a horrible, crystal-clear feeling in her head. As if her head is two wide-open eyes with a cold wind blowing into them. She shakes her head. Your husband has fucked another woman this evening. She wants to laugh. And so we have to stop thinking symbolically! Ha ha. Jesus! she mumbles. And then she laughs again. What a thing to mumble. In fact she wants to cry. She has to pull into a bus stop and cry. Imagine, she thinks as she leans forward over the steering wheel, crying, imagine if it's not what I think, but that he's been in an accident. She looks over her shoulder at Thomas, he's asleep, lying with his face to the back of the seat, she can only see his hair sticking up from the duvet, a small fan that spreads across the pillow, and she thinks: Then he will be fatherless and I will be a single mother, and she leans over the wheel again.

Alvin cannot quite understand what has happened. He drives home along the fjord, it has stopped snowing, the branches on the trees on the mountainside are weighed down, the road is white, no one has driven here since the snowplow swept past, no tracks in the snow. The street-lights stand silently with bowed heads off into the distance, he imagines the noise that is made when the light from each streetlamp hits the roof of his car as he drives past, *bzzzzzzzzzt*, he imagines that they are X-ray beams that penetrate the roof of the car and illuminate him, so that if you were looking in from the outside you would see a skeleton sitting there holding the wheel and driving along the road. Out of the light: a man. In the light: a skeleton. On, off, on, off. In a kind of corny, gray light, you can now see his right hand with all its white bones moving like tentacles, gripping the stick shift and changing gears. And then he dresses the skeleton up in bluish-red muscles, veins, and sinews, at the very moment he remembers a picture in the anatomy book at secondary school that made a lasting impression on him: a person without skin, only muscles, veins, and sinews. Teeth without lips, eyeballs without eyelids. Sometimes it comes back to him, like when Edel was shouting and screaming and saying it was over, he could barely hear what she was saying, he just stood there staring at her, imagining her as a face without skin, only bluish-red, knotted muscles in her cheeks, over her lips and teeth. He feels hot, flushed, conspicuously flushed, and it will not have died down by the time he reaches home, he knows that, because he has done it before, he should really take a long detour when he gets to the village, but it will not be of much help, since he will get home even later and Edel will know, maybe she'll have packed the suitcase on wheels like she did the last time—the good, big, red suitcase with wheels—and then remembered that it was a gift from him and stopped right in front of the front door, opened the suitcase, and taken out all the clothes, then kicked the suitcase across the floor so that it hit the chest of drawers and lay there open like a gaping mouth, just like last time, and then run up into the attic and searched and searched until she found the old bag that she had brought her clothes in when she moved in with him, as she had last time, to make a symbolic point to herself that she was on her own again, and then woken Thomas up and gone down to the hotel; maybe he smells of perfume, he thinks, thank God he took her from behind, touching as little skin as possible from the waist up. It was really only the lower part of his stomach that had touched her hips. He pictures Susanne's salsa-rolling hips and feels sick. He stops the car in the middle of the road, gets out, and leaves the door open, walks to the edge of the road, turns around, stretches his arms out from his body, and allows himself to fall backward into the snow. It is soft. If he lies here for a while, he will cool down. He will lie here and slowly but surely erase Susanne from his mind. Because now he can feel it in his bones, it is over.

Susanne pulls on some sweatpants and opens a bottle of wine. She sits down on the sofa and tries to think that she has just had a visit from her lover and that she is a grown woman with a rich life. She managed to get him to come. He could not stop thinking about her. He could not get her out of his mind—that's how strong the power is that she is fortunate enough to possess. But she knows there's no point. She tries not to think about the desperation that drove her to dance for him. She tries not to think about the embarrassed look on his face when she wanted him to dance. She drinks the glass of wine in one slurp, swallowing only a couple of times. It tastes of alcohol. Susanne purses her lips and goes over to the phone, looks up the number of a travel agent in the directory. She just doesn't understand, she thinks, how Alvin, the best person she knows, so sensitive and observant, who has told her the strangest things about what he thinks, could just come like that and fuck her and then leave with an embarrassed, hard expression on his face. She feels it, deep down, that he will not come back. This time it's over. She hopes he has an accident. She hopes he has an accident and ends up in the fjord. She dials the number for the travel agent. He could quite possibly have an accident with all this snow. The travel agent is closed and will open again tomorrow morning at eight. She throws herself down on the floor. She wonders if she should slide her way over to the sofa, she pictures herself wriggling, exhausted and doomed, like a soldier on a muddy battlefield, over to the sofa—but she knows it isn't true, the truth is that she's lying on her back on the floor, she's looking up at the ceiling, the back of her throat is burning and the tears are running from her eyes down into her ears.

"*Please*," says Thomas. The missing rhino has not come back and Thomas is not allowed to leave the ark. Noah is so big that he nearly reaches the ceiling and he says firmly that it is not possible to go out, it has started to rain so they have to shut the door soon. Thomas tries to get to the door all the same, but the floor is heaving with baby crocodiles, so he slips and falls and doesn't make it. He notices that there is an elevator like the one at the hotel beside the door and he can see that it is on its way down, the floor numbers are showing on a panel above the door, and he thinks that maybe it is the rhinoceros, *2*, *1*, *pling*: it is two lizards. The lizards waddle over the baby crocodiles. Edel lifts her head from the wheel. She starts the car and swings out into the road. "Bloody shit," she mumbles.

Bloody, fuck, shit, *shit*.

Alvin has made an angel in the snow, which he realizes is a great paradox, symbolically. It makes him think about Edel, it makes him want to cry, but he fails, so he sits up, pulls up his knees, and crouches huddled in his own angel. A pathetic, overly symbolic position, Edel thinks as she pulls up beside him before he has looked up. He looks up. He is not surprised to see her there. She stops the car, gets out, and stands in front of him. "What happened?" she says. He shrugs his shoulders and opens his hands. Closes them again. "This," he says. "I made an angel in the snow." "You little shit," she says, and nearly starts to laugh. She isn't reacting the way she thought she would. She had imagined the scene and it was not like this, she shouted and cried and then he fell to the ground, but now it almost feels as if she isn't here at all. The whole scene is slightly comical. "We're finished," she says, without feeling anything, and then goes back to sit in the car. Her head feels crystal clear and cold, almost light. Her feet feel light as well. "The car broke down!" he shouts, coming after her. "Bloody hell, Edel! I've been standing here for nearly an hour! And I couldn't phone you because I couldn't find my mobile! I've been sitting here waiting for help but no one came." The crystal-clear, weightless Edel smiles. "I would have liked to see that," she says. Alvin says nothing, just gets into his car, and his hands shake as he turns the key, because now it *is* over.

But the car doesn't start.

The car just manages to splutter a few times but will not start.

"There you go," says Alvin. Edel says nothing. The blood is about to leave her legs and rush to her head, her cheeks. She looks at him, coughs. Nothing of what is happening now is as she'd imagined. She does not know whether it's true or not. "Get out of the way," she says, and sits down in the driver's seat of his car, it's cold, so he can't have stopped, he must have been there for a while. It is cold in the car. She turns the key, the car barely reacts. It's true. The car has broken down. She does not know what to do. She has driven along the fjord to collect him, to shout at him and leave him, and her side of the road was cleared of snow first, and then his side was cleared, it hits her, all this actually happened. It literally happened. She goes round to the boot and gets out a towrope and hands it to him. Alvin stands looking at Thomas, who is sleeping in the backseat of Edel's car, and tries to behave like someone whose car has broken down and who has been waiting in the snow for an hour. "What's he been up to today?" he asks, casually, and coughs. "He learned about Noah's ark and sold raffle tickets," answers Edel. "Come and look at him," says Alvin. Edel stands beside him and looks at Thomas. He's lying asleep with his arms stretched out above his head, along the back of the seat. In the same position that Susanne is now lying on the floor, without knowing that the painful pressure she feels in her heart is the same pressure that is in Edel's and Alvin's hearts right now, as they stand there side by side.

Edel drives the small car and tows the big car, which Alvin is steering. She refuses, she thinks, to interpret this symbolically. It's just the way things have turned out. They drive along the fjord. It's night. There are three of them. And the fact that there is a rope between the cars has no significance other than the physical fact that when a car breaks down it needs to be towed. I just don't understand this, Alvin thinks. He feels that he is being watched, as if someone is laughing at him; he said the car had broken down, and that's what happened. He got exactly what he asked for. He leans forward toward the windshield to see if he can see the stars, but is blinded by the light from the streetlamps, which stand silently with bowed heads, illuminating the cars as they pass. At regular intervals along the road you can see a skeleton, an adult, sitting at the wheel of a car, then a child's skeleton lying across the backseat, and then finally another adult skeleton sitting more or less directly behind the first. The adult skeletons have their arms in front of them, holding their steering wheels. The child skeleton is not holding anything but has his arms stretched out above his head.

You can also see a larger skeleton, standing on all fours, which has a huge horn on its snout; it is standing beside the child skeleton. A similar skeleton now appears from the left, to the surprise of the first, which lifts its head and looks at the approaching skeleton expectantly. They stand for a moment staring at each other, and then the one rhinoceros rubs up against the other. A couple of antelope skeletons wander past, and farther along a tiger skeleton and a lion skeleton can be seen, and two small cat skeletons and then dogs and a mass of small crocodile jaws that nibble the child skeleton's legs, making it laugh and wriggle. And if X-rays could also show the contours and shape of other things that were not of solid, indisputable mass, you would be able to see the outline of an enormous wooden boat, with pairs of skeletons, two by two, arranged on many levels, two skeletons for each sort of animal. A big human skeleton lifts its arm and then everyone feels the boat leave the ground and float through the air.

Translated by Kari Dickson

SMALL WORLD

by FRODE GRYTTEN

ONE EVENING, YOUR BEST friend tells you about Google Earth. With Google Earth, you can choose a city and then you can fly there. You can dive down from outer space to street level, and you can see every house and building in 3-D. But the best thing of all, your best friend says, is that you can see women sunbathing topless. Your best friend tells you that Google Earth is pure genius. He has done this very thing, dived down and looked at women in his neighborhood. You know he's telling the truth. You heard another kid, from another class, talk about how he'd found a topless woman on Google Earth, only to realize that he was staring at his own mother. You don't mention this to your best friend. You're not sure why. Instead, you think about what it would be like to fly even farther down, into her body, to see how everything inside is connected, the stomach, the intestines, the lungs. You wonder what it would be like to fly into her heart at dusk.

Translated by John Erik Riley

LIKE A TIGER IN A CAGE

by PER PETTERSON

WHEN ARVID WAS outside playing he would sometimes go quiet, hunker down, and think about his mother. Then he would try to draw her with a stick in the sand the way he was used to seeing her, standing in front of the kitchen work-top wearing one of her three striped aprons. She would lean against the sink with one hand while holding a cigarette with the other, and when, absentmindedly, she ran that hand through her hair, there would be a hiss and then the smell of burning. Arvid often sat waiting for that moment.

She'd looked as she always had for as far back as he could remember, and still did right up until the day he happened to see a photograph of her from before he was born and the difference took his breath away. He tried to work out what could have happened to her and then realized it was *time* that had happened and it was happening to him, too, every second of the day. He held his face as if to keep his skin in position and for several nights he lay clutching his body, feeling time sweep through it like small explosions. The palms of his hands were quivering and he tried to brake, to resist and hold back. But nothing helped, no matter how hard he squeezed, and with every bang he felt himself getting older.

He cried, and said to his mother:

"I don't want to get older. I want to be like I am now! Six and a half is a good age, no?" But she smiled sadly and said to every age its charm. And time withdrew to the large clock on the wall in the living room and went round on its own in there, like a tiger in a cage, he thought, waiting, and Mum became Mum again, almost as before.

She had worked at the Freia chocolate factory, and those were the good days, for no one could deny that quite a bit of chocolate found its way from Grünerløkka to their home in Veitvet. But all good things must come to an end and now she had a cleaning job at the music school in the evenings and that was not quite the same. Once, when Arvid was allowed to come with her even though it was late, he searched for things she could take home, but you didn't get fat on sheet music, and the pianos were too heavy.

Now it was Dad's job to sing Arvid to sleep in the evening, and that was nowhere *near* as good. He sang the same song every night, the one about the cat getting stuck in the spruce tree or something like that. Arvid never understood what it was really about, and anyway he couldn't care less. It didn't take him long to realize that the only way he could be spared the song was to go to sleep as quickly as possible, and of course Dad boasted and said it was his talent as a singer that made him a success. There was only one song that was worse, and that was "When the Fjords Turn Blue," but that one Dad only sang when there were guests and they had had a dram or three. Then Mum went into the kitchen and waited there until he had finished.

Sometimes Dad went out onto the balcony when his yodeling was at its worst, for he wanted a view of the land as he sang. *"When the fjords turn blue!"* he would roar, though not counting the bullfinch tree there was nothing out there to roar about, only the terraced houses and the tenement buildings, and then Mother would drag Dad back into the living room with a snarl:

"Now you damn well pull yourself together, Frank!"

And he did, too, at least when he had had no more than three drams.

But there were other things afoot. Arvid could sense that, because he didn't always go to sleep at once, he just pretended to so that his father would stop singing. Voices seeped up from the kitchen. They slipped out through the crack under the kitchen door, glided along the rag rug in the hallway, over the worn carpet in the living room, and up the stairs, wearing themselves shiny and sharp on the way. Sitting at the top of the stairs, Arvid could feel the voices skid off his body. He was cold, but inside him there was a heat, like a little flame only he could put out, and one day he would do that, he thought, put it out when they least expected and turn to ice, but he would never let someone else make the flame go out, nor even let them come near.

The voices grew louder, the kitchen door must have been open now, and then he heard a bang followed by the sound of something breaking. He knew what it was, it was the last plate in the set they had brought with them from their life in Vålerenga, and it was a sound Arvid knew well because it was he who had broken the last but one, when he had tried to carry a knife, a fork, a glass, and a plate to the worktop all in one go. The plate had slithered out of his hands and smashed into a thousand pieces on the kitchen floor, and it startled Arvid and he was afraid his father would get mad since he was so fond of that set, or so he said, but only Mum saw what happened and she said:

"Don't worry about it, Arvid. I couldn't be more pleased." And she looked pleased as she swept up the pieces and threw them in the rubbish bin.

Now Arvid could hear someone clattering around in the hall, and then Mother stormed into the living room at full speed in boots, rain-coat, and gloves, tying her headscarf in a furious knot under her chin. With one ill-tempered movement she snatched the pack of Cooly ciga-rettes from the coffee table, turned, and saw Arvid sitting on the second step from the top.

"So that's where you are, is it, Arvid?" she said in an unfamiliar voice.

"Yes."

"Aren't you cold?"

"Yes." He huddled up and was truly cold now.

"You go upstairs to bed. I'll be back soon. I'm just going out for a lit-tle walk."

He got up and his legs hurt, they had gone quite stiff, and as he was about to enter his bedroom he heard the front door slam.

In the room next to Arvid's his sister, Gry, was in bed asleep. He went in and shook her by the shoulder.

"Gry! Wake up!"

Gry twisted away and buried her face in the pillow.

"What is it?" she mumbled from the depths.

"Mum's off out again."

Gry rolled out of bed and together they went to the bedroom win-dow. Outside, night was drawing in and it was wet and they could see their mother striding out beneath the streetlamp on her way up the slope and the raindrops were twinkling in the light above her green headscarf. She was the only person out in the street, and when she was gone, past the shopping center and toward Trondheimsveien, it became totally deserted again, just streetlamps and rain.

They knew where she was going, even though they were never allowed to come with her, and anyway she walked so fast there would have been no point, but she had told them. She walked up Trondheimsveien, on the left-hand side, as far and as fast as she could. When she reached Grorud or thereabouts, she crossed the road and came all the way back at the same insane tempo, smoking nonstop. Arvid had seen how the pack of Coolys dwindled.

"Why would she want to go out in weather like this?" Arvid said.

"She has to, don't you see?"

"How do you know?"

"We women know that sort of thing, Arvid," Gry said, laying her hand on Arvid's shoulder.

"Jesus," Arvid said, wrenching himself away. "You're only in the fourth grade, you are."

And then he went back to his room. He had decided to stay awake until his mother returned, but then he fell asleep and when he woke up he had wet the bed. His mind made a halfhearted attempt to remain in the trough of sleep, but in the end it had to surface and he sensed the all-too-familiar, freezing-cold sensation around his hips.

He lay quite still and tried to go back to sleep, squeezing his eyes shut and thinking of sheep and clouds and all those things that Uncle Rolf had once taught him, but it was rubbish and it didn't help and he had to get up. Carefully he took off his sodden underpants and put them under the dresser. This was his secret trick and it always worked. Every time he had wet himself he put the clammy underpants under the dresser and the next night they were gone. It was like magic, but he tried not to think about it. He didn't want to break the spell.

Mum was back. He could hear her light steps on the stairs and he jumped into clean underpants and got back into bed, close to the wall, he seemed to curl around the wet patch that he could do nothing about, but he knew it would be gone by the morning. Mum came in to see if he was under the duvet. He pinched his eyes shut to show he was asleep, but she came up close and said:

"Are you still awake, Arvid?"

"Mm."

"You should have been asleep hours ago."

"Mm. I know. But I *have* slept." He wondered if he should open his eyes, and then he did, and she perched on the edge of his bed and stroked his hair.

"Were you afraid for Mummy, Arvid?"

Afraid? No, he hadn't been. She always went for these walks when there was something up, and even if he didn't like her going out when the weather was really bad, he had never been afraid. He shook his head, but then he remembered something.

"Mum?"

"Yes?"

"Why do you cross the road? I mean, why do you cross the road when you're almost in Grorud and you're on your way back?"

"Because I don't want to walk with the cars heading in the same direction as me."

"Why not?"

"Because it makes me feel like they are all leaving me and I'm standing there, going nowhere. D'you see?"

"Mm. But what do you do?"

"I don't do anything. I think."

"About what?"

"Nothing you have to bother your little head about."

They all thought he didn't understand. Everyone thought he was stupid just because he was only three feet seven inches tall. But he was not stupid, and he knew well enough what went through her head while she was out there walking, and when she said "Goodnight," turned off the light, and went downstairs he was absolutely sure, because then he could hear them down below.

"You've let off some steam, then, have you?"

"Oh, that's so typical of you, Frank! You don't understand a thing! You just say wait and we have to think this over, but I don't want to wait, do you understand? I'm not twenty anymore!"

Next morning when he awoke he had slept longer than usual, the room was light and he had a clean sheet underneath him. How that could have happened he didn't know, it was more magic, and as soon as he realized that he tried to think about something else.

Everywhere was strangely quiet, he could not hear a sound and he was the early riser, he was always awake before Gry, while Mum lay in bed reading, as she often did no matter what time he poked his head round the door, and Dad would be in the kitchen making himself breakfast before leaving. Then Arvid used to sneak down and eat a slice of bread, trembling with cold until Dad tousled his hair and left with a bag under his arm.

Now Dad was at work, and when Arvid peeped into Gry's room, her bed was empty. He quietly tiptoed down the stairs to the living room, and that was empty, too, but the cellar door was open and if he listened carefully he could hear a faint splashing of water he knew came from the laundry room and that meant his mother was down there.

He was all alone in the flat and it gave him such a chilling sensation of freedom that for a while he just stood still, it was so unexpected, he could do whatever he wanted and then he knew what he wanted. He quickly fetched a chair and placed it by the bookcase, stepped up onto it, and started to climb. He knew it was all right, the shelving was screwed into the wall. When he swung himself up to the very top he almost knocked off the old vase they had brought with them from Vålerenga, and even though Mum might have been pleased about that too he managed to catch it at the last moment.

Cautiously he straightened up. It was a long way down to the floor, and for a fraction of a second he balanced on the edge and felt the rush of fire in his stomach. Then he raised his arms as high as he was able, which was not really all that high, but it was enough to touch the bottom of the large clock. He pushed it off its hook, held it in his hands for a moment, and Jesus it *was* heavy, and then it tipped over and sailed through the air and landed on the floor with a crash that was a hundred times louder than he had expected.

He stood on top of the bookcase in no more than his underpants, which were slowly getting wet, and he looked down at the splinters of glass, the scattered cogwheels and the two clock hands wobbling round in a functionless void. From the cellar he heard his mother's hurried *click-clack* steps, *"Arvid! Arvid!"* she cried, and then he faced the wall and cupped his hands over his ears.

COMPUTER LOVE

by NILS-ØIVIND HAAGENSEN *and* BENDIK WOLD

D O COMPUTERS SHAPE new literary forms? Fifteen or twenty years ago, during the early days of the internet, that question was debated intensely. People without their own Hotmail addresses raved enthusiastically about "hypertext" and "non-linearity."

But then the IT bubble burst, and that early enthusiasm faded. Maybe professional authors remembered that, above all, it was bound books, not freestanding text, that kept debt collectors at bay. In any case, experts on the media continued to develop concepts for new literary forms—"cybertext," "interactive fiction," "ergodic literature"—but increasingly longer periods of time passed between the appearances of examples of such texts.

Only toward the end of the first decade of the twenty-first century did it again become possible to mention "the internet" and "literature" in the same breath without sounding like a futurist dressed in a corduroy suit. The reason? Hordes of "digital natives"—twenty-somethings who had never lived in a world without Nintendo consoles—began to publish literary texts. We're talking about a generation that did not get their education from Joyce and Proust, but from the Wachowski and Mario brothers. This generation does not make a point of its familiarity with file sharing and hypertext; the existence of YouTube, Hype Machine, and Urban Dictionary is an undramatic premise for everything they write (just like previous generations of authors could take the existence of pagers, magazine file organizers, and dual-cassette decks for granted). Put simply: the digital world exists, and so authors write about it.

In little Norway, a snow-covered petroleum state with 99.9 percent broadband coverage, the "digital turn" is changing literature. At Flamme Forlag, a small press based in Oslo, we want to embrace these changes. What follows is a selection of poetry and short prose by four Norwegian authors born in the early- to mid-1980s. These are people writing for the contemporary *data sapiens*. They do this, paradoxically enough, on printed pages, in a format as old as Gutenberg.

NOBODYREADSPOETRY2.DOC
[COMPATIBILITY MODE]
Audun Mortensen

Reply to all
Forward
Reply by chat
Filter messages like this
Print
Add to contacts list
Delete this message
Report phishing
Report not phishing
Show original
Delete this message
Show in fixed-width font
Show in variable-width font
Message text garbled?
Delete this message
Why is this spam/nonspam?
Reply to
Me

EVERYTHING I SAY IS A EUPHEMISM
Audun Mortensen

i have a suspicion that my parents were hippies
damn what should i do
e-mailing my mom, cc-ing my dad
"hi, were you a hippie"
waiting for reply
is this something i shouldn't "fuck with," maybe
researching a little while i'm waiting
hippie van
cannabis
flower children
the vietnam war
lsd
bob dylan
jimi hendrix
janis joplin
grateful dead
woodstock
hm, what else
Thanks for following!
IMAGINE PEACE: Think PEACE, Act PEACE, Spread PEACE
love, yoko
[via twitter]

THE SONG "AS WE GO UP, WE GO DOWN" BY GUIDED BY VOICES

Audun Mortensen

i wake up late and check my inbox
without glasses
seems like i almost have to put my face against the screen
Gmail—inbox (4)—audun.mort...
yes!
sweet
what am i supposed to do this summer
am i just going to wake up late and check my inbox
this summer i want to go waterskiing
i want my dad to drive the boat
will my dad ever buy a boat
i doubt it
i need a new bicycle

READING THE WIKIPEDIA ARTICLE ON AGYNESS DEYN IN THE LIBRARY AFTER THE LIGHTS HAVE BEEN TURNED OFF

Audun Mortensen

i walk into the reading room with my thermos
and begin to play air guitar on my thermos in front of a study group
    that is discussing intertextuality
one of them wonders which song i'm playing
i pretend i don't hear the question
one of the librarians comes over to me and tries to give me
    a sarcastic high five
i pretend i don't see his hand and continue playing air guitar
    on my thermos
wonder why nobody says that it reminds them of my bloody valentine
    etc.

EXTREME MAKEOVER SIMS EDITION
Rannveig Revhaug

THE YOUNG MAN:
(Enters house through front door.) Hello.

(The action speeds up.)

(He hangs his overcoat on the coatrack, listens to music, dances. Moves into the kitchen. Prepares food on the most expensive stove there is. Gets points.)

(The young woman twirls out of the shower. She has changed clothes.)

THE YOUNG MAN (CONT'D):
(Sits in an armchair eating steak.) I can telephone the whole city. I am megapopular.

THE YOUNG WOMAN:
Oh.

THE YOUNG MAN:
Is there any coffee?

THE YOUNG WOMAN:
No—

THE YOUNG MAN:
(Cuts her off.) The food was delicious, thank you. *(Gets up.)* Do I smell? No? By the way. The faucet in the kitchen is dripping. See you later. *(On his way out the door.)* I'll stay platinum all day. *(Exits.)*

(The action slows down to normal speed again.)

KID ICARUS (1987)
Ole-Petter Arneberg

I try to pull the curtains closed. Grab the controller again and peer at the TV screen. I see myself, the reflection from the screen makes it hard to control the little guy with wings. Arrows and monsters appear dimly while he jumps farther upward. The controller gets sweaty in my hands, the buttons are slick. I move closer and closer to the screen [←] or [→] (A) (A) (A) *ENEMIES* [↑] (B) [→] *flying eyes* [←] (B) *blue skeleton* (B) *scythe* (B) *a new heart* (A) [→] (A) [→] (A) [↑] *flies* [↑] *clouds* [↓] [↑] *flies* [→] EYE [→] (B) (B) (B) [↓] *dies*—suddenly I feel the static electricity against the tip of my nose, and I pull back, swearing out loud to myself, and I turn off the machine.

BANJO
Ole-Petter Arneberg

[→] stops me (LAUGHS) continues the hand a banjo (NO) a ukulele continues running (NEW) person stops me (HAPPY) sit down (PLAY) on the ukulele stops (NOT) ukulele (LAUGHS) holds me (HAPPY) continues my hand [→][←] her hand (NO) fall lifts me [↑] [→] holds me continue fall [↓] (BAAARRRFFF) [↓] [↓] [↓] holds me [↑] [→] holding sees (NO) me (KISSES)

XLIII. LE GALANT TIREUR DE "DUCK HUNT"
Ole-Petter Arneberg

On the way through the funfair I stopped by the shooter in the arcade, thought it would be nice to take a few shots to kill Time. When I stretched out my hand to drop in a coin, she came and stood right next to me, she who always came along and with whom I was in love— and the reason that I was so good at this game.

I didn't hit a single duck, one of my shots even went outside the screen. And when she began to laugh raucously, gloating over my uselessness, I suddenly turned to her and said: "Do you see that dog that appears and chuckles every time I miss one of the ducks? Watch this! Now I'm imagining that it's you." I closed both eyes and squeezed the trigger. Hit the dog right in the head.

Then I leaned toward my programmed companion, kissed her, and said: "Thanks for making me such a good shot!"

CREATE A PROFILE
Victoria Durnak

YourName
Connect
choose password
create profile

we are eleven years old, on the internet
at the desk under the stairs of the house in Lillestrøm
her parents are still together
the father hasn't mailed, met, married Anna
we're eating cheese sandwiches
every day after school
come from Oslo: Majorstua, Frogner, Bislett, Aker Brygge
like shopping, to be with friends, listen to music, work out,
use color codes, write every other letter as a capital

met a guy once
he was so ugly
the first thing she tried to do was kiss me
I didn't dare talk to him at school
sent a note to

how many friends on MySpace
        comments, entries

a couple I know goes to Japan
he refuses to speak to her from Gardermoen to Nagoya
she has flirted with someone on the net

should we hug?
hold hands?
I've never chatted

we say we're seventeen

CONTRIBUTORS

HILTON ALS is a staff writer for the *New Yorker*. His work has also appeared in the *New York Review of Books* and the *Believer*.

INGVAR AMBJØRNSEN is a novelist, short story writer, and commentator. He has also written acclaimed books for children, and his tetralogy about Elling was made into a series of feature films. He lives in Hamburg, Germany.

OLE-PETTER ARNEBERG is a writer living in Oslo. His first book, a short prose collection entitled *Upforit*, was published by Flamme Forlag in 2008.

ROBERT BARNES fought his way to the top of Chicago's flyweight boxing ranks in the early 1950s, winning the Golden Gloves before retiring at age sixteen. His paintings are in the collections of the Museum of Modern Art, the Whitney Museum of American Art, and the Art Institute of Chicago. He lives with his wife in a one-hundred-and-eighty-year-old house on the coast of central Maine.

BRIAN BEATTY's jokes, poems, and stories have appeared in numerous print and online publications.

BENJAMIN COHEN teaches at the University of Virginia and lives nearby with his wife, Chris, and two children. He is the author of *Notes from the Ground: Science, Soil, and Society in the American Countryside*.

PATRICK CRERAND lives in Dade City, Florida with his wife and son. His work has appeared in *Barrelhouse*, *Conjunctions*, *New Orleans Review*, and other magazines. He teaches writing at Saint Leo University.

RODDY DOYLE lives and works in Dublin. His latest novel is *The Dead Republic*.

VICTORIA DURNAK is a Norwegian artist and writer living in Stockholm. She is a member of seven internet societies, and every day she decides to reduce her email checking to once a day. Her first collection of poetry, *Stockholm Says*, was published by Flamme Forlag earlier this year.

BEN GREENMAN is an editor at the *New Yorker* and the author of several books of fiction, including *Superbad, Please Step Back*, and *What He's Poised To Do*. He lives in Brooklyn.

FRODE GRYTTEN worked as a journalist for many years, and now works as a writer full time. He has received numerous awards, including the Rivertonprisen for the crime novel *Flytande Bjørn* (*The Shadow in the River*).

JOHAN HARSTAD has written short stories, plays, and three novels. His first novel, *Buzz Aldrin: What Happened to You in All the Confusion?*, is being adapted into a television series for Norwegian broadcasting.

HANS HERBJØRNSRUD works solely in the short story genre, and has received several awards for his work, including the Norwegian Critics Prize for Literature. He lives on a farm in Heddal, Norway.

ROY JACOBSEN is the author of numerous novels, short stories, and works of nonfiction. He is a two-time recipient of the Norwegian Booksellers' Prize.

ELLIE KEMPER plays Erin Hannon on NBC's *The Office*. She is also a contributing writer for *The Onion*.

DAN KENNEDY is the author of *Loser Goes First*, and a contributor to *GQ*.

PASHA MALLA is the author of *The Withdrawal Method* and *All Our Grandfathers are Ghosts*.

STEVEN MILLHAUSER is the author of eleven works of fiction, including *Edwin Mullhouse, Martin Dressler*, and *The Knife Thrower and Other Stories*. His most recent book is *Dangerous Laughter*, a collection of stories.

AUDUN MORTENSEN maintains audunmortensen.com, lives in Oslo, and is the author of *Everyone Tells Me How Great I Am in Case I Turn Out to Be*.

GUNNHILD ØYEHAUG has published poetry, short stories, essays, and a novel. In the mid-2000s, she co-edited *Kraftsentrum*, a literary journal, with the author Olaug Nilssen.

PER PETTERSON's most recent novel is *I Curse the River of Time*. He is a recipient of the International IMPAC Dublin Literary Award.

RANNVEIG REVHAUG is a young woman. "Extreme Makeover Sims Edition" is taken from her novel *IRL*.

MIKE SACKS has written for the *Believer*, the *New Yorker*, *Esquire*, *Vanity Fair*, *Time*, *GQ*, *Salon*, *Vice*, *MAD*, and other publications.

LEON SANDERS is an activist living in Cambridge, Massachusetts.

JIM STALLARD is a science and humor writer. His story "No Justice, No Foul" was published in the second issue of *McSweeney's Quarterly*.

LAILA STIEN mainly writes short stories; she is a recipient of the prestigious Aschehoug prize for fiction. She is from Rana, in northern Norway, and has lived in Finnmark for much of her life.

TOR ULVEN published a novel, short stories, and various essays; he is remembered, too, for his short prose and poetry. He died in 1995, at the age of forty-one.

SARAH WALKER is a writer and comedian living in New York City. Her column, "Sarah Walker Shows You How," appears on the *McSweeney's* website.

TEDDY WAYNE is the author of the novel *Kapitoil*.

KENT WOODYARD lives in Southern California, and blogs at *fiveminuteanswers.net*.